PRAISE FOR STINA LINDENBLATT

Decidedly Off Limits

"...I was captivated by the shenanigans of this duo. Not to mention laughing out loud and blushing. Boy do these two turn up the heat."—*The Subclub Books*

"A feel good, sensual, intoxicating and sexy love story; if you love contemporary romance you do not want to miss Decidedly Off Limits." —*Slick, Guilty Pleasures*

"Sweet, sexy and invigorating, Decidedly off Limits is a friends to lovers story that is truly a breath of fresh air!" —*Read & Share Book Reviews*

Decidedly With Baby

"So many laugh out loud moments that you do not want to be reading it in public or be ready for some weird looks. I speak from experience here."—*The Subclub Books*

"Oh my goodness this book was so much fun!!!"—*For the Love of Books*

"There are steamy moments but you are just left with feel good melty moments more"—*Books Are Love*

"Once I started, I couldn't stop reading it!"—*Blog on the Run*

Decidedly With Love

"Be warned dear reader, this book will have you giggling and blushing as you devour it"—*The Subclub Books*

"I laughed with this book, but also cried a lot"—*Blog on the Run*

Other Books By Stina

"Everything – the plot, the characters and the dialogue – made this story captivating"—*Harlequin Junkie* (5 star Top Pick review for *My Song For You*)

"A well-written story that kept me entertained from start to finish."—*Harlequin Junkie* (4.5 star Recommends review for *This One Moment*)

"I love that Stina Lindenblatt was able to layer this book with so much depth, mystery, hurt, friendship, and of course love."—*Four Chicks Flipping Pages*

"I loved this book; this is romance at its best, this is that perfect ending we all read romance for, this is an absolutely beautifully told love story."—*Guilty Pleasures Book Reviews*

"Very satisfying . . . Stina Lindenblatt is a new author to me and a very good one I may add. . . . I will sure keep an eye on her in the future. She is really worth it!"—*Collector of Book Boyfriends & Girlfriends*

"Filled with emotion, intensity, a lot of sexual tension and the perfect amount of heat."—*About That Story*

ALSO BY STINA LINDENBLATT

COWBOY MOST WANTED

STINA LINDENBLATT

*To the readers who never grow tired
of falling in love with book boyfriends.*

COWBOY MOST WANTED

1

H e who has the best sperm wins the race.

Or so it seems when you're trying to breed future winners of the rodeo circuit. Not just any sperm will do. It has to be the sperm of a winning quarter horse. A champion.

Am I thankful the same rules don't apply to me when it comes to getting laid?

You'd better believe it.

I lean against the wooden fence, forearms folded on the top railing, and watch the three colts chase each other across the pasture. My cowboy hat blocks the late afternoon sun.

Gravel crunches behind me, and I turn to find my two brothers approaching. Behind them are Sophie and Aubrey. Sophie is our brilliant horse trainer. The woman Jake gets a hard-on over—but you didn't hear that from me.

Aubrey is our equally brilliant vet.

Who I grew up with.

She's like a sister to me and my brothers.

The two women are chatting and not paying attention to Jake and Noah. Jake says something to Noah, and my youngest brother laughs. Whatever Noah says in response has Jake laughing even harder.

"What's up?" I ask once they're only a few feet away.

"Nothing," Noah says, still chuckling.

Jake's barely contained smile betrays the laughter still simmering under the surface. He parks himself next to me, gaze on the pasture. Noah props his forearms against the fence, sandwiching me between him and Jake.

Those two are keeping something from me. Possibly something to do with today and their plans for my birthday. A secret that's hopefully nothing like last year's...with the stripper. Named Roxy Bliss.

Formerly known as Robert.

But whatever it is, it's nothing compared to the secret that has poked, poked, poked at me for the past twelve years. A secret that has me lusting over my best friend's sister.

"So, what do you think, TJ?" Jake gestures to the colts. "Are we looking at future winners?" His all-business tone is echoed in the words. The tone he always uses when he talks about the ranch.

"With Thor as their father, how could they not be winners?" I say.

Fortunately for us, my horse isn't the type to settle down with one mare. When it comes to females, he's a player like the three of us. And the more mares he knocks up, the greater the chance we'll end up with future champions.

Jake folds his arms across the top railing. The girls stand on the other side of him and look out at the pasture. He tap-tap-taps the fingers of one hand against the wood. "You think they'll put the ranch on the map?"

"It's already on the map," Noah says. "Just the wrong map when it comes to us being a horse ranch."

"Well, this is what we get for switching from cattle to horses." Jakes uses his I-knew-this-was-a-bad-idea tone. The same tone

I've heard for the past two years, ever since our grandfather died and we inherited the ranch.

"But you have to admit that while Granddad might have lived and breathed and dreamed cattle," I say, "cows were never our passion."

"True—except cattle brought in the money." Jake's words hit straight to the core. Do not pass go. Do not collect two hundred dollars. This is not the first or second or tenth time that he's told us switching to horses was a bad idea.

I push back from the fence. "Give it time, Jake. Thor proved himself as a rodeo champion. We can't do any better than using him to build our reputation."

"Plus he's healthy," Aubrey says. "He's in prime reproductive health."

"Do you usually bring guys to their knees with all that sexy talk?" Noah says with a laugh, next to me.

She grins at him. "Don't you know it?"

"Hope you're right." Jake's tone warns me I'm in for a lifetime of "I told you so" if the ranch doesn't make money.

But he has a point. The ranch is my life. If it goes down, Jake, Noah, and I have no backup plans for our futures. The ranch is our past and our present and our till-death-do-us-part.

Or rather, *I* don't have a backup plan. Jake has a business degree to fall back on.

Noah peers at the blue sky above us. "You think Grandpa's looking down on us, grumbling that we're dumbasses for tossing away all his years of hard work?" He salutes the sky like it's an army general. "You're welcome, old man."

"He's probably thinking he's the dumbass for leaving the ranch to the three of us. He could have just left it to Jake and me to manage while you were off partying."

"At least I was enjoying myself. You turned thirty today, and you're still miserable." Noah's smirk contains a better-you-than-me attitude and I-can't-believe-you're-still-alive awe.

"I'm not miserable."

"Well, you're not happy."

Before I can deny the truth in Noah's words, I catch Jake's expression. The expression claiming Noah has a point. "Sure, I am." I shift my mouth into a two-parts-genuine, one-part-whatever smile. "I'm very happy. Why wouldn't I be happy?"

"You haven't been truly happy since you fucked up your knee," Jake says.

Both Sophie and Aubrey nod in agreement. *Traitors.*

I scowl at my brothers. "You two are beginning to sound like a couple of old women. I don't need to be smiling and laughing and breaking out in song to be happy."

"When exactly was the last time you broke out in song?" Noah doesn't snort a laugh but it's there in his tone.

"What? Am I supposed to spontaneously start dancing too?"

Jake lets out short, loud laugh. "Now *that* I'd like to see."

"So, Mr. Happy, are we still on for tonight?" Noah slaps my back. "Now that you're an old man, you think you'll be able to stay awake long enough to hit the bar?"

"I'm not old."

At what is no doubt a pout in my tone, both men crack up, laughing loud enough to startle a herd of cattle to stampede.

Sophie walks over to me, her long, blonde ponytail shining in the summer sun. She settles her arm on my shoulders. "Don't worry about TJ. If he gets too tired, I'll tuck him in bed."

That gets me a fuck-you glare out of Jake. I return it with a *What-can-you-do?* shrug. Sophie is oblivious to our silent communication.

Her hands are covering her face.

"Oh, God," she groans. "That didn't come out right."

Aubrey and Noah laugh.

"I know what you meant," I tell her—mostly so Jake doesn't clobber me, even though he knows I'm not interested in her.

She's the kind of woman who you imagine one day having a husband and kids and a white picket fence.

That life's not for me.

And it's not for Jake either.

Hence his hard-on problem.

"Good," Noah says, "then you have no excuse. We'll see you tonight." He starts to walk away but then adds over his shoulder, "Eight o'clock. Don't be late."

"What the hell are you guys planning for tonight?" I ask Jake.

He laughs, the sound far from reassuring. "Guess you'll find out tonight." He moves away from the fence and heads toward the stable.

"You know I don't like surprises, right?" I call after him.

"Yeah, might have heard that somewhere." He doesn't even bother to look over his shoulder when he says it.

"Just tell me Roxy Bliss won't be there tonight," I call back.

I climb the bungalow's recently painted porch steps and knock on the front door. From the other side of it, Killer lets out a high-pitched, come-play-with-me bark.

A moment later the door opens, and a bundle of white fuzz comes barreling out. Killer jumps up, parking his paws against my legs, yapping for me to pet him. I oblige the furry little beast's request.

The name Killer? You can thank Noah for that. We bought Grandma Meg the dog for Christmas a few years ago to keep her company. Noah thought it was the perfectly ironic name for something that was quite the opposite.

But when Grandma Meg tried to give the dog a new name, he

gave her a haughty bark, making it clear that there was only one name to which he would respond.

A bright smile slides onto Grandma Meg's face. Her long, gray hair is pulled back into a loose, puffy bun. Stray strands frame her weathered but still-beautiful face. She's wearing loose leggings and an oversized light-blue T-shirt with a cartoon Jersey cow on the front.

Grandma Meg is not really my grandmother, but she might as well be. My brothers and I have known her forever.

I straighten, remove my cowboy hat, and enter the house. The smell of freshly baked chocolate chip cookies greets me.

I've barely crossed the threshold before she throws her arms around me in a massive hug, catching me off guard. I stumble back a step.

"Happy birthday, TJ. I can't believe you're now thirty." She releases me. "Goodness. It feels like just yesterday when you were a little hell-raiser in diapers."

I chuckle, mostly because it's the same speech she gave Austin —her grandson, my best friend—last month when *he* turned thirty. "I can guarantee it's been a long while since I was in diapers."

My gaze shifts to the wall where the photo of Violet still hangs. My best friend's sister. Aubrey's best friend. It was taken over a year ago—ten years after she moved away to attend college.

Memories of when we were growing up replay in my head. Hanging out with her and Austin. Biking together. Swimming in the river. Riding horses. Back when I thought Violet was the coolest girl around. Back before I became aware of her as some-thing more than Austin's little sister.

I've seen that photo so many times, and the reaction is always the same.

My insides twist into a knot—the kind you get when you miss someone.

"She's doing really well," Grandma Meg says. "She's still working for a fancy marketing and publicity firm in LA that specializes in the entertainment industry. She's also been doing some work as a professional photographer."

I smile because even back in high school, Violet's photos were amazing. "I'm not surprised she's doing well. She's worked hard for both."

Grandma Meg's face glows like a peacock on parade. Her smile widens. "I've got a gift Bert left explicit instructions to give you on your thirtieth birthday. But first I have something in the kitchen for you."

The kitchen is bright and cozy, with the white cabinets and the white walls and the white-tiled floor that Austin and I installed last year. The curtains, towels, and seat cushions are a chaos of yellows and blues and florals. It's nothing like the kitchen at the ranch she and Bert lived on when he was still alive, but the place fits Grandma Meg perfectly.

On the table is a big, squishy package. My stomach slouches in my gut, much like it did when I was a kid. Every Christmas. When I got a gift from Grandma Meg.

She hands me the present. "Here, I made it for you."

After saying a quick prayer for the gift not to be as bad as the one from last Christmas, I rip off the wrapping paper and remove the blue cable-knit sweater. Relief rushes through my lungs. The last sweater she knitted for me had a picture of Thor—my horse, not the god—on the front. Decorated with Christmas ornaments.

I still wear it with pride...whenever Grandma Meg is around.

"This looks great. Thanks." I hug her because I am genuinely happy with the gift, even if it is the middle of June.

I release her and my gaze lands on the brochure next to the plate of cookies. Frowning, I reach for it. "Skydiving lessons?"

"Yes. Tilly, Gertrude, and I decided now is a good time to work on our bucket lists."

"Bucket list?" I echo, even though I know what the hell it is.

"Why does an eighty-year-old woman's bucket list include skydiving lessons? And more importantly, does Austin know about it?"

I already know the answer. Do you really think the brochure would be on the table if he did? He would've sped back to his sheriff's office—lights flashing, siren blaring—and shredded it. Several times.

"No, he doesn't. And you, TJ Christopher Daniels, won't be telling him either." She says it in her I-mean-business voice. The same voice she used when I was ten years old, and she caught me smoking.

That was the last time I put a cigarette in my mouth.

Granddad made sure of that.

"Yes, ma'am." I might have said it, but I sure as hell didn't mean it. "But you aren't seriously thinking of taking skydiving lessons, are you?"

She lets out a heavy sigh. "Apparently not. The place has an age restriction, and the girls and I exceed it. Just by a little, mind you. So don't you go thinking that I'm ready to be put out to pasture with the old crows."

A laugh erupts from deep in my chest. "I wouldn't even think about it."

"And if they didn't have the age restriction"—she wags her finger under my nose—"you can guarantee the girls and I would've done it, no matter what my grandson said."

"Even though you could end up breaking every single bone— or worse yet, die?"

"But at least I'd go out with a bang. Well, more likely a splat." She claps her hands, the sound more like a loud slap than a splat.

"It doesn't matter if you go out with a bang or a splat or any other way. Neither Austin nor Violet will appreciate you dying before you're supposed to."

"Ha! Maybe our maker has plans for me to go out in style. Have you even thought of that? And as for my grandson, he's just too protective for his own good...or in this case, for my own good. I can see why he's that way with his sister. But even then, he has to remember Violet's a grown woman. A grown woman with a—" Her words come to an abrupt halt, and her mouth forms an O.

"With a what?"

She waves her hand, as if swatting a fly with the back of it, and shuffles toward the doorway. "Never mind that. Bert's gift is collecting dust as we speak."

I grab a cookie from the plate and follow her from the kitchen. She walks down the hallway with me trailing behind, chomping on the sweet treat.

My gaze flicks to the wall covered with photos. Violet's photos. The photos she took, not the ones she's in. They're action shots taken a few years ago, just before the accident that ended my rodeo career. I'm riding Thor as he gallops toward the calf I'm about to lasso.

Pretending I don't notice the photo, I enter the guest room. I miss competing almost as much as I miss Violet. It's hard seeing those photos without feeling like regret has kicked me in the nuts. With spurs on.

The same piles of unopened boxes that have been here since Grandma Meg moved into the cottage five years ago still crowd the room. There's also a twin bed with floral bedding and a few antique pieces from the old ranch house.

Grinning her mother-bear smile, she points to a medium-sized cardboard box on the floor. "It's in there."

I kneel, my bad knee telling me to go to hell. Nothing new there. It's been that way since the accident. It doesn't always act up, but after a hard day of work, it's as grumpy as a bull in a hailstorm.

I place the sweater on the floor, open the flaps, and peer inside. The pain in my knee is instantly forgotten.

No.

Fucking.

Way.

"Is this for real?" I remove the old Thor Marvel comics one by one from the box. Yes, I'm a Norse mythology freak—and these comics are responsible for that.

"Bert knew how much you loved them," Grandma Meg says.

"But why wait until I'm thirty?"

"No idea. Even after being married to him for forty-six years, I didn't always know what he was thinking. But I do know he was hoping that one day you'd share these comics with your own kids."

My laugh comes out as a God-you're-hilarious snort, and I straighten to my feet. "He definitely got that wrong. There won't be any kids in my future."

Her eyes go wide, crinkles forming across her brow. It's the early warning signal that I'm in for a lecture: the sweet-grandma-guilt-you-up-the-ass lecture. "How can you say that?"

Has she asked her own grandson that question lately? He and I are both in the We're-never-going-to-be-fathers club—new members always welcome.

"Because I'm not interested in settling down."

"And why not? You're young and virile. What woman wouldn't want you?"

"I have a busy ranch to manage. I don't have time for a girl-friend." I kneel again next to the box of comics, set the sweater on top of it, and stand, hoisting it all in my arms. I head for the bedroom door.

"Why?" Grandma Meg says from behind me as I walk down the hallway. "Because it didn't work out with She Who Shall Not Be Named?"

I can't help but grin. It's a very apt name. My ex-girlfriend and Harry Potter's nemesis have a lot in common. Although in Katherine's case, the last I heard, she's married to some tech whiz in Silicon Valley.

Killer barks.

"See—even Killer thinks my single status is a good idea." I pause at the front door.

The little white fluff ball barks again.

"No, what Killer said is, you should sing at the senior center during our next bingo night."

"I don't sing," I deadpan.

Grandma Meg rolls her eyes like she's a teenager instead of a senior citizen. "Remember, I've known you since you were in diapers, TJ. I know you sing. You have a beautiful singing voice."

"That still doesn't mean I sing." At least not in public.

"That's too bad. Violet always loved it when you sang."

I ignore her—while battling the urge to look at Violet's photo.

Too bad my heart and cock rule my brain at the most inopportune times.

Traitors.

2
____

"What do you think?" Jake asks as he and I study the computer screen. It's been four weeks of avoiding Grandma Meg's house and Violet's picture on the wall.

Four weeks of not jerking off in the shower because I knew I'd be thinking of Violet if I did.

All right—there might have been the one time last week.

And a few times before that.

But I swear I wasn't imagining Violet's sweet lips trailing down my pecs, down my abs that flexed and relaxed at her touch, down the V formation leading to my cock.

I wasn't imagining her tongue licking the sensitive spot under the head. And I wasn't imagining her lips wrapped around my superhard length.

My dick twitches at the memory of what I hadn't imagined, and I mentally curse myself for going there.

My birthday party? It was uneventful—so I'll spare you the details.

Jake is sitting at the antique oak desk in front the picturesque window. It's the same antique oak desk and antique oak furni-

12

ture, the same deep burgundy curtains and deep burgundy rug that have resided in the office since Granddad was alive.

For the past few minutes, Jake and I have been clicking through the pages of our website.

"It's boring," I say on a sigh.

"Exactly. It worked fine for Granddad. He'd already earned a reputation in cattle ranching long before websites were necessary." And long before social media was a thing. As it is, none of us have social media accounts. We don't have time for them.

And it's not like we need Instagram accounts to get laid.

Jake enters "Scottsdale Ranch, Montana"—our rival—into the search engine and clicks on the link. The website pops up on the computer screen.

And shit, it's good. Better than good.

I lean in closer to the screen. "Do you think if we update ours, it will make that much of a difference?"

Jake heaves an I-knew-this-was-a-mistake sigh that has nothing to do with the website. "It couldn't hurt. But it definitely won't be enough to get the word out about our ranch. We need to do something bigger. Something that will get us noticed."

True. "The best way to do that is to have our horses compete in rodeo events and consistently win. We have the champion sperm, thanks to Thor and Odin. It will just take time to get there."

At sperm, my cock sends an SOS message, reminding me just how long it's been since my last fuck. The rate I'm going, I'll die of a brutal case of blue balls in no time. Won't that make quite the RIP on my gravestone?

Jake opens his mouth to say something—the something I recognize in his expression. It's the look he always gets when he's about to try to convince Noah and me to switch back to cattle.

I don't give him a chance to speak. "And if worse comes to worse, I can return to the rodeo circuit and prove how great our horses are."

Jake gives me a dubious smile. "So, how's the old knee doing?"

"It's fine."

"Right, it is. You know what the doctor said would happen if you blow your knee out again."

"That I'm fucked." Not his exact words—but the sentiment was the same. "Fine, we'll call that plan B."

"What's plan A?"

I go back to studying the screen. "You'll be the first to know once I figure it out....The good news is, Sophie said two of the colts show promise."

I glance at Jake in time to see his face soften at her name. It's my secret weapon that works every time. With Jake.

"And in the meantime, we need to fix our website." I gesture toward the computer, with the Scottsdale Ranch website still on the screen. "But I'd prefer to hire someone from town than to trust it to a stranger online."

"Any suggestions?"

"Not a one. But we can get word out that we're looking for someone." I back away from the desk, only for a scary thought to stop me. "And it's probably best we don't hire anyone who you, Noah, or I have screwed. The last thing we need is to give a woman who was hoping for more than a one-night stand access to our account. Who knows what might happen?"

"Good point."

I turn to leave. "If you need me, I'll be in my workroom."

"Sounds good. Oh, before I forget, Noah called and said there's something he needs to discuss with us. He said it's really important."

I glance over my shoulder in time to catch Jake's *God-what-kind-of-trouble-did-he-get-into-now?* expression.

With Noah, it could be anything.

"How did he sound?" I ask. "Was he happy, or did it sound like he was shitting his pants?"

"Ecstatic."

"Shit. That can't be good."

"Don't I know it."

MY FAVORITE SCENT AFTER THAT OF STRAW, HAY, AND HORSES IS THE sweet smell of freshly cut wood. Maybe that's why I prefer spending the evenings in my workroom, located in an old hut on our property.

With my goggles on, I grab the fine sandpaper and rub it along the wood grain of the horse's leg. The rocking horse is big enough for a five-year-old child. Or a five-year-old girl, in this case.

I continue sanding until the wood is smooth, blowing away the sawdust that clings to it as I work. Then I clean the wood and apply the conditioner.

An hour or so later, someone knocks on the door as I'm staining the wood dark brown.

Without looking up, I call out, "Come in."

The door softly creaks open and I glance up.

Noah is in the doorway, Jake behind him. "Is this a good time?" Noah asks.

"Sure." I lay the brush on top of the can as they enter my cave. Only those with man cards are permitted inside.

"Who's that for?" Jake points at the wooden horse.

"Katie Higgins. Her mom wants to surprise her when she comes home from chemo tomorrow. I just have to varnish it."

Noah bends down and picks up a toddler-sized rocking horse. "Who's this one for?"

"No one yet. I'd planned to finish it, so Grandma Meg could show it at the farmer's market last weekend, but I didn't have time."

Noah's eyebrow lifts. "You do realize we are trying to gain a reputation as horse breeders, right? Shouldn't we be marketing our real horses instead of your wooden ones?"

"Hey, don't mock my strategy for gaining future customers. In a few years, the kids with my rocking horses will be wanting a real horse, and we'll be ready for them." I was joking, but now that I think about it, it's not a bad idea. "I just need to include a plaque on the rockers, so the kids know where they got the horse from. It's a brilliant plan." I give Noah a smug grin, daring him to come up with something better.

"Fortunately, I came up with a fucking awesome idea to promote the ranch, and it will give us results much sooner."

I look at Jake. He shrugs, appearing as clueless as I feel.

"So, what's the idea?" I ask.

"Ever heard of *The Bachelorette*?"

"Isn't that the female version of a bachelor party?"

"I'm talking about the reality show."

Both Jake and I give him an identical expression. The *What-the-fuck?* expression.

"Exactly how many reality shows do you think we have time for?" I ask. That's zero, in case you're wondering.

"It's the show where the hot chick spends time getting to know twenty-five single men. At the end of each episode, she selects the men who will continue on to the next one. At the end of the season, one man is left, and he proposes to her."

"Do I even want to know how you know this?" Jake asks at the same time as I say, "What kind of desperate idiot does that?"

"Sophie told me about it," Noah explains.

"All right," I say, "we've established that of the three of us, you're the one holding the estrogen card. But what does this have to do with promoting the ranch?"

"Because Sophie told me about a new reality show."

"That's it...no more talking to Sophie for you." Grinning, I smack him on the arm.

He ignores me and powers on. "It's called *Cowboy Most Wanted*. The idea is that the star of the show—a hot chick like on the other show—wants to fall in love with a cowboy. The production crew will go to the ranch of each participating cowboy, and spend a few days there, filming him in action. The viewers then vote which cowboys should go on to the next round."

"That's nice," Jake says in a tone implying that what Noah told us is anything but nice; Jake is just humoring him. "But what does that have to do with anything?"

That's when I put it all together. "You're seriously thinking of applying to be on the show?"

"I figured it would be great publicity for the ranch," Noah says, once again ignoring me. Warning sirens blare in my head, but apparently Noah isn't the only one good at ignoring things.

"Even if the contestant doesn't go all the way to the finals," he adds, "the ranch will be showcased. And if he does go all the way, it could lead to social media brand endorsements, which can only further benefit the ranch."

"Except, how do you know that viewers who want horses will be watching the show?" More than likely, Noah has come up with a new way to get laid. A brilliant way, if he's lucky.

"It's not guaranteed, but nothing in life ever is."

Jake laughs. "You sound like Granddad."

"That's because both Granddad and I are geniuses. Or was in his case."

"Well, genius boy." Jake slaps Noah's back with enough unexpected force to cause Noah to take a step forward. "The odds of being selected are pretty slim. Do you have any idea how many cowboys will be applying?"

"No, but I'm guessing thousands," Noah says. "Of course, most won't qualify because the show is searching for good-looking men. The hotter the better."

At least Noah will get points for that. No one can claim he's not good-looking.

"When do you find out if you made it in?" I ask.

"They've already contacted me."

"And?"

The corners of his mouth tug up in a smooth movement. It's the smile I recognize. The smile that is the equivalent to a huge neon sign. It warns you that his news is about to flip your world upside down and inside out—and not always in a good way.

Noah holds out a piece of paper to me. "Congratulations, TJ. You're a contestant on *Cowboy Most Wanted*."

My stomach nose-dives onto the sawdust-covered floor.

Holy fuck.

3

I pull away, as if the paper in Noah's hand is a glowing hot branding iron, and pace around the room. I want to yell at him. I want to shake some goddamn sense into him. I want to strangle him.

The overhead light in my workroom flickers. Despite the sweet smell of pine in the air that usually soothes me, a forest fire burns inside me—complete with scurrying woodland critters trying to escape its rage.

My gaze darts to Jake. "Did you know anything about this?" But even before the words stomp from my mouth, I know the answer.

It's painted on his face like graffiti.

Jake shakes his head. "No, I had no idea what he was up to."

"Why the hell me?" I ask Noah. "Why not you?"

He answers with his patented Your-guess-is-as-good-as-mine shrug. "Because you're the oldest."

"That's your fucking excuse?"

"Sounds like a good reason to me." Noah grins. "Look, I swear once you hear me out, you'll realize I'm right."

I doubt that. "Right about what?"

"That you being on the reality show will help us. It will help the ranch."

"Help us?" I intone.

"Help us put the ranch on the map."

Both Jake and I exchange looks.

"What the fuck are you talking about?" Jake asks, echoing my own thoughts.

"We agreed that we need to do something to get our name out there—"

"Right, to get our name out as a ranch that sells winning horses." My tone is as tight as a glued-shut jelly jar. "Not so we can become the butt of a joke."

"You won't be a joke, TJ," Noah says.

"Yes, because the reality show will gain me a shit-load of respect."

"I think you're looking at this the wrong way," he says.

"There's another way?" Jake asks. I can't tell if he's amused or siding with me or inwardly doing cartwheels that Noah didn't submit *his* name for the show.

"*Cowboy Most Wanted* could do big things for us," Noah says. "And it's a lot cheaper than anything else that might get our name seen. Millions of viewers could potentially watch it...like with the other reality shows similar to it."

"He has a point," Jake says.

Easy for him to say.

"Great, then *you* do it."

Jake chuckles. "Hey, keep me out of this. You guys wanted to switch to horses when I thought it was a bad idea. So it's only fair that the unlucky contestant is one of you two."

All I can say is, those two had better watch out. It won't take much for me to accidentally spill a bottle of hot sauce in their chili tomorrow—when it's my night to cook.

I turn to Noah. "What makes you so sure the viewers are even looking to buy a horse?"

"I'm not saying we'll get rich. But you never know. This might lead to the word-of-mouth we need. I looked at the demographics for *The Bachelor* and *The Bachelorette*. They're impressive."

"What do you mean impressive?" Jake asks, always the businessman.

"A high percentage of the viewers come from households with an excellent annual income. Those viewers might not want to participate in rodeos, but some of them might be interested in owning a horse. We can't just rely on the rodeo circuit to market our horses."

Which is something we already know.

"As for why Jake or I can't do it..." Noah says, "the show's producers picked you, TJ. They didn't pick me, and they didn't pick Jake. They picked *you*."

"Are you saying you also submitted your name and his?" I point at Jake.

"Well, no. I only submitted yours. No point in us looking desperate."

"Yeah, heaven forbid that ever happens." I shove my fingers through my hair, mostly to keep them from going around his neck. For now. "So, what? You just woke up one morning and decided to submit my name for the show because—what? You were fucking bored?"

His mouth twists into a smirk, and I upgrade my desire from strangling him to punching him in the face. Let's see what the women think when he's missing a few teeth.

"For your information," he says. "I wasn't bored that morning. Fucking, yes. Bored, no."

I don't even want to know who he was screwing. Like Jake and I, Noah isn't interested in settling down.

"But why the hell submit *my* name?" I say in what comes out as a growl. Satisfaction slithers through me at his sheepish reaction. *Good, I can work with that.* "What was wrong with submitting your name? And don't give me that crap about me being the oldest."

"It can't be me," Noah says. "I'm not looking at settling down."

I fist my hands on my hips to keep from grabbing the paint brush and drawing a brown stripe across his face. Immature? Possibly. But you can't say he doesn't deserve it. "And when exactly did I say I want to settle down?"

"Really? Because the way I remember it, you had a serious girlfriend at one point. Sounds to me like you were willing to settle down."

"A serious girlfriend who I found in your arms one day, kissing you. Or are you forgetting *that*?"

He cringes at the not-so-pleasant reminder. Score one for me. "I told you it wasn't my fault. Katherine was the one who came on to me, not the other way around."

I slap my forehead. "That's right. How could I be such an idiot?" There's more sarcasm in that than there is horseshit in the stable. "I forgot how you were pushing her away and telling her 'no.' "

He grimaces at that reminder, too. He had done nothing to dissuade her. He had been getting into it as much as she was.

"How many times do I have to tell you why I did that?" He's not mad, just exasperated.

I on the other hand...

"Right, because you thought I didn't deserve her."

"Damn straight you didn't deserve her. You're a helluva lot better than Katherine will ever be. You just didn't want to see it."

If this were a boxing match, he just scored a direct hit. He's right. I didn't want to see any of that. Like Violet, Katherine never had the desire to stay in Copper Creek permanently. Like Violet, she never had the desire to be a rancher's wife.

Katherine saw my being an up-and-coming rodeo-circuit star as her eventual ticket out of town—with me going with her.

Noah raises his hands like a criminal caught stealing fruit-flavored condoms. "Look, I realize now that I handled it badly. I could have told her to fuck off when she came on to me. You're my brother, and you'll always come first. I thought I was doing you a favor." He grins—a warning that we're about to be hit by Noah Logic. "And you have to admit, I did do you a favor. If you ended up marrying her, your marriage was already doomed to fail. At least I saved you from paying alimony."

That's Noah for you—always finding the twisted bright side to everything.

"Okay, so you did me a favor with the whole Katherine fiasco. But where the hell did you get the impression I want to settle down? She was my girlfriend. That's all. We weren't engaged or married. And where the hell did you get the idea I'd want to marry a screwed-up version of a mail-order bride?" I fold my arms, my muscles overwound rubber bands, ready to snap at even the slightest breeze.

Noah makes a sound that's a cross between a grunt and a groan. "She's not a mail-order bride."

I don't say anything. I just narrow my eyes at him.

He shifts on his feet and sidesteps, possibly inching his way to the door, and lets out a long hard breath. "Because this ranch means as much to you as it does to Jake and me. Maybe even more so. Jake and I have options if we decide to walk away from it. What do you have?"

He has a point there, but that doesn't mean I have to like it.

And it doesn't mean I have to do the show. I'll find another way to save the ranch.

I snatch up the paintbrush and stalk to the sink. "You'll just have to tell the producers that after some consideration, I'm withdrawing my application."

Problem solved.

"Can't do that."

"Fine, then I'll do it." I turn the water on a little too forcefully. *Clunk eek boom* is the only warning I get before my T-shirt becomes a casualty of this discussion. Cold water sprays at me from the tap and seeps through the fabric.

Fuck.

"Because there's no way in hell I'm going through with it," I say without missing a beat...and as if my T-shirt isn't clinging to my abs.

Both brothers snicker but are smart enough to contain their laughter.

"You don't have any choice in the matter," Noah says.

"Sure, I do." I don't bother looking at him as I focus on cleaning the brush.

"Not unless you want to be sued."

My head jerks around and I glare over my shoulder. "Why would they sue me for changing my mind?"

"Because it's in the contract you signed."

My gut sinks faster than Thor's hammer in quicksand.

I spin around to face Noah so rapidly, I'm surprised the friction between my boots and the wooden floor doesn't spark a fire. "I didn't sign a contract." How could I have signed a contract for something I didn't enter?

The realization as to who did sign it hits me, and my gut finishes its descent to the floor. "You forged my signature?" And more importantly, how many other times has he done that?

Noah snorts. "As if I can forge that mess. No, you signed it yourself."

"No, I didn't." I would remember something like that, and I definitely wouldn't have signed it.

"Sure you did, but you were in a rush and didn't bother to read what you were signing." He shakes a finger at me. "You really should read everything you sign. You never know when someone is trying to screw you over."

Given the circumstances, what are the odds the Montana courts will let me off on justified homicide if I strangle my brother? Because right now, that's exactly what I'm planning to do.

"Why don't I remember signing it?"

"You might have been a little distracted at the time. I told you it was for horse feed, and you signed it."

"And you saw nothing wrong with lying?"

"I was thinking about how this would benefit the ranch."

I can only roll my eyes at that. "Let me get this straight…if I win, I have to get married? And that's in the contract?"

"It only states that the winner agrees to propose to the woman after she chooses him. And I did some research on the other two shows. Most of the couples split up a few months after the final episode airs. They don't get married. At least not to each other."

Jake rubs his thumb against his jaw—the look he gets when he's contemplating something. Except in this case, I have a feeling I won't like what he's considering.

"It might work," he says.

"What will work?" I ask.

"This lame-brained scheme of his." He nods at Noah. "It might be worth a try. What's the worst that can happen?"

I raise an eyebrow with a silent *Do-you-really-want-me-to-answer-that?*

Right—I thought not.

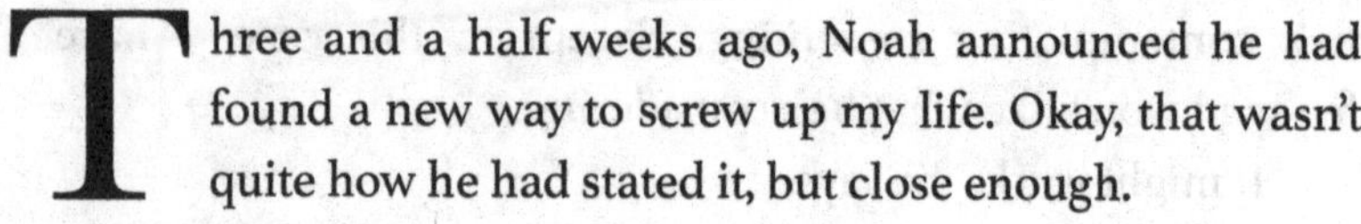

4

Three and a half weeks ago, Noah announced he had found a new way to screw up my life. Okay, that wasn't quite how he had stated it, but close enough.

Dread now plays an out-of-tune wedding march in my veins. The day I had prayed would never come is unfortunately here.

The good news? Well, for Noah anyway. I haven't tried to kill him. Yet.

It's still early.

Usually, riding Thor soothes me. But not this time. This time as my horse walks along the path to the ranch house, I'm feeling the opposite of soothed.

Normally, I love the two-story house my brothers and I live in. Stucco and stone and wood and windows comprise the building that is as grand as the Bitterroot Mountains. I spent so much time here as a kid, it felt like home even before it officially became our home.

Yes, normally I love this house—but right now, it looms ahead of me like a carnival funhouse. A carnival funhouse complete with a scary-ass clown.

A group of cars and vans that weren't on the long, curved

driveway a few hours ago are parked there now. We stop our horses several yards from the edge of the driveway.

"You ready for this?" Jake gestures to the group with a nod.

"They're early." I dismount from Thor. What I really want to do is turn around and gallop off. Become a mountain hermit for a few months. Anything to escape this.

Jake laughs down at me from his saddle. "Try not to sound too excited about meeting the people who are introducing you to your future wife."

I glare at him with a grunt. "You're not as funny as you think."

That causes him to laugh harder. "Sophie seems to think I'm funny."

"I'd say that's because she's an idiot, but lightning might strike me for lying." The last thing anyone can call Sophie is an idiot. She's smart as all hell. "So...I'm going with horse manure must have temporarily messed with her brain."

That would also explain her reaction whenever she sees me since she found out I'm participating in the reality show. Every time she looks in my direction, she bursts out laughing. The same deal with Aubrey.

"Guess I should get this over with. The sooner we start this, the sooner they can leave."

"Just remember what's at stake here," Jake says, dismounting from Orion.

"My sanity?"

"No—that I'm sure you lost a while ago. I'm referring to our reputation. I've been watching old episodes of the other two shows and reading about them in general." Holding Orion's reins, he walks around the front of his horse to join me between Orion and Thor. "The producers like to turn some contestants into villains, even though in real life they're nothing like how the show portrays them. The last thing we need is for the producers to paint you as an asshole."

"Is it too late to kill Noah?"

He laughs again. This time the level of humor isn't quite what it was before. It's taken a quick dip in the pool of reality. "Probably."

Jake and I lead our horses over to the group. Asgard, my two-year-old Aussie shepherd, follows next to me.

By the time we reach the driveway, everyone is out of their vehicles and convening as a group, along with Noah, in front of a black car.

Well, not everyone.

"Hey, what are you two doing here?" I ask Sophie and Aubrey as they walk up to us.

With Sophie, it's not a big surprise that she's here. She works at the ranch. But as far as I know, Aubrey should be at her clinic.

"We're here to be supportive friends," Sophie says, grinning. It's Aubrey's smile that has me frowning. It's one of those smug I-know-something-you-don't-know smiles she used to give me when we were teens.

The one that always surfaced right before I got in trouble at school.

"Why do I have a hard time believing that?" I say.

"All right, we're curious as hell."

"You do remember what happened to the curious cat, don't you?" I mime a slicing motion across my neck.

Both women laugh. "I'm sure we'll survive," Aubrey says.

The sole woman with the group on the driveway is nothing like Sophie or Aubrey—nor is she similar to the girls who hang out at Joe's and the rodeos, hoping to hook up with a cowboy. She's wearing a tight, gray skirt that stops just above her knees, a white blouse, and heels. Her light blonde hair is pulled back in a low bun. She looks like she'd be more comfortable in an office than on a ranch.

Jake gives a low whistle of appreciation, unheard by the group on the driveway or by Sophie and Aubrey. "I don't suppose that's your intended bride."

"Thought I wasn't meeting her unless I make it to the next round."

"Maybe she changed her mind about waiting. She certainly seems to like what she sees." He chuckles, keeping the smirk in his laugh off his face.

Asshole.

But he's right about the way she's checking me out. Her gaze slowly skims up my body: boots, jeans, black T-shirt, and cowboy hat. She gives a slight nod, as if answering a question in her head.

She then says something to Noah. I can almost imagine him rubbing his hands in glee at how his dumbass plan is coming together. I bet Violet, with her marketing degree, wouldn't have dreamed up anything as crazy as this.

The woman's gaze lands on Asgard, and she takes a wary step back. "Oh, what an adorable dog."

From her reaction, you'd think she was expecting him to turn into a doggy vampire, launch himself at her, and dig his fangs into her neck. Instead, he barks his agreement that he is indeed an adorable dog and sits.

He glances up at me, with his typical doggy grin, waiting for me to agree with her.

"Yes, Asgard," I say on a sigh and scratch him behind the ear. "You're an adorable dog."

He barks again, pleased.

"Asgard?" the blonde says. "Isn't that from the movie *Thor*?"

"It's from Norse mythology." My gaze flicks to Noah. His eyes are slightly wide, and he gives a small shake of his head. In other words, he never mentioned my love of Norse mythology on the application, and he never mentioned my love of Marvel comics.

Because what grown man still reads comics?

Ignoring Noah's warning, I rub Thor's muzzle. "And this is Thor."

The stallion nods his head and whinnies at her. The woman

lifts an eyebrow—possibly because of his reaction or because of his name.

"That's his way of saying hi," I explain. "He can be a bit of a flirt." Especially when it comes to Sophie and Aubrey.

"Well, hi to you, too," she says to him, then extends her hand to me. "I'm Camilla Collins, the show's creator and one of the co-producers."

I shake her hand and introduce her to Jake, Sophie, and Aubrey. In turn, Camilla introduces me to the director and the group of eight or so men standing behind them. All are dressed in either jeans or shorts and sneakers. None look like they've grown up on a ranch.

They're the crew who will be following me around for the next seven days. "...showing the world how sexy you are," Camilla says with a confident smile.

The eyes of some of the men mock me with a better-you-than-me smirk. I'd be surprised if my own don't say, *I'd rather jab my foot with a pitchfork than do this.*

But since I need my feet so I can do my job—and sticking a pitchfork into my foot won't help promote the ranch—I don't have a choice but to suck it up.

And spend the next seven days cursing Noah.

"We want you to just go about your normal day-to-day routines and ignore the camera," Camilla explains.

"That's it?"

"I'll also be interviewing you so that Natalie and the audience can get to know you better. Plus we have a photographer who will be shooting both action shots and portraits of you, to post on our website and social media sites."

I fire Jake a look that can be roughly translated as, *I bet their website is a helluva lot better than ours.*

"Do you usually wear T-shirts while working?" Camilla asks matter-of-factly. She says it at the same moment the sound of a car engine yanks my attention away. I glance to see who's coming up the driveway but don't recognize the vehicle.

"That would be our photographer." Camilla gives the driver a friendly wave.

The car parks behind a white van and the driver cuts the engine. The door opens, and the driver climbs out.

Holy. Shit.

At the sight of the woman who I've secretly wished for the past few years would move back to Copper Creek, my heart picks up its pace...and my cock says, *Hot damn!*

5

I've never done drugs.

Okay, let me change that to, I've never done illegal drugs—the kinds of drugs that alter your perception of reality. I've never felt the need to.

But at this moment, my first thought is that God has rolled a massive joint and is blowing smoke in my face.

That's the only explanation for why Violet is standing there, wearing cowboy boots and a lacy white dress that reveals mouth-watering long legs. Long legs that when I was a teen caused many a morning wood.

It's all a delusion.

And since it is just a delusion, why shouldn't I get to enjoy it some more?

I go back to checking out the view.

Violet's shiny brown hair brushes against her bare shoulders. The hair I long to run my fingers through, to see if it feels as soft as it looks. The shoulders I crave to kiss, to lick, to taste.

Around her waist is the gift I gave her for her seventeenth birthday: a western leather belt with a horse's head engraved on the buckle. In retrospect, the gift might not have been a good idea

—if Austin's comments back then were any indication. After he witnessed her innocently kissing my cheek, he pulled me aside and interrogated me. Interrogated me as to why I gave her the present. Interrogated me as to my intentions when it came to his sister—only he didn't state it quite so nicely.

And then he made it clear what he would do to me if my thoughts about her were less than brotherly.

That was before he spent eight years in the military.

I'm sure he has since added to the list. Added newly acquired torture techniques. All with the Navy SEALs' stamp of approval.

Let the fun times commence.

"This should be interesting," Jake says, low enough so only I hear him. His tone is sitting on the fence. Cracking up is on one side, concern on the other. And right now, his tone is tottering more on the laughter side of things. "And by the way, you might want to close your mouth before it fills up with horseflies."

I snap my mouth shut.

Guess that clarifies some stuff. I'm not suffering from a delusion.

I wished that Violet would return to Copper Creek and *bam!* My wish came true.

Except...I also prayed that the show would be canceled. So maybe my guardian angel or fairy godmother—or whatever the heck it is—is only a rookie. She could only finagle the first wish.

Oh, well. One out of two ain't half-bad.

"What should be interesting?" I ask, unable to take my eyes off Violet, even though my brain is screeching, *Mayday, mayday, mayday* and demanding I look away.

"TJ," Camilla says before Jake can reply. "This is Violet Brooks, our super talented photographer. Violet, this is our cowboy, TJ Daniels, and his brothers, Jake and Noah." She points to each of them in turn.

That explains why Aubrey is here. She and Violet have been

best friends as long as Austin and I have been the same. She knew Violet was part of the TV crew.

"We actually know each other," Violet says. "TJ has been my brother's best friend since we were kids." Her gorgeous brown eyes, alive with flecks of amber, slide to me—and just like that, my knees have trouble remembering their function.

She smiles. Christ, how could I have forgotten what her smile does to me? Between that and those eyes, I'm surprised I remember how to speak.

Wait—I do remember how to speak, right?

"It's great seeing you again." *Yes!* I can still form a coherent sentence.

"You too." She steps in for a hug and wraps her arms around my shoulders. Her breasts press against my chest, and I inwardly groan. Luckily, Austin isn't here to witness this, or else the reality show would have some serious entertainment for its viewers.

My arms loop around her and threaten to never let go.

"I can't believe how long it's been since I last saw you," she says so only I can hear her. Her arms remain around my neck. "I've missed you."

"I've missed you, too. I was beginning to think the only way I'd ever see you again would be if I went to LA."

The feel of her soft body against mine and the smell of her vanilla and rose perfume sparks a memory I've kept close all these years.

I had gone to her house to hang out with Austin. He was held up at his grandfather's ranch, where he was working that summer. I was nineteen; Violet was seventeen.

She was dating a guy at the time. Some loser, if memory serves me correct. They were supposed to go out that night, but the dumbass forgot and stood her up for his buddies.

Violet was sitting on the porch steps, her shoulders slouched forward, her heart in her hand. I sat next to her, and she told me what happened.

"What's wrong with me?" she whispered once she was finished.

My heart pinched at her words. How could she even believe for a second that something was wrong with her? Everything about her was right. The way she smelled like vanilla and roses. The way the world seemed a thousand times brighter whenever she smiled. The way she made *me* smile even when I was having a crappy day.

But I couldn't tell her any of this.

Not if I valued my life and my friendship with Austin.

So I did the second best thing: I hugged her.

It only lasted a few seconds, but the memory of it has clung to me all these years like well-chewed gum on the bottom of your boot.

I reluctantly release Violet, who goes on to hug Jake and Noah.

Camilla's face lights up. "You must have some juicy stories about TJ growing up," she says to Violet. "What was he like?"

Amusement flares briefly in Violet's eyes. But it's gone too quickly for Camilla to notice. I only recognize it because I'm more than familiar with those juicy stories. Stories my old teacher Miss Truby would be delighted to share—if she was still with us.

Although now that I think about it, Miss H *is* still around. She was my high school English teacher.

Jake's warning from earlier comes back for an encore.

Note to self: Make sure Camilla doesn't track down Miss H. If my old teacher is given the chance to talk about my mischief-making days, I'm sure I'll be painted as the villain on the TV show. While that would be a great way to avoid advancing to the next round, it won't help us promote the ranch.

For a moment, Violet seems to consider Camilla's question. "I'm assuming he hasn't changed much since back then." Her gaze sweeps over my body, much like Camilla's did earlier. Except when her eyes land on my face, there's a heat in them that wasn't in Camilla's.

But then it flickers away faster than a flame in a blizzard, and I can't be a hundred percent certain I didn't imagine it. I mean, we're talking about Violet. I've never been anything but a big brother to her.

I brush the heat in her eyes off as nothing more than a hallucination—a hallucination brought on by seeing her again after she's been away for so long.

Sounds like a reasonable explanation, right?

"He's a sweet, hardworking man who is liked by everyone." The corners of Violet's mouth twitch up.

I choke back a laugh at the "sweet" part. I can't remember anyone ever describing me as that. I'm not an asshole, but I'm about as sweet as frills are manly.

I'm not the only one trying to keep from laughing. Jake is rubbing his hand across his mouth, as if erasing the laugh lurking there.

Thor nickers—giving into *his* need to laugh. And to remind me that he's still standing there, and if I'm not riding him now, he would like to check on his mares.

"Jake and I need to tend to our horses." And maybe after that, I can leap into the cold river. Because if I don't do that soon, everyone is going to discover the effect Violet has on me.

Not to mention, jumping into the cold river might knock some sense into me. I need to play things cool. No point revealing just how much I've missed her friendship and her humor.

No point revealing how much I crave seeing if her lips are as soft as I've imagined they would be.

"How about Noah gets you all settled in the meantime?" I say.

Camilla and several members of the crew are staying with us for the week—another surprise that Noah sprung on us a few days ago.

The rest of them will be in Copper Creek's one and only hotel. Thank God for that.

And when I say hotel, I'm referring to the tiny hotel in the heart of downtown. Hence the reason some of the crew has to stay at the ranch.

A new thought almost levels me onto my ass. Does the list of guests at the ranch include Violet? Having a house full of people keen on videotaping my every move will be bad enough; having the girl who I'm not supposed to touch stay under the same roof will be a new lesson in torture.

"You have a gorgeous place," Camilla says, admiring the two-story building with the wraparound porch, large picturesque windows, and the pointed roofs over the various wings that comprise the upper level.

"It was our grandparents' home before they died. Jake, Noah, and I inherited it and the ranch."

Our grandmother had died ten years before that, and for whatever reason, Granddad never willed it to his only living child. Deep down, he was probably still angry that she hadn't married Walter Scottsdale's son like Granddad and Walter had planned.

That was back before the ranches became rivals. Back when our ranch focused exclusively on cattle and theirs on horses.

"Did you live here while you were growing up?" Camilla asks.

"No, we lived on the other side of town." In a small but nice house.

"Do your parents still live there?"

"No, they moved to Helena a few years ago when my mom was offered a nursing job there."

"What does your father do?"

"He's an author of thrillers."

That was another point against Dad as far as Granddad was concerned. Being an author wasn't a job for real men—as Granddad liked to frequently point out.

"Are you telling us that Christopher Daniels—*The* Christopher Daniels—is your father?" Wilson the director asks, practically fanning himself in excitement at that little detail.

"That would be him."

"Can Noah deal with your horse while you show us around, TJ?" Apparently Camilla doesn't share the same enthusiasm as Wilson about my father's career and books.

But if showing them around means I get to talk to Violet, then I'm all for it.

Even better if it means getting to kiss her senseless.

But since I know that won't be part of the tour, I open my mouth to suggest Noah show them around instead.

"That's a great idea," he says, halting my words before they can form. He flashes me a dog-eat-dog grin.

Asshole.

It's only then that I realize a large portable camera is perched on one man's shoulder. Guess that means the tour will be videotaped.

My gut clenches into a tight fist, reminding me how much I hated doing interviews back when I was competing. It's not that I sounded like an idiot in them. I didn't. It's just I had better things to use my adrenaline high on than being interviewed on TV.

I hand Noah Thor's reins. "Did you know Violet was part of the show?" My voice is low enough so no one else can hear me.

I don't have to ask Aubrey if she knew. Of course she knew. The question is why didn't she tell me?

Noah chuckles, the sound a quiet rumble. "Not at all. But it will definitely make things more interesting," he says, echoing Jake's earlier comment.

"Interesting for who exactly?"

"I guess we'll find out soon enough." And with that, he and Jake lead the horses back to the stable. Sophie joins them.

Shit. Has Noah figured out my illegal feelings toward Austin's sister? Right, they aren't technically illegal. But try telling that to Austin, the town's sheriff.

Mr. Follow-The-Rules might not feel the same way.

Aubrey, who has been grinning like the cat who ate a pet store's worth of canaries, tells Violet that she'll call her later and leaves.

I gesture for the group to walk up the porch steps. Violet is ahead of me, chatting with one of the men. I'd like to say that jealousy doesn't pitchfork me in the ass, but that would not be accurate.

So instead, I appreciate her fine ass from behind. It's better than I remember. Rounder.

Sweeter.

Now, that's a more appropriate use of the adjective than what Violet used sweet for.

An image flashes in my head of me pounding into her from behind, of her sweet pussy devouring my cock, and I barely keep from groaning out loud.

No more looking at her ass. Move your eyes away from her ass.

My eyes do a piss-poor job of listening to my brain.

We step into the house and I begin the tour: The main foyer large enough to party in. The grand living room with the huge stone fireplace. The numerous windows spanning two walls. The dark, honey-colored overhead support beams with the matching ceiling and floor. The iron chandelier above the dark green couch that forms an L-shape in the middle of the room.

The many cathedral ceilings.

The kitchen.

"If I cooked," Camilla says as she takes in the massive room with the black granite counters and stainless steel appliances, "this would be my dream kitchen. Do you guys have a cook?"

One would believe that from looking at the room. "My grandmother did all the cooking. That's why the kitchen is so big. It was her dream kitchen." Our grandfather made sure she got exactly what she desired when he built the house. He loved her that much.

"As for having a cook—no, we don't have one. My brothers and I take turns cooking." Fortunately, the show hired a local caterer to provide lunch while everyone is here. Otherwise, I'd make Noah do all the work.

"You enjoy cooking?"

I chuckle. "I enjoy eating, and since none of us really enjoy cooking, we take turns."

Besides, hiring a cook costs money, and it's an expense we aren't interested in taking on. Of course when it comes to hiring someone to keep the house clean, that's a different story. "Let me show you to your rooms."

After I direct the three men staying with us to their bedrooms, I open the door to Camilla's room. If I had a choice, I would've given it to Violet. It's the largest guest room in the house, with huge windows overlooking the meadows and the mountains. Violet had always loved this room.

Camilla steps in and her breath hitches. "Wow. This is gorgeous."

I have no idea if she means the rustic antique furniture or the four-poster bed with the lacy white bedding or the view.

Don't think about Violet spread out on the bed, gazing up at you with those beautiful, soulful eyes. Her soft lips parted, waiting for you to—

The ringing of a cell phone intrudes on my thoughts, and I shake myself back to reality.

"Roger, I'm so glad you called," Camilla says. The vowels are dragged out longer than normal, and there's an almost sing-song quality to her tone.

I turn to Violet—and my mouth curves into what I hope comes off as an I'm-happy-to-see-you smile. Better that than the smile betraying my I-want-to-do-you-on-this-bed dirty thoughts. "Let me show you to your room."

My cock not-so helpfully points out she can always share my bed.

Yeah, I'm sure that will go down well with Austin and the show's producers, I remind it.

"I'm not staying here," Violet says. "I'm staying at my grand-mother's."

Even though that makes a helluva lot more sense, I blurt, "We have plenty of room, and staying here will make your job easier."

"I'm the photographer, not the videographer. I don't have to follow you around all the time like the guys do."

That's a good thing, I tell myself. And then, because I've done a piss-poor job convincing myself of that, I imagine Austin discovering me fucking his sister in my bed, followed by him demonstrating some SEAL-approved moves on me.

That argument is more convincing.

Besides, Camilla and the crew might find it odd if I invite Violet to my room just so that we can catch up on the past ten years. In private. Because as great as Grandma Meg has been at keeping the town up-to-date on what Violet's been up to, I want to hear it from Violet.

"I'll call you right back." Camilla ends the call. "Violet's right," she says to me. "She isn't needed here all the time, so I'm fine with her not staying with us. But since we have the afternoon of shooting ahead of us, let's get started. We can shoot some photos of you shirtless. You have a barn, right?"

"Yes, ma'am." Not that I have time for a photo shoot. I've got my own work to do. But since Noah got me into this mess, he can do my chores.

Sounds only fair.

"Your application mentioned you sing," Camilla says.

That's right. Noah's toothpaste is about to have extra-hot chili paste added to it.

"He has a beautiful singing voice." Violet's tone is soft. Soft in a way that makes my stomach do several impressive somersaults.

I let my gaze drop to her lips.

Not a good idea, the know-it-all voice in my head snaps. *Eyes up.*

"We can light a fire by the lake in the evening and shoot the video there." The way Camilla says it, you'd think she was planning to shoot a music video for an up-and-coming country singer.

But since that's not going to happen if I can have any say in this, I do my best to redirect her from the campfire idea. "I'm singing at the senior center tomorrow night."

Now I just have to hope Grandma Meg can pull it off on short notice. Ever since the afternoon almost two months ago, when she gave me the Marvel comics, she's been hinting—loudly— about me entertaining the seniors.

Camilla taps her finger against her lips. "I don't suppose that will entail you being shirtless?"

I laugh. "I'm not sure the seniors would go for that."

"I don't know," Violet says. Her tone holds a giggle, her eyes an unexpected heat. An unexpected heat directed at me that no one else notices.

I'm hallucinating things. That must be it.

My cock one hundred percent disagrees with me.

"Grandma says Gertrude has a framed, shirtless picture of Ryan Reynolds on her nightstand," Violet explains. "Gertrude claims it ensures happy dreams."

Why doesn't that surprise me?

6

―――

"Ooh, I'm going to be famous," Gertrude says.

"You're not going to be famous," Grandma Meg replies.

"You don't think us being on a reality show will make us famous? Maybe we can be the next Kardashians."

"We're not going to be the next Kardashians."

"Why not?"

Grandma Meg lets out a long, I'm-going-to-hit-my-head-against-the-table sigh. The same round table Gertrude, Tilly, and Violet are also sitting at. "Because we're old and we're not rich," she says. "That's why not. And we won't be famous just because we're here while they videotape TJ singing to us." She gestures to the twenty or so seniors sitting around the six other tables in the rec room.

"You're such a killjoy," Gertrude grouses. "So, to bring joy back into my life," she says a little louder in case I couldn't hear her before, "I think TJ should perform without his shirt on. In fact, I think TJ should do a benefit concert while shirtless to help save Mavis's store."

I roll my eyes because this isn't the first time Gertrude has

43

made that request. About going shirtless—not the concert part. She tried last week to sell me on the virtues of me grocery shopping shirtless. "Sorry, ladies. The shirt's staying on." Then I frown. "What's going on with Mavis's store?" She sells antiques. Has since before I was born.

"Not enough business these days." Gertrude says it quietly, as if telling me a secret no one else is privy to.

"Why?" Andrew says loudly from their table. The eighty-five-year-old war veteran's hearing isn't all that great. "Are you afraid they won't be as impressed with your body as they are with mine?"

Gertrude snorts. "Like that will ever happen. I'd say our TJ's body puts even Ryan Reynolds's to shame." Which is saying a lot given she has his picture next to her bed.

"If you'd like," Violet says, "I can give you a shirtless photo of TJ from the photo shoot I'm doing for the show."

"Oh, Violet." Gertrude practically claps her hands in glee. "You always were one of my favorite students."

"I thought *I* was your only favorite student." Austin steps up to the table. He's wearing his sheriff uniform, so he must be on a break and here to witness my humiliation.

Grinning, he bends down and kisses Gertrude's cheek. She giggles and blushes like a sixteen-year-old who is crushing on the starting quarterback.

"And whose shirtless photo are we talking about?" Austin asks.

"TJ's, of course," Gertrude not-so-helpfully points out.

"From the reality show." And in case he hasn't noticed them, I indicate to the TV crew setting up the lighting equipment.

"Violet's taking the photos," Gertrude once more not-so-helpfully points out—and I calculate the odds of getting in trouble if I duct tape her mouth shut.

But then I remind myself, *What's the big deal?* Austin has no idea about my fantasies that star his sister. Do you think I'd be standing here if he did? That's right—I would be six-feet underground.

Of course, that applies to any guy who thinks about Violet that way.

"Are you going to take a picture of *me* shirtless, young lady?" Andrew asks Violet, then laughs a deep, rough sound.

Violet smiles my favorite grin and pats Andrew's hand. "If you would like me to, Mr. O'Henry."

Austin leans down and exchanges words with his sister, but I can't hear what he's saying. She replies and points to the nearby hallway entrance. He nods and parks his ass on the chair across from her and next to where I'm sitting.

"Hey, less talking and more singing," a man, from a few tables over, grumbles loudly. He gestures at me with the cupcake in his hand.

"He hasn't started singing yet." Gertrude's voice is equally loud and has a singsong tone to it. I almost expect her to add "Na-na-na-na-na," as if they are five-year-olds on a playground.

"Then it's about time he does," the man shoots back. "I'm not growing any younger."

"No, just grouchier." Tilly winks at me, then reaches for a cupcake on the plate in the middle of our table. A thick swirl of green frosting and a woodland critter sits on top of her cake. "I so do love Cora Lee's cupcakes. Especially her cute little marzipan animals."

Violet stands and moves away from the table. This is my chance to talk to her. Alone.

And hell if I'm missing out on that.

She heads toward the hallway she indicated to a moment ago. I leave my seat and easily catch up to her, placing my hand on her arm to stop her.

She turns around and I smile. "Hey, I really want to know what's been going on in your life since you moved away," I say, giving her arm a light squeeze. "When are we gonna have a chance to catch up?" So far, we haven't been able to. We're never alone. And when I finally get some space from the TV crew, Violet isn't around. She's gone back to Grandma Meg's house.

Violet smiles at me. "I would like that too. I've just been really busy. But there is something I should probably tell you. Something Granny and Austin have kept quiet—"

"All right, TJ," Camilla says through the microphone, interrupting Violet. "We're ready for you."

I indicate for her to give me a minute. "What do you want to tell me?" I ask Violet.

She glances toward the hallway. "You know what? It can wait. Camilla can't." She doesn't give me a chance to tell her that I don't give a damn what Camilla wants. She hurries off.

With a grunt, I walk to my guitar case next to the stool in the middle of the floor, remove my guitar, and make myself comfortable on the seat.

With all eyes and camera lenses on me, I strum the opening bars of an upbeat country song and begin singing. It used to be my grandmother's favorite.

Not once during the song do I look at the video camera. I'm not doing this for the reality show. I'm doing it for Grandma Meg and her friends. Violet returns to her seat halfway through the song.

After I'm finished singing it, I sing a few more country classics I know my audience will enjoy. Then, without realizing what I'm doing, I start singing a song I haven't sung in thirteen years.

The last time I sang it was while Violet had been recovering from the flu. She was tired and had asked me to sing. So I did. I sang a popular ballad that she loved. It was a song about taking a chance on love when circumstances were against it.

Even though I have the urge to look at her, I close my eyes so Austin doesn't get the wrong idea.

With my eyes still closed, I visualize in my head that I'm singing directly to her and only her. I visualize her smiling my favorite smile. And I visualize her running the tip of her tongue along her lower lip as she watches me.

Which might explain why my voice turns husky at the beginning of the song and remains that way for its entirety.

The final bars of the song fade to a mess of clapping and hoots and whistles.

I reopen my eyes and quickly glance at Violet to see what she thought of the song. She's chewing her lip, her telltale sign that she's contemplating something. But since it could be about anything, I mentally shrug it off and return my guitar to the case.

A childish giggle comes from the hallway. A moment later, a senior in a motorized wheelchair comes speeding into the room. On his lap is a toddler with short, messy brown hair and a familiar grin.

"And the winner of the Kentucky Derby is Deacon on Sir Apple Pie," Arnold says in a fake announcer voice and cheers. The little boy also cheers and raises his arms in the air.

The pair comes to a stop next to Grandma Meg. She helps the toddler off Arnold's lap.

The boy walks over to Violet and lifts his arms. "Mommy! Up!"

Holy. Shit.

Without missing a beat, the woman I've been inappropriately fantasizing about hoists the boy up and hugs him.

What else have Austin and Grandma Meg kept me in the dark about without even a sliver of a hint?

"You've got a great boy, Violet. He's going to grow up to do amazing things." Arnold holds out his hand and helps the toddler bump fists.

"I agree, but that's 'cause he has an amazing mother." Grandma Meg beams at her granddaughter, but Violet is too busy talking to her son to notice.

"Hey, Deacon," Austin says in his friendly sheriff voice. The same voice he uses with kids because he doesn't want them to grow up afraid of cops—unless they've done something wrong. "Aren't you going to say hi to your uncle Austin?"

Deacon grins and squirms on his mom's lap. She whispers something to him and lowers him to the floor.

As soon as his feet touch the ground, he toddles over to his uncle. The ex-SEAL, who easily intimidates most people without even trying, scoops up his nephew and parks him on his lap.

I can feel my eyebrow slide up. "So?"

Austin looks over the boy's head, his expression that of a cop, not giving away anything. "So—what?"

Now that the show is over, some of the seniors have vacated their seats to participate in other activities. I sit on the empty chair next to him.

"When did you become an uncle, and why is this the first I'm hearing of it?"

And why doesn't Grandma Meg have pictures of her great-grandson all over the house? Hell, why doesn't she have even just one on display? The Grandma Meg I know would.

Or maybe she does, but they're in her bedroom. It's not like I've ever gone in there.

"Because Violet asked Granny and me not to say anything, and I have to respect my sister's wishes."

Ha—I bet that isn't entirely true. I bet if Violet decided to have wild sex with me, Austin wouldn't be okay with that.

I open my mouth to ask another question.

Austin cuts me off at the pass. "Whatever she wants you to know, she'll be the one to tell you, not me." But from his tone, it's clear he doesn't think she'll tell me anything when it comes to her son. It's also clear Austin's lips are sealed shut with extra strength superglue.

That's one thing I appreciate about him: he's loyal.

Without looking obvious about it, I check for an engagement or wedding ring on Violet's finger. Just like I did yesterday when she showed up at the ranch.

Her finger is still bare.

Camilla joins us and sits on an empty seat between me and Grandma Meg. "TJ, you failed to mention on the application just how talented you are."

"I'm always telling him that he should sing more," Grandma Meg says. "But he never believes me when I gush about how amazing he sounds."

"I take it you know TJ well, then?" Camilla's expression reminds me of a lioness on a nature show...right before she charges at her prey.

Grandma Meg smiles proudly at me, revealing her not-so-pearly-white teeth. "I sure do. I've known him since he and Austin here were little kids. I've always considered him to be one of my own grandsons. Him and his brothers."

"Cookie?" the little boy asks, still on Austin's lap. He points to the plate with the chocolate chip cookies that I recognize as Grandma Meg's recipe.

"I don't blame you for wanting one," I tell him. "Grandma Meg bakes the best cookies in the entire universe. Do you know what the universe is?"

The boy shakes his head so fast, I'm surprised his head doesn't fall off and roll across the tile floor.

"It's a very big place." I stretch my arms out to the side. "So they must be awesome cookies. By the way, Deacon, I'm TJ. Your mommy and Uncle Austin's friend. Nice to meet you."

Deacon bounces on Austin's lap. "Horsie!"

"You like horses?"

He bounces again. "Horsie!"

"I take it that's a yes."

"He's never seen a real horse before," Violet says. "But there are pictures of them in one of his favorite books."

"Would you like to meet some horses?" I ask him. "Your mom can bring you to the ranch and I'll introduce you to my horse,

Thor." *And then your mom can explain why I didn't even know about you until now.*

I mean, why the big secret?

Deacon nods, his baby teeth all revealed in a smile.

"Do you have any kids?" Grandma Meg asks Camilla, who is studying the little boy like he's a science experiment gone wrong.

"Kids aren't my thing. My career is more important. Kids would only get in the way." She turns to me. "Which I believe is pretty much what you stated on the application."

Grandma Meg shakes her head, looking both amused and disapproving. "You say that now, TJ. But you just wait. You'll change your mind."

Right. After what happened with my ex-girlfriend, I swore never to make that mistake again. So unless I randomly get some woman pregnant—which isn't likely given I practice safe sex—I'm not planning to have kids.

But despite this, I would never have said on the form that I don't want kids because they only get in the way.

Of course if I'd had *my* way, the form would never have been filled out to begin with.

"Hey, Craig." Violet's tone is mother-wolf-fang sharp. "You aren't allowed to shoot footage with my son in it."

He lowers the video camera. "Sorry."

If that's what it takes to get a break from the camera, I might have to recruit Deacon. Wherever I go, Deacon goes.

Especially if Violet is part of the package.

Sexy fantasy or not.

7

"We got great footage yesterday of TJ singing to the seniors," Camilla says the next morning. The world outside the kitchen window is still dark. "That's bound to melt viewers' hearts. So today we need to focus on what makes TJ hot."

Camilla is definitely a morning person—although that might have to do with the two cups of coffee she has consumed since getting up an hour ago.

Which is more than I can say for the two cameramen who are supposed to follow me around. They look ready to crawl back into bed—right after they nail Camilla on the side of her head with their own coffee mugs.

The remaining members of the TV crew haven't staggered into the house yet. They're still at the hotel.

Or they were.

They're supposed to be on their way since my day starts regardless of when they show up.

It's five thirty a.m. and we're sitting at the kitchen table, eating the bacon and scrambled eggs I cooked.

Well, my brothers, the two cameramen, and I are consuming

51

the eggs and bacon. Camilla is eating a container of yogurt and granola.

Violet hasn't arrived yet.

But that doesn't mean I didn't dream about her last night. Naked. On my bed. Tied to the headboard with a bandana. Knees apart. My head between her legs.

And because of that, I woke up with the worst case of morning wood. It took a long cold shower to deal with it—and that was only after my hand took care of the job.

I swallow hard, pushing down the memory of the dream before my cock can advertise it to everyone in the room.

I'm sorting the last of the dirty dishes in the dishwasher when the front doorbell chimes. Noah disappears from the kitchen and returns with Violet.

Asgard migrates over to her. Even without seeing his face, I know he's giving her puppy dog eyes. It's his special superpower.

Violet kneels next to him. "Aren't you just the sweetest thing? Like a big bear."

"The big bear is hoping you brought him some bacon since he didn't get to steal ours."

She laughs and throws her arms around the big goofball of a dog.

And damned if a shot of jealousy doesn't pulsate through my veins. At least *he* doesn't have to worry about Austin kicking his ass into Wyoming. Kicking his ass for touching Violet.

As if sensing the emotions I have no right feeling, Asgard gives me one of his big doggy grins.

I mentally flip him the finger.

"I think you have a new fan, Violet," Noah says on a chuckle.

Camilla noticeably shudders. She's no longer eyeing Asgard as though he were a two-headed monster, but she still gives my dog a wide berth.

The same goes for Loki, my cat.

The feeling is mutual, but that's nothing new. The only use Loki has for humans is when they feed him.

The devil himself strolls into the kitchen as if lording over his peasants. He makes a beeline for Asgard, ready to begin his daily ritual of tormenting the dog.

But at the last moment, he changes course. He struts over to Violet, rubs against her leg, and releases a rumbling meow.

She scratches him behind the ear, eliciting the purr of a tractor engine. "Yes, Loki, you're the sweetest kitty ever. If I could bring you home with me to LA, I would."

Loki meows again, which I loosely translate as, "Great, let me get my stuff now."

It's hard to believe those two only met yesterday. You'd think they were lifelong buddies.

"I take it you're not a fan of small animals." Craig, the cameraman, is referring to Loki's size. My cat is what some people would refer to as big-boned—but he's not fat. He just looks that way because of his chubby face. It's part of his breed.

All right, I'll admit it—he is a little chunky. Not quite the image of a Norse god.

"I love British shorthairs," Violet says, now standing. "They're so cute and cuddly."

I nod, more so to appear like I'm listening than what I'm really doing: appreciating how hot she looks in her clothes. Although I can guarantee she's equally spectacular out of them.

As if you'll ever find out.

She's wearing cowboy boots and slim-fitting jeans that hug her never-ending legs just right. A white tank top peeks through the opening of her light blue plaid shirt. The shirt is unbuttoned to just below her breasts, the hem loose against the mouthwatering swell of her hips.

Like yesterday, she's the complete opposite of Camilla. But at least this time, the producer is wearing jeans. Designer jeans. And this time she's wearing boots—just not cowboy boots. The black suede reaches to a couple of inches above her knees, and the heels are taller than Violet's. She also has on a wraparound cardigan in a southwestern theme.

Most guys would think she's incredibly sexy. I'm not one of them. Violet wins it for me double hands down.

And not just because I'm a horny bastard when it comes to her.

She's the full deal and more.

A slap on my back snaps me from my thoughts. "Okay, time to get to work," Jake says, "Or posing for the camera. Not quite sure what you're doing today." The last part he says directly to me.

This time I do physically flip him the finger. He knows I'm doing this to benefit the ranch. I'm taking one for the team. He could be a little more supportive—like, for starters, begging to take over the role of the cowboy desperately hoping to find true love on reality TV.

Noah and Jake leave to do their morning chores. Today it's my turn to clean the stables.

Asgard trots alongside me as Violet, Camilla, the crew, and I head to the barn. A sliver of pink sits low in the distance as twilight makes its presence known. But as beautiful as the sky is, it's nothing compared to the brunette beside me.

Camilla *oohs* and *ahhs* at the view. Violet pauses. Before I can blink, she has her camera on the tripod and is capturing shot after shot of the slow-coming sunrise. Everyone except me watches the pink deepen to red, lighting the thin strip of clouds along the horizon.

Instead, I watch Violet's excitedly thoughtful expression.

And damned if a thrilled tremor doesn't go through me.

Even though I have to start on the stables, I wait until she finally stops. As we walk to the barn, gratification on her face smiles back at me, making me glad I waited until she was finished before moving on.

At the stable, I slide the main door open and step inside. The familiar scent of pine shavings, hay, and horses greets me. Though based on the wrinkles near the bridge of Camilla's nose, "greets" is not the verb she would use. Violet, on the other hand, smiles like she's home after being away for so long. But I guess that's true in a way. When she and Austin were younger, they used to go riding with me several times a week. They're as comfortable around horses as I am.

"Do you miss riding?" I ask her. "Or do you get to ride in LA?"

What I really want is to find out about Deacon's father.

Or maybe I don't want to know about the man who got to fuck her when all I have are my fantasies. Fantasies that Austin would kill me for possessing.

"I've ridden a few times in the past couple of years, but not as much as I would like. So yes, I miss it very much." She inhales deeply, as if filling her lungs with the outdoorsy scent to enjoy once she returns to LA. "I miss all of this very much."

"You miss the smell of horse dung?" If disgust could generate electricity, there's enough in Camilla's sentence to power Copper Creek for a month.

Violet laughs. "Well, not that smell specifically. But I miss the rest of it."

One by one, I remove the mares and the colts from their stalls and lead them to the pasture where they'll spend the day. Thor, Odin, and Orion are taken to another pasture.

And so begins the cleaning of the stable.

For the next while, I don't pay attention to the TV crew. To be honest, I can't see how watching a cowboy shoveling horseshit would get any woman excited.

"You must be getting hot." There's a hint of hopeful impatience in Camilla's all-business tone.

"Nope, I'm good."

"Wouldn't you feel better without your shirt on?"

I barely restrain an eye roll.

"Not to say that you don't look great with your clothes on," she says, "but you need to sell yourself more."

Sell myself more? What am I? A male prostitute?

I open my mouth to argue but then remember why I'm doing this.

While I inwardly curse Noah in a thousand possible ways, I unbutton the shirt and jerk it from the waistband of my jeans.

And because I know that won't be enough to appease her, I toss it aside, reach back to the collar of my T-shirt, and yank the fabric over my head.

My gaze falls on Violet, and satisfaction parades through me. Her eyes are wide and focused on my stomach. *Yes, Violet, not quite the same abs I had when we were teens.*

The tip of her tongue smooths along her lower lip, and the satisfaction transforms into something scorching. It's like she's imagining running her tongue along the ridges and valleys of my stomach, tasting me. Exploring me.

And shit if my cock doesn't appreciate the thought.

She's not thinking of you that way, I remind myself.

My cock doesn't believe me, so before it can get any harder and betray my secret, I visualize the potential torture techniques Austin might use on me.

That works.

"Well, that's more like it." Camilla studies me like I'm live-stock waiting to be sold. If I were a horse, she'd been checking my teeth.

Violet lifts her camera, and I take that as my cue to start working again. The clicking of her camera, the scraping of the shovel's metal edge against concrete, and my slightly labored breaths are the only sounds filling the stable.

The cool air kisses my sweat-covered body as I work hard to finish the job.

Over an hour later, the stalls are clean and fresh shavings cover the floor.

"Do you guys offer riding lessons?" Camilla asks once we're outside. "One of the ranches my team visited is a dude ranch. You know, where city folk spend a week working and pretending they're real cowboys. Your house is definitely large enough for numerous guests."

Granddad would haunt us for all eternity if we turned his ranch into, as he put it, a fancy-ass resort where idiots paid for the privilege of doing the work that he and his men did. And after that, he and his men would have to waste time redoing everything.

Granddad didn't have much respect for those types of ranches.

"We've considered offering lessons." Well, not so much considered. More like Sophie mentioned it one day, and Jake said no. "We're just not interested."

Camilla tilts her head to the side like girls do when they're flirting. Except there's nothing in her expression to suggest that's what she has in mind. "So there's no chance you'll take me out on the trail?"

"Do you ride?"

Or more importantly, has she even sat on a horse before? And I don't mean the kind on a carousel ride.

"No, but I'm a quick learner."

"Do any of you ride?" I ask the TV crew. I'm guessing not, but maybe they'll surprise me.

They shake their heads.

Violet's lips tug up at the corners. She might be smiling, but her eyes are saying so much more. They sparkle with desire.

No, not the kind of desire where she wants me to bend her over a bale of hay and do her from behind. Although I would be all for that.

It's the kind of desire I've seen growing up with her. She wants to ride a horse more than she wants to breathe. She wants to feel the smooth firm muscle between her legs.

My cock seconds that vote—getting it all wrong as to which muscle I'm referring to.

But it does give me an idea—which would be even better if Camilla wasn't so keen on learning to ride.

"If you would like, I can take you both riding." As I say it, I silently will for Camilla to say no.

"I would love that," she says.

Clearly I didn't will hard enough.

There's a longing in Violet's eyes as well as another emotion I can't peg. She bites her lower lip—a sign I know well.

My gaze appreciates her mouth for another moment, then unwillingly moves away. "What about you?"

Her expression rivals that of a lightning storm, with all its thrilling, awe-inspiring beauty. "That sounds great."

Now if only I could ditch the producer and camera crew—then we'd be all set.

Not that I can act on my lust when it comes to Violet. But I wouldn't mind spending time with her, just the two of us.

Camilla helps me partway, telling the guys they don't have to join us. "There's no point in shooting footage of TJ hanging out with single women. We don't want him to come off as a playboy. We want him to come off as a down-to-earth cowboy and ideal boyfriend."

None of the crew appears disappointed at that.

"All right," I say. "I still have work to do, but why don't we plan to ride later this afternoon?"

And if I'm lucky, something will happen to keep Camilla from tagging along.

8

The sun is still high in the sky by the time I introduce Violet to Valkyrie, a mare with spirit in her—but a horse I know she can handle.

Thor, Valkyrie, and Frieda—Camilla's horse—are standing at the hitching post outside the tack room. Sophie is helping Camilla with her horse, a quiet, mild-mannered mare.

"Valkyrie?" Violet says with a laugh, stroking the horse's nose. "Still in your comics and Norse mythology phase, I see."

"Hey, there's nothing wrong with geeking on that stuff. Only real men can admit it." I wink at her, then check over my shoulder to ensure no one can hear us. Even then, I keep my voice low. "How come Austin and Grandma Meg never mentioned Deacon—or that you have a man in your life?"

All right, that was a stretch when it comes to her brother. It's not like he would ever discuss his sister's dating life with me.

But Grandma Meg is another matter.

Violet pretends to adjust the stirrup that we both know is fine. "They don't tell you *everything*."

I snort a laugh. "Hello, have you met your grandmother?

59

There isn't a person in town who doesn't know about your great job and how well it's going."

She smirks, then gives in to the laugh she was holding back. "Okay, you've got a point there."

"So, does Deacon's father treat you well? Do you love him?" I didn't mean to ask the second question. It bulldozed its way out of my mouth, needing to wreck everything in its path.

"There's nothing to tell. Suffice it to say, he's not part of Deacon's or my life. End of story."

Is there a man in your life? Those are the words I should ask—because if there is, then it's time for me to hop off this lust train.

Yes, I know I should ask the question—but I can't seem to shape my mouth around the words.

"Noah looked pretty grumpy when I saw him a few minutes ago," Violet says.

I chuckle. "That's 'cause he got stuck doing my afternoon chores, so I can take you riding."

"And I'm guessing he wasn't happy about it."

"He didn't complain—not much anyway. But I can't imagine he's doing backward somersaults over any of it." I, on the other hand, walked away from the conversation grinning. Especially after I told him what needed to be done.

Let's just say he's going to be busy for a while.

"But you have to admit it's sweet of him to do your chores, so you can take Camilla and me riding."

My chuckle is heartier this time. "There's nothing sweet about it. He's doing it to make up for—"

"Hey, look at me," Camilla says. "I'm on a horse. Are you guys ready to go?" And then in a quieter voice, she asks Sophie, "So how do I get it to start moving, and how do I steer it?"

"Spoken like a true animal lover," I say under my breath. People who aren't animal lovers tend to refer to them as "it."

Violet giggles. Thor whinnies and nudges my back.

I turn to him. "Okay, boy, we're going."

Violet and I mount our horses, and the three of us set out. Because of Camilla's lack of riding experience, I lead the way and Violet brings up the rear.

At one point, as our horses walk along the dirt path that travels parallel to the river, I twist around in my saddle. Camilla's gaze is taking in the breathtaking view: the mess of pine and cottonwood trees, bushes, wild grasses, bitterroot flowers. Her horse is long forgotten, plodding along, following Thor.

Violet is behind her, looking completely at peace, like she always did whenever she used to ride. She glances in my direction, smiles, and my heart acts like a newbie line dancer, stumbling a few beats.

That's new.

I brush it off as the result of the perfect summer day, the perfect scenery, and the not-so-perfect sexual response to the woman I can't have.

We've been riding for forty-five minutes by the time I steer Thor down the worn path to the riverbank. I dismount and lead him to the water, confident he won't bail on me. While he's drinking, I help Camilla down from Freida.

She sighs, content. The view has that effect on people. The grassy bank. The shallow stony beach. The pine trees following the curve of the river. The Bitterroot Mountain range. This is nature at its finest.

"I forgot how beautiful it is here." Even though I can't see Violet's face, I can hear the relaxed smile in her voice.

"It's so quiet." From the way Camilla says it, I can't tell if that's a good thing or not.

"I bet it's not like this in LA," I say as I walk Frieda down to the water to join Thor.

Violet does the same with Valkyrie. The three horses drink from the river while I fight against the itch to touch Violet. To run my fingers through her hair. To taste her.

The next few minutes are spent with me asking Camilla and

Violet questions about LA. Safe enough topic. Although from the way they talk, I get the impression Camilla loves the big city more than Violet. But Violet must love it enough to stay there.

That's because she has a job she loves in LA. It's not like she can do it here, I remind myself.

"So how did you get involved with the reality show?" I gesture toward Camilla because I'd rather do that than say *Cowboy Most Wanted* out loud.

I do have some pride after all—although after this episode goes live in a few weeks, I might not have much left.

"The marketing and publicity firm I work for specializes in the entertainment business. My boss had seen some of the portraits and horse photos I've shot over the past few years. She thought it would be a good idea to include professional photographs from the show for publicity purposes. But I'm also involved in the social media side of things."

"You are?" Do I know what that means?

Not at all.

"That's my usual job. Or part of it. I work with some of our clients when it comes to their social media accounts. Make sure they're not putting themselves in the worst possible light."

She doesn't roll her eyes, but I know Violet. That's exactly what she wants to do when it comes to some of her clients. I might not pay attention to social media, and I might not care two shits about what happens in Hollywood, but that doesn't mean I missed the recent controversy. What happened? According to gossip around town, a celebrity went apeshit on Twitter.

Maybe the actor is a client of Violet's company—and someone swooped in and cleaned up his mess.

"I don't suppose you know anything about website design?" My tone is off-handed, but there's a shitload of hope bubbling beneath the surface.

"I do know a thing or two. Nothing high tech like you'd find with a big-name company, mind you. But I have helped a couple of clients with their websites."

Camilla, who wasn't paying much attention to us while we talked, pulls out her phone and checks the screen. "Damn it. I'm not getting any reception." She holds it up high, as if that will solve the problem.

When that doesn't work, she paces back and forth. She grunts, then starts walking along the trail we just came from, gaze still on the screen. "I'll be back in a minute."

Hopefully, we're talking figuratively, not literally.

"My grandfather set up a website for the ranch," I tell Violet, "but other than changing a couple of things, we haven't done much with it since he died. Could you look at it for us?"

Violet steps closer and brushes a stray strand of hair behind her ear. "Do you want my honest opinion? Or would you prefer I pander to your ego?" A smirk slides onto her face.

I was always a sucker for that smirk. "My ego can take a beating."

Most of the time.

Her gaze drops to my mouth. Her lips part slightly, and my heart does a quickstep.

She doesn't want to kiss you, idiot, the rational voice in my head says. *So don't even think about it.*

Her eyes flick back up to mine. "Before I say anything, let me preface this with a reminder that I'm not familiar with marketing horses. I'm more familiar with marketing people in the entertainment business to their target audience."

"Understood."

She nibbles her lip for a second. "All right. To be honest, your website is boring."

"Yeah, I kind of figured that." And then what she *really* said hits me. "You've already checked it out?"

"I might have looked up your website a while ago. After Austin told me you and your brothers had inherited the ranch. I might have been curious." She turns on the brilliant smile that always leaves my legs a little bit wobbly.

"Do you think you can help us make it better? We'll pay you, of course."

She glances at the horses, who are busy eating the grass near the water. It takes her a few seconds before she finally nods. "Okay, but I'll also need to shoot some photos of your horses and the ranch. And of you and your brothers, too. To give the website a personal touch."

Now it's my turn to smirk. "Will that be with or without our shirts on?"

She laughs. "Either way is fine with me. But I wouldn't mind taking photos of you, this evening, before the sun sets. For the show." Her gaze drops to my lips again and stays there for longer than considered normal—unless you're lip reading.

Without thinking things through, I lean in, the scruff on my jaw scraping her soft skin. "Will it be just you or will we have an audience?" The words come out low and husky.

Not exactly how I had planned to say it, but at this point I don't care.

Her breath hitches, but she doesn't move away. "It depends if Camilla wants to videotape us or not."

It's a good thing we're standing near the river, because my body temperature just climbed a thousand degrees. I know what she said isn't how she had intended for it to sound, but my brain instantly jumped to the land of sex videos.

"TJ, do you mind if we head back now?" Camilla's voice breaks through my desire to brush my lips against Violet's. The same desire is mirrored back at me in Violet's eyes.

We turn away from each other and pretend to pay attention to our horses. I'm one step away from whistling a happy, carefree tune.

If I knew any.

Camilla enters the clearing, her focus still on the phone. "I've got something I need to discuss with the show's marketing team, but I still can't get a signal."

"Not at all," I say, silently cursing her untimely return.

Now I just have to hope she doesn't decide to videotape Violet taking photos of me this evening. Because Violet and I have things to discuss. And our conversation being aired on national TV is *not* part of my plans.

9

Deacon races through the front entrance of the ranch house. "Horsie."

Behind him, Grandma Meg enters, carrying a portable high chair. Slight exhaustion lines her otherwise smiling face. She's babysitting her great-grandson while Violet is staying in Copper Creek.

"TJ doesn't keep the horses in the house," she calls after him as I take the high chair from her.

He stops abruptly in the middle of the foyer and scans the area. "Where horsie?"

Asgard barks his answer.

"They're in the fields until we bring them in for the night." Which I'm sure is roughly what Asgard woofed. "Would you like see them?"

"Horsie."

"How about we check on your mommy first?" I say. "She's helping make dinner. Then we can go see the horses."

Where's Camilla and the crew? Camilla is in her room, catching up on her phone calls and emails. The only other person around from the TV crew is Craig. The rest left as soon as they finished videotaping me make the chili.

"Viewers love it when the cowboys are domesticated," Camilla had explained earlier before disappearing into her room. And before the act of cooking dinner became a made-for-TV production.

Deacon nods so fast at my question, he could be mistaken for a bobble-head figurine. I remove his sneakers, then he and Grandma Meg follow me into the kitchen. Violet is standing next to the island sink, rinsing the spinach.

"Mommy!" The little boy rushes over to her as she turns off the water.

She scoops him up and plants a big kiss on his cheek. He giggles.

"My mommy," he declares for my benefit.

"Is that so?" I say. "She's a very pretty mommy."

What I was going to say is that she's gorgeous—as in the-star-of-my-sexual-fantasies gorgeous. But fortunately, my brain hijacked my mouth before it was too late.

A light blush sweeps across her cheeks, and she's catapulted to a new realm of hotness.

One that my cock fully appreciates.

Until...

"Rumor has it TJ's making his infamous chili." The cheerful sound of Austin's voice sends my cock into hiding.

Violet's brother and Noah enter the kitchen.

Deacon bounces in his mom's arms. "See horsie. See horsie."

"I told him I'd show him the horses before dinner," I say.

"Can I come, too?" she asks her son.

If I had my way, she'd be coming several times in my bed tonight. But instead of slipping that into the conversation, I ask Deacon, "What do you say? Can your mommy come see the horses with us?"

"See horsie."

"I'm taking that as a yes," I say to Violet. "Why don't I finish making the salad? And then we can head to the paddock to see the colts."

It takes all but ten seconds before the toddler starts squirming in her arms. She lowers him to the floor. He scampers away to join Noah and Grandma Meg at the kitchen table.

Violet hugs her brother. "I thought you were working tonight." Which would explain why he's wearing his uniform.

"I am. But even as sheriff, I get to have dinner. Funny how that happens." A chime pings from his pants pocket. He pulls out his phone and reads the message.

"That isn't a call, is it?" Violet asks.

"No, a text from a friend of mine from the SEALs. Liam and I served together until I left. Now he lives in San Francisco and owns a security and investigation firm. He's been trying to recruit me to work as part of his team for a few months now."

"You're leaving Copper Creek?" She sounds as surprised as I feel. This is the first he's mentioned it to me.

He shoves the phone back into his pocket. "I have a job here that I enjoy. So that would be a no. Although if I did, it'd only be a six-hour drive to see you and the little squirt."

Which is better than the eighteen hours from here to LA.

"Awww," Violet says as I pick up the small knife and begin slicing the strawberries. "Didn't realize you missed me so much."

"Hey, you're my baby sister. Of course I miss you. I hate that you're not here. At least then I can make sure you don't hook up with any more dumbasses."

Naturally, that would include me—if he knew how she was frequently featured in my thoughts.

His comment does, though, pique my interest about what dumbass he is referring to. *Deacon's father?*

I pause, the knife blade resting on the strawberry, watching how this will play out between them. Even when we were kids,

Austin took on the role of protective older brother—a role that Violet, time after time, disagreed with.

Violet rolls her eyes. "I'm a big girl now, Austin. You don't have any say in whom I date."

"You wanna bet?" is his muttered reply before he heads to the table.

"I didn't know you were quite the cook," Violet says to me as though Austin hadn't said anything.

I lean closer to her. Close enough to appreciate her vanilla and rose scent—but not close enough to have her brother in my face. "Wanna know a secret?"

She turns around, the curve of her back pressing against the kitchen counter. And like earlier by the river, her gaze lowers to my lips, and she holds it there for a heartbeat.

Her brown eyes, with mischief dancing in them, flick up to meet mine. "I like secrets."

For a second, I forget where I am. I just get lost in her eyes, and I'm more than happy to stay there.

Until Austin's loud laugh booms through the kitchen, reminding me exactly where I am and what I shouldn't be doing.

I swallow back the lust that's eager to be my downfall. "I'm not all that good a cook. Just ask my brothers. But they aren't much better. Chili's about the only thing I can make well. And Sophie gave me the recipe for the salad."

Violet laughs, the sound soft and breathy. "Why does that not surprise me?" Then after a beat she says, "She's really nice, by the way. Sophie, I mean."

"She is."

She pops a strawberry slice from the cutting board into her mouth. "Have you guys dated?"

"You mean each other or dated in general?"

"Each other."

I shake my head. "Sophie is more like a sister to me. So that would be a no." She and Jake were friends in college before she moved to Copper Creek. He was the one who suggested we hire her—and then came up with his "No Dating Employees" rule.

"Are you seeing anyone?" Her tone is casual, like when asking someone if they prefer coffee or tea. But the same casualness is not mirrored in her eyes or her partially parted lips.

My fingers crave to pick up a strawberry slice and trace it along her plump lower lip like I crave to do with my tongue. I curl my fingers into a loose fist, reminding myself that none of it would be a smart idea.

"If I were," I say, "I wouldn't be doing this stupid show."

Her eyebrows raise in question.

"I don't think this kid is going to last much longer before you take him to see the horses," Noah says, intruding on the moment between Violet and me. The moment between us that shouldn't be happening.

I step back, putting some much-needed distance between us.

"He might just explode if he has to wait another second. *Kaboom!*" Noah's arms shoot up for added emphasis.

Deacon copies the sound and arm actions, although his make for a much smaller explosion.

"All right, Deacon," I say, setting the knife down. "Let's go see those horses."

I don't have to say that twice. He runs over as fast as his two-year-old legs can carry him.

"We won't be long," I call over my shoulder. "But, Noah, if you feel compelled to finish making the salad, don't let anyone stop you."

This is met with a hearty laugh and a "Nice try."

I'd like to say that Austin stays in the kitchen with Grandma Meg and Noah. But at least Craig does stay behind since there's no point videotaping me showing Deacon the horses. It's not allowed to be aired.

Outside, Violet helps her son down the steps, then the four of us make our way to the corral where the colts are waiting. Asgard follows us.

Curious if I have any treats for them, the three colts trot over.

I remove an apple slice from the plastic bag I brought with me and place it on my hand, palm flat. Austin picks Deacon up, so the toddler can get a better view.

With my fingers straight, I offer the apple slice over the metal gate to a colt. He sniffs it and greedily gobbles it up. Deacon giggles.

The little boy reaches out to pat the horse, and I show him how to stroke the colt's muzzle. The horse whinnies. That gets another giggle from Deacon.

The other two colts attempt to nudge their half sibling out of the way, annoyed that he gets to have a treat when they presumably don't.

"Okay, Oaklie, let Max and Whiskey have their turn." I feed them their apple slices. They then allow Deacon to pat them.

While this is going on, Violet takes photos, capturing Deacon's pricelessly awed expression. And for the first time, ever, an image pops into my mind of a little boy watching me feed the horses. A little boy with my own dark hair.

I quickly squelch the image and step away from uncle and nephew.

"I guess this means you need to get a horse," I say, standing beside Violet.

She keeps clicking away at the camera. "Something tells me my apartment in LA won't allow me to keep one. They won't even let me have a dog or a cat."

I grunt, the noise a mix of what-the-fuck and teasing. Mostly teasing. "What kind of hellhole do you live in?"

The corners of Violet's mouth twitch. "Welcome to apartment living. I'll admit that's the one thing I miss about living here. I miss having a pet." Her parents also had a dog.

Bored of the attention and disappointed at the lack of more apple slices, the colts walk away from the fence.

"Do you want to meet my horse, Thor?" I ask Deacon. "He's black and was named after the Norse god of thunder. And when you're older, I'll let you read my Thor Marvel comics and you'll see exactly why I named him that."

He nods, his attention still on the colts.

But instead of taking him to the field where Thor is hanging out, I lead Deacon, Violet, and Austin to my workshop. It's located on the other side of the barn where Violet took photos of me yesterday—with Camilla and the TV crew looking on.

And where we plan to take some more after dinner.

Hopefully without Austin in tow.

"You're taking my sister to your man cave?" Austin's tone borders on horrified, as if I had just offered to castrate him.

"I'm making an exception. This one time." I unlock the door and flick on the light as I enter.

Violet steps inside and I take in her expression as she scans the space: the workbench, the various tools stored on the wall, the jigsaws, power sanders, and router on the side bench, the piles of wood next to the shop vac in the corner.

"What is this place?" she asks.

"My workshop. By day, I'm a rancher—by night, I do woodwork. And more specifically, I make horses." I stride over to where the toddler-sized rocking horse awaits.

I pick it up and return to where mother and son are standing. I set it in front of him. "Deacon, meet your very first horse." I pat the seat that makes up the horse's back.

The only parts of the horse that aren't made of wood are the fake leather ears, the plastic eyes, and the mane and tail, which are made from cream-colored wool.

Deacon steps forward and looks at me. I nod, understanding his unspoken question. I assist him onto the horse and instruct him to hold on to the handlebars. Then I show him how to rock it. Back and forth. Back and forth. Back and forth. He giggles the entire time.

"You made that?" Violet's voice is low and slightly rough.

"Damn straight he did," Austin says. "He's been giving them away for a few years now to kids who are undergoing chemo."

Violet crouches next to me and touches the wooden head. "This is beautiful, TJ. It looks like an antique."

Deacon giggles again, getting the hang of rocking the horse on his own.

"Thanks. I think he likes it."

An intoxicating warmth fills me at the happy expression on his face. This isn't the first time I've witnessed a child's reaction after they've received one of my horses, but this is the first time I have felt this way about it.

The downside?

The pride on Violet's face leaves me craving to pull her into my arms and kiss her.

Which might have been okay if Austin wasn't standing behind me.

"We should go back to the house for dinner," I say while reminding myself that I'm being an idiot.

Violet isn't interested in me that way.

I'm just her brother's best friend.

The guy you don't kiss.

The guy you don't fuck.

The guy you don't imagine naked.

But then I remember how she was looking at me in the kitchen and by the river...like she did want to kiss me, like she did want to imagine me naked, like she did want to think of me as something more than her brother's best friend.

And I have no idea what to make of it.

10

"Well, that can't be good."

No five words are truer than when Grandma Meg and the co-producer of a reality show are sitting together at the kitchen table, chatting.

And based on Violet's comment and her expression, she agrees with me one hundred and ten percent. "I told Granny to be careful what she says about you. The last thing you need is for Camilla to get any real dirt on you."

"You mean, how I like dirty talk?" All right, that one slipped out, unabashed. Reckless.

Luckily, Austin and Deacon didn't hear it. They're next to the stove, checking to see if Jake and Noah have finished making dinner.

Violet's current smile now appears at the top of my list for upcoming fantasies. There's nothing innocent or sweet about it. Every curve is seductively shy.

"That wasn't quite what I meant, but you have me intrigued," she says. "Have you ever watched a reality show?"

"Do you really not remember me that well?"

"Right. Of course not. Well, if a show doesn't have enough

74

conflict and drama, viewers will quickly grow bored of it, and the viewership will drop. A drop in viewership means advertisers will redirect their money to other time slots for the next season. All of this is a kiss of death for the show, and it's something producers try to avoid—especially if they want to keep from joining the unemployment line."

"And you're worried Camilla will dig around and find something to add conflict to the show?"

"Exactly. I mean, I'm sure they'll find something anyway. You haven't exactly been a perfect little angel your entire life."

Unfortunately, Noah didn't consider that when he submitted my name for the show.

"Is that horse for Deacon?" Grandma Meg asks, spotting the rocking horse in my arms.

Nodding, I lower it onto the floor and instantly Deacon is on it, rocking and giggling.

"TJ made that," Grandma Meg tells Camilla. "He donates them to kids undergoing chemo."

Camilla's eyes widen—but not in surprise. The cogs in her head are spinning. Spinning as she plots how to use this new information. Spinning as she calculates a way it can benefit the show. "Really? How come you didn't mention it on the application form?"

I shrug because it's not like I filled it in. "That's because I didn't think it was important. Not for the show anyway. Creating rocking horses isn't your standard cowboy duty."

"True. But it's a great angle to your story."

"My story?"

She pushes away from the table and stands. "Yes, your story. It's what makes each cowboy unique," she says, walking toward me. "The show is more than just about hot-looking men."

Could have fooled me, given how much she's been pushing for me to be shirtless. And yes, she actually suggested I go shirtless when Craig videotaped me cooking the chili.

"Do you have any more?"

I shake my head. "I usually give them away as soon as I finish making them."

"How long does it take you to make one?"

"About two to three weeks." Depending on how busy I am.

"Do you think you can have one ready for the next round?" she asks. "It would make a great segment to have you and Natalie present the horse to a kid in the hospital."

"You mean *if* I advance to the next round."

Camilla pats my arm in a way that I'm not sure how to read—other than it's not seductive. "I'd bet money that you'll make it, no problem. Of the men I've met so far, you're definitely the one our audience will be lusting over. And I'm sure my fellow co-producers who have met the other contestants will agree."

Oh, joy.

"So, can you have a horse ready by then?" Her tone is all business, further confirming my original suspicion. She's only thinking of the show. She's not thinking of the sick kids I make the horses for.

"Sure." Somehow, I sound more enthusiastic than I feel. Maybe way, way, *way* deep inside me, there's an actor waiting to break free.

I inwardly snort at that.

After dinner, Austin, Grandma Meg, and Deacon drive back to town.

Violet glances out the living room window. "TJ, we should head out now. The lighting will be perfect soon for what I have planned for the photos."

"Craig," Camilla says, standing from the couch. "We might as well join them and get footage of TJ modeling for the camera."

Disappointment kicks me in the ass. Violet has been sending me unmixed signals, and now I want to find out if I've been reading them correctly. Find out if they're what I'm hoping for.

Find out if they're what I *shouldn't* be hoping for.

But I can't do it with Craig and Camilla tagging along.

"That's probably not a good idea." Violet says it a little too quickly, gaining a few surprised looks. "I mean, I'll be shooting photos with low, directional lighting. It will look great for what I have in mind. It won't look so hot for the video camera." If the speed of words spoken was a rodeo event, Violet just won top prize.

"She's right," Craig says. "Depending on where she plans to do it, I'll need the lighting guys back to add diffused lighting to help soften the shadows."

"Which will ruin the effect I'm after," Violet says, going in for the final kill.

After a moment, Camilla nods—and I release the breath I didn't realize was lodged in my lungs. "Okay. We'll sit this one out. I've got some work I have to do anyway."

Violet gathers her gear and we walk to the barn.

"Shirt on or off?" I ask once we get to the spot where she plans to shoot the photos.

Her mouth takes on a mischievous grin. "On for now."

"Where do you want me?" I have a few suggestions, but they aren't appropriate for family-friendly photos.

She points to the side of the building, softly lit in the sun's golden glow, then sets up her tripod and camera.

She then walks to a bale of straw that she had asked me earlier to put there. She bends down and starts dragging it toward me.

"You need help?" I say, making a move toward her to do exactly that.

"No, I'm good."

Yep, from the prime view of her ass I'm getting, I'd say she's more than good.

"Keep wiggling your ass like that and I'll be so hard, you won't be able to take photos for a while." My voice comes out low and sandpaper rough—not at all like my usual voice around her.

She peers over her shoulder and her gaze lands on my package—which doesn't help my present situation. "Oops, sorry."

Except she sounds far from sorry.

And that gets my cock even more worked up.

Which is definitely an issue for the photo.

I recite the chili recipe in my head. Not the most effective image but it's preferable over the other option: dwelling on the ex-SEAL who shares her genetics.

Once the bale is positioned near the wall, she straightens. "Put your foot on that."

I do as she asks, and she explains how she wants me to pose: one hand resting on my upper thigh, my head tilted slightly forward, hand on the rim of my cowboy hat.

She gently places both of her hands on either side of my face. My heart hammers against my chest like a swarm of dragonflies trapped inside.

She repositions my head, the movement negligible. "That's perfect." Her voice is soft and breathy, the sound of an angel's song. "Don't move, and I'll get a few shots with you like that."

She lightly caresses her thumb across my cheek, further hyping up the dragonflies. Then she removes her hands from my face and measures the light falling on me—her explanation—with some weird-looking handheld device.

Violet returns to her camera and starts clicking away. The entire time, she directs me on how to move.

And when I say move, I'm talking tiny adjustments. Tiny adjustments in the way I'm standing. Tiny adjustments in the position of my head. Tiny adjustments in the way I breathe. I couldn't imagine being a model and doing this full time. By the end of it, I'd resemble a crazed monkey caught in a factory of fake bananas.

After she's been snapping photos for several minutes, she asks me to lower my hand and look up at the camera.

Those dragonflies in my chest? They go berserk at the vision in front of me. I suck in a sharp breath.

The sun is shining on her dark hair, setting strands of it on fire with bursts of red. Her bare arms and shoulders also glow in the warm light. She resembles a dark-haired angel—and damned if I don't need saving.

"Oh, that's perfect." Her tone is more strained than it was a few minutes ago. "There's going to be a lot of exploding ovaries from women checking out your pictures on the show's website."

"Sounds painful," I say, doing my best not to move, my eyes still locked on Violet.

Her mouth slides up to one side. "Fortunately, it's not fatal."

"Are your ovaries exploding?" My voice is even rougher than before. Rougher and heated.

She walks slowly toward me, the way you do with a colt you suspect is going to bolt. Only she doesn't have to worry about me going anywhere.

She stops in front of me. "Maybe a little."

I smirk. "Just a little? I must be losing my touch."

She laughs. "Somehow I don't think you're losing anything." She runs her hands along the collar of my white western shirt, brushing her fingertips against my skin.

A shiver of anticipation rolls through me, but I don't move. I just gaze at her, barely breathing.

"I'm going to undo your shirt now, but keep still."

I couldn't move if I tried. I'm starving for more of her touch. Starving to inhale her sweet scent. Starving to spend more time with her, to enjoy her company.

Because that part hasn't changed over the years. I love hanging out with her. Not because she's sexy and gorgeous and gets every part of me running hot. She's funny and smart.

She's Violet.

With slow, measured movements, she slides the top button through the hole. Her fingers slip beneath the shirt's edge and skim along my skin. A tingling I've never experienced before vibrates from the spot, leaving my body humming with need.

While I watch her face, she continues unbuttoning my shirt. My fingers itch to touch her skin, but I keep still, worried that if I even flinch, she'll vanish.

Her breath comes in fast, much like my own. I feel like I used to, seconds before a rodeo competition, when I was on my horse, waiting for the calf to be released from the shoot. My body strums with anticipation, strums from both nerves and excitement.

Once she's finished unfastening the final button, she glides her hands between the fabric of my shirt and my abs. Her thumbs trace over the ridges of my muscles.

Her face turns up to mine, her lips parted. Her eyes are now dark with need, dark with challenge. "Stay exactly like this."

She then pulls her hands out of my shirt and walks back to her camera, the swell of her hips taunting me as they move.

At the absence of her hands on my body, disappointment crashes into me like a rogue wave. But as much as I want to complain, I can't. These photos are important to her. Not because of the show, but because of what they mean for her career.

She shoots more pictures and then returns to stand in front of me. "Now you can remove your shirt."

"What—you're not gonna help me?"

I smirk. She rolls her eyes.

"You're a big boy, TJ. I'm sure you can figure it out yourself."

"You don't know what you're missing." Like she did when she unbuttoned my shirt, I take my time, shrugging it off my shoulders.

I drop the shirt to the ground.

It's not like Violet hasn't seen me shirtless. But the way her gaze is drinking me in, it might as well be the first time. The girl is practically panting at the sight of me.

And that's not my ego talking.

"I didn't plan to be part of this show," I tell her after she's taken a few more photos.

The clicking pauses. "So why did you apply? Because I'm thinking that if you apply to be on a reality show, it means you're hoping to be selected."

"I didn't apply. Noah applied on my behalf and didn't tell me until it was too late."

She bites her lip, clearly struggling not to laugh.

I frown. "It's not funny."

She bursts out laughing, my words having the opposite effect of what I'd intended. "You have to admit—yes it is."

"How exactly do you think it's funny? What happens if I make it to the end of the season, and the woman expects me to propose to her?"

"You don't have to worry about that, TJ." Her mouth twitches as she fights back another laugh.

Her comment only makes me frown again. "Why not?"

I have no clue why I said that or why I frowned, because proposing to anyone—never mind a stranger—isn't on my to-do list. Ever.

"I didn't say it to hurt your ego," Violet says. "This show isn't like *The Bachelorette*, where the woman and the men spend maybe six or more weeks together. And during that time, the woman is expected to fall in love with one of the men...and he her. That's bad enough. In *Cowboy Most Wanted*, you only get to spend a total of five weeks with her. One week alone with her on your ranch—well, as alone as you can be with a camera crew following you everywhere. And then the final five guys will spend four weeks on a ranch with her—vying for her attention.

"So first there have to be sparks between the two of you before you even advance to the final round. And the odds of her falling in love with you and you with her are extremely low."

"But she still has to pick one guy from the final five," I point out. One out of five is a lot worse odds than one out of fifteen.

"That doesn't mean you have to marry her. You propose to her and a few months later, you guys break up."

"You sound like Noah."

Violet laughs. "I'd say Noah is a smart guy, but since he signed you up for the show when you obviously don't want to do this…" She leaves the sentence hanging, letting me fill in the blanks.

"So why did he do it anyway?" she asks. "Did you guys have a brotherly spat and he entered you as payback? Because if that's the case, I'd hate to see what the fight was about." She visibly shudders—faked of course.

I remove my foot from the bale of straw and place it on the ground. "Sorry to disappoint. There was no fight. The dumbass just figured it was a great way for people to find out about our ranch. He thought it would be great marketing." I grab my shirt off the grass.

This time when Violet bursts out laughing, tears fill her eyes. I grunt, which only makes her laugh harder.

I slip my arms into the shirt sleeves. "Glad you find it so amusing." How did we go from things getting heated between us to this? I'd rather go back to when I was seconds from kissing her senseless.

"I'm sorry," she says, appearing anything but apologetic. "It's just I never would've guessed that as a reason for why you decided to be on the show. And when you think about it, it's not that great a plan."

"You don't have to tell *me* that. I'm the one who has to be something he isn't."

"And what's that?"

"Eager to settle down."

She nods thoughtfully. "I can see why that would be a problem. Thanks to the show, people around here assume you're looking for love. So if you don't end up with the girl, and unless you look broken up over her picking someone else, I'd say you're screwed."

She tilts her head slightly to the side. Not in flirting mode. More like she's figuring out what makes me tick. She then removes her camera from the tripod. "If you want, I have time right now to look at your website and discuss some ideas with you."

"Even though Jake and Noah are heading out after they get the horses in for the night?" I'd go with them, but I'm not in the mood to go to Joe's with cameramen in tow.

Violet grabs the brim of my hat, lifts the Stetson off my head, and sets it on her own.

And the image of her wearing the hat and only the hat now keeps me company.

"What's wrong, cowboy?" Violet asks. "Don't you trust me?"

I jerk the brim of the hat down over her eyes.

"The question is...do you trust *me*?"

T he house is quiet when Violet and I enter.

We head to the office and close the door behind us.

A few minutes later, the computer on the oak desk is booted and the ranch's less-than-stellar website is on display.

Only a couple of inches separate us. A rose-and-vanilla-scented heat rolls off Violet, mixing with my own body heat...like lovers getting all hot and heavy.

A battle wages in my head, debating the pros and cons of touching her. Of kissing her. Of telling her how much I want her.

Right now, the sides are evenly matched, but I suspect the pro side is planning a sneak attack to takeover logical reasoning. And the con side will be left waving the white flag.

"I haven't had a chance yet," Violet says, "to tell you how sorry I was to hear about your knee."

I shrug as though it's no big deal when in truth, it is. I miss the competition within the rodeo circuit.

"Injuries happen all the time," I say. "It's the nature of the sport. It's not like I would've been able to do it forever. There's a reason you don't see ninety-year-old cowboys sitting on the back of some crotchety old bull during a rodeo event."

Violet laughs. "I guess you have a point there. But I'm still sorry. I know how much you loved the sport." My favorite sweet smile slides onto her face. "I used to love watching you compete. The way you were one with the horse. The way you were able to block out the entire world like nothing else mattered. The excitement in your eyes when you won or did really well. I miss all of that...I've missed you." The last part is said on a whisper.

"I've missed you, too." My words come out strong, husky. Not the way you would sound if you missed hanging out with someone who is just a friend.

Our gazes remain locked for a heartbeat, and my breath stalls. I could get lost in her beautiful brown eyes.

But then she blinks and turns back to the computer as if the moment between us never happened. She clicks on another website page. "Granny said you're hoping to appeal to customers interested in buying horses that have the potential of becoming champion rodeo horses. You should mention on the website that you were a state champion calf roper. And you should also mention Thor's and Odin's pedigrees and winning titles."

I nod, even though I'd rather be tasting her lips for the first and second and fourth time than discussing the website.

"I've studied the websites of your competition within Montana and Texas. The solid ones state the horse breeds that are part of the ranch's program and the roles they're being trained for. That needs to be part of your mission statement on the first page. And that's a great place to include a photo of you competing."

Can you tell that Jake is more a numbers guy than a marketer? From what he told me, marketing hadn't been his thing back in college.

Hence our website.

"Except I don't have any photos," I say.

"That's not a problem. I have some I took at the rodeos I attended. You can use those."

An unfamiliar heat flickers inside my chest. Was I aware that more photos existed, other than the one on Grandma Meg's wall? Not at all. I also wasn't aware that Violet had attended other rodeos where I'd been competing, or that she'd kept track of my career.

"We'll make sure you get credit for the photos," I tell her, channeling my inner Jake...complete with his all-business tone. "That way you can benefit, too."

The smile she gives me is soft and shy. A craving to pull her into my arms dances through me—pull her into my arms and kiss her sweetly on the temple, on the tip of her nose, on her lips.

"Thanks," she says. "Right now, my photography career is based on word of mouth and the right people at the right time seeing the photos I've taken."

"And that's why you agreed to work for the show? So the right people see your photos?" It makes sense.

"Yes. It would've been different if one of those other reality shows had asked. I still want to focus on horse photography—both the ones where the horses are running free and the posed shots with their owners. Even with the cattle ranches on the show, I've been able to do that. The photos will be on the website and in a special edition magazine that will be released. I'm hoping both will help me out."

"There's going to be a special edition magazine?" That's news to me.

"After seeing my photos from the earlier ranches, the executive producers decided they could do something with that. It's not to promote the show's drama, but rather to highlight the beauty of the land and the horses." She shrugs, but her excited tone has already betrayed her lack of indifference. "They're trying to broaden their target market by focusing on more than just the hot men on the show."

An eye-rolling laugh escapes me. "I was beginning to think

that's all the show was about. A bunch of shirtless men looking for love." Despite what Camilla told me earlier.

Violet's mouth curves into a smirk. "Well, that's the major gist of it. But they want it to stand out from *The Bachelor* and *Bachelorette* a bit more. I was hardly going to argue with that when it could help my photography career. Especially when it's a chance for me to showcase parts of America that people don't know about."

"Does that mean you plan to pursue it full-time now?" Because once upon a time, she believed it wasn't an option. Let's just blame it on her lawyer father. To him, being a photographer was akin to being a starving artist.

"I still believe it's hard to be a full-time photographer and make a steady income," she says, echoing the same thoughts her father had hammered into her head. "Plus all the traveling I'd have to do wouldn't be fair to Deacon. He was staying with a nanny who agreed to be live-in while I was gone for the show. But that's expensive, and I miss him like crazy when I'm not around."

She clicks on another website page. "This is slightly better. But the horse photos aren't great. They're stagnant. Anyone can shoot a picture of a horse just standing there. It's fine for a few photos. But it gets boring when they're all like that."

"So, what are you suggesting?"

"Horses in motion." She grabs her phone from the desk and taps on it. "Something like this." She holds it out for me to see. On the screen, a white horse is frozen midmotion while cantering in a field. There's a wildness about the photo that is captivating.

I take the phone from her and continue studying the picture. "You took this?" I already know the answer. I just want her to admit it out loud.

She smiles, but it's not a full out smile. It's trampled on with uncertainty. "Yes."

"It's perfect. You always were an amazing photographer back in high school. But this is a whole new level of amazing."

Her smile becomes less uncertain and more relieved. And then it's the sun at sunrise. Stunning. Gorgeous. Breathtaking.

I can't help but absorb its heat, greedy bastard that I am.

I'm storing it for when she's gone again and I'm back to missing her.

I return the phone to her. "Do you have a website?"

"That's the funny thing…despite doing this for my clients and despite my marketing background, creating a website is still on my to-do list. Once I get home from work, Deacon is my number one priority."

"That doesn't surprise me. I always knew you'd be a great mother." Except not once did I imagine she'd be raising a child by herself. "Does his father at least provide child support? Or will I have to get Thor to kick his ass?"

Violet rolls her eyes and sets her phone back on the desk. "One thing you guys should consider is to pick a color scheme and maintain it throughout. Same goes for the font. Select something that speaks to the underlying message you wish to convey."

I might have just suffered whiplash from the abrupt change of topic.

I test my neck, turning my head from side to side. Nope, it's all good. "Does Thor need to kick Deacon's father's ass?"

Violet let's out a long, *Can-we-just-drop-this?* sigh. "I already told you I don't want to talk about his father. He's not in the picture and that's all there is to it. Now about your website's underlying message…"

"I'm a cowboy, Violet, not a freaking designer. I didn't understand a single thing you just said." Letting her have her way for now, I bump her with my hip. Like I used to do back when I teased her. Back before I got hard-ons at the sight of her.

Except unlike then, my body feels like it's been zapped. The electricity zinging through it leaves me even more hyperaware of her. Aware of her sweet scent, of the light splattering of freckles on her nose, of her begging-to-be-kissed lips.

I touch her cheek as if to wipe away a stray tear that isn't there. Her skin is as soft as I'd imagined it would be. She doesn't move. She just stares up at me, her eyes dark and heated. Like earlier by the barn, her breath comes in faster, shallower than normal.

I start to move my hand away from her face. She places *her* hand gently over mine, turns her head, and kisses my palm.

Heat radiates from the spot. If this is what it feels like with her just kissing my hand, what would it be like if we actually kissed?

Would it be everything I've ever imagined it would be?

"I'm really hoping you're going to kiss me now." Her voice is low, breathy. "Because that's all I can think about."

I don't wait for another invitation. I lower my head to hers. The touch of our lips is teasing. Questioning. Tender.

My heart beats loudly in my chest, *Don't stop, don't stop, don't stop.*

Half listening to it, I pull back ever so slightly. "I probably shouldn't be doing this," I murmur.

"Why not?" The sound of her voice has shifted. It's now rough, a sliver more than a whisper.

" 'Cause your brother will kill me."

"Why would he kill you? You're his friend. He knows you and he trusts you."

I snort a quiet laugh. "That's probably why he wouldn't trust me. He knows me too well."

"Well, for the record, despite what my brother believes, he doesn't get a say in who I date or kiss or have hot, dirty sex with." She moves her head back and locks her gaze with mine. "And also, for the record, I'm all for kissing you and having hot, dirty sex with you."

I stroke the pad of my thumb across her lip. She nips my thumb between her teeth and my entire body hums for joy. I can't remember a time when it's reacted this way to a simple kiss—not even with my ex-girlfriend.

A voice in my head tells me to go ahead and kiss the girl again.

So I do.

I press my lips against Violet's once more. A stuttering sigh releases from her, then she opens her mouth and welcomes me in.

I thread the fingers of one hand through the soft strands of her hair and cradle her head. The other hand presses against her lower back, bringing her closer.

Our tongues slide together, tasting, teasing, getting acquainted. I could spend a lifetime doing this with her and never grow tired of it.

Heaven? This is it.

Unfortunately, I don't get to enjoy even a minute of it, never mind a lifetime. A knock on the office door brings our kiss to an abrupt, I'm-going-to-kill-whoever-that-is end.

We separate, our breaths ragged and not sounding too innocent.

"Yes?" I call out. Violet goes back to studying the computer screen.

The door clicks open and I turn around to see who it is.

Camilla walks into the office, smiling like she has discovered buried treasure. "There you are, TJ. Your brothers said you weren't going to the bar with them, so I was wondering where you had disappeared to."

"Violet and I were just discussing the ranch's website."

"Good idea. You might want to add something about being on the show when it airs in three weeks. Violet can assist with that if you need help."

As if being on the show wasn't bad enough, now I have to announce it to the people who wouldn't have otherwise known? *Excellent.*

Naturally, that doesn't count anyone in Copper Creek. Thanks to Tilly, everyone who follows her Facebook page is aware of it.

And for those who don't follow her page...the old-fashioned gossip mill is always hard at work.

"I can do that," Violet says, sounding less breathless than she did a moment ago. Enthusiasm is a pale ghost in her tone—and I'm not referring to Casper the Friendly Ghost.

Hopefully her reaction is because Camilla interrupted our kiss and not because of her request.

Camilla joins us and peers at the computer screen. I half expect her to suggest shirtless photos of me on the site. She doesn't.

Well, there's a first.

"You should also include a page about you and your brothers," Violet says, as if our original conversation hadn't been intruded on by either the kiss or Camilla. "Make it personal, but not too personal. Potential buyers will develop an emotional connection to you, especially if one of you shares a similar interest to them."

"That's a good idea." I might have said that, but what I really want is to touch Violet again.

Touching does happen, only it's not my fingers tracing along the tantalizing skin on Violet's neck and shoulder. And if Camilla hadn't interrupted us, that's exactly where my lips would be right now.

No, this touch is Camilla's hand on my shoulder, like we're business partners. "I was thinking that you and I should discuss the plans for the next few days," Camilla says, fortunately oblivious to my thoughts about my best friend's sister.

I'm about to say okay, since the moment between Violet and me is now over, when my cell phone pings. I read the text from Aubrey.

> Aubrey: Get your ass down here and bring my
> girl with you or else there will be hell to pay. :)

I mentally chuckled at Aubrey's text. "Actually, Violet and I are supposed to join my brothers at the bar. But you're more than welcome to discuss the plans with me there."

Violet looks slightly confused, a wrinkle sitting adorably between her eyes. I show her my phone. She picks up hers from the desk and walks away while tapping on it.

"I'm going with Violet in her car," I tell Camilla. I can always get a ride back with my brothers. "Did you want to follow us in your vehicle? We'll be leaving in a minute."

And if the Norse gods are shining down on me, I might be able to finagle a slow dance with Violet.

Because after the kiss that rocked the ranch's foundations, I can't wait to get her in my arms again.

As it is, it will be a little trickier than I'd like.

And I'm not talking about Austin.

I'm talking about the contract I signed that prevents me from being involved with another woman while I'm part of the show.

It's a good thing I had lots of experience sneaking around as a teen.

That skill is about to come in handy.

12

For a Wednesday night, Joe's is busy. Well, busy for this town. The local country band currently playing might have something to do with it.

Violet, Camilla, and I weave our way through the crowd. Empty peanut shells crunch underfoot. A protective need surges through me to settle my hand on Violet's lower back, to make sure the guys eyeing her know they're entering dangerous, you're-about-to-be-torn-apart territory. But that's not exactly feasible with Camilla tagging along.

Especially since she's also gaining the same attention from the men.

We join my brothers at our regular table near the dance floor. Jake is busy watching Sophie and Aubrey line dance.

Or more specifically, he's busy scowling at them.

Sophie is laughing and smiling at Chase Scottsdale. He's the grandson of Walter Scottsdale...the owner of Scottsdale Ranch. Our rivals.

Jake's scowl deepens.

"She's just dancing with him," I helpfully point out. "She's not running off to marry him."

That gets my brother's attention. He levels his ticked-off gaze at me. *Ouch.* "What does that have to do with anything?"

"And even if she is," I say, ignoring his question, "that's her choice. She can do whatever she wants. But I doubt she's into him that way. She doesn't stumble over her words with him."

I forgot to mention that Sophie has an issue when it comes to talking to men she's crushing on. The issue? Her ability to form coherent sentences. It vanishes every time. It's always a riot watching her flirt.

Or attempt to.

Jake's scowl upgrades to a level four hurricane. The kind of hurricane that could wipe out islands. And it's all directed at me.

Double ouch.

"Besides, the last I heard, you weren't interested in her that way. Because she's our horse trainer and therefore our employee...and dating her is against company policy."

Because apparently we have company policies.

That was news to both Noah and me when Jake sprung it on us over a year ago. Shortly after Sophie began working for us.

My voice is nonchalant, but there's no hiding the full-out smirk in my tone. "Christ, do yourself a favor, and get laid tonight." I slap him on the back.

"What the fuck are you doing here anyway? I thought you weren't joining us." He then notices Violet and Camilla and nods at them.

"Aubrey texted and told me to bring Violet. So here we are." I spread my arms wide open.

He dips his head slightly, eyebrows raised. It's his signal. Like Batman's signal. Only in this case, it means he's calling me on my bullshit.

But really, what is he expecting? I'm hardly admitting to my brother that I'm here to spend time with my best friend's sister because it's impossible to do that at home with Camilla there.

A new song starts. Jake stands. "Ever line dance before?" he asks Camilla before she has a chance to sit.

"Country music isn't my thing." The comment is echoed in her clothing. She's wearing a knee-length skirt, stilettos, and a sleeveless silk top. "So I haven't had a chance to try it."

"Well, you are about to have your first lesson."

She barely has a chance to agree before he's leading her to the dance floor.

Violet starts talking to Sophie and Aubrey. I talk shop with Noah about one of the colts...while he surveys the area to figure out which girl to go home with tonight.

The fast-paced song ends and a slower one takes its place. Jake and Camilla are returning from the dance floor.

"Can I steal Violet for a few minutes?" I ask her two friends. "I'm in the mood to dance."

More like in the mood to touch Violet, but since I can't exactly do that here with Camilla watching me, dancing is the only excuse I can come up with that allows me to touch her.

Is Camilla the only person I have to worry about here?

Not at all. Let's just say that Tilly isn't the only gossip in Copper Creek. The last thing I need is for a friend of a friend of the police station's secretary to be here. Experience is a bitch, and that bitch has slapped me in the face at least once.

It's one thing to have Austin find out about what almost turned into a bar brawl—the start of which was completely not my fault, mind you. It's yet another to discover that I'm touching his sister in a way he won't approve of.

I lead Violet to the dance floor and take her in my arms. Hers go around my neck and we sway to the beat.

"What are the chances of us escaping without Camilla and the TV crew wondering where we've disappeared to?" I ask.

"I doubt the guys will care. They're just here to do their job. It's Camilla who won't be so understanding if she puts two and two together."

"That's too bad." My voice is low and gravelly against Violet's cheek. " 'Cause I want to taste your pussy. It's all I can think about. I want to taste you when you come against my mouth. I want to hear your sweet moans as you fall apart in my arms."

It's a good thing I'm holding her. Her body dips slightly, as if her knees buckled under the erotic weight of my words. Her swallowed whimper also gives away that she craves for me to follow through on my promise.

We finish dancing to the song and return to the table. Luckily, my cock realizes being hard after dancing with Violet isn't the wisest course of action.

It behaves—for now.

My beer is on the table when we arrive. I pick up the glass and chug back the cold liquid.

Jake leans closer to me. "You need me to distract Camilla, so you and Violet can go fuck somewhere?" He says it low enough to be heard over the music, but not loud enough for anyone else to overhear him.

Shit. Are we that obvious?

On instinct, I glance around, searching for Austin.

When I don't see him, I swivel back to my brother. "No idea what you're talking about, man." I gulp back more beer.

"No? Is that why you're heading toward hangover-ville? Which, I might add, won't look too great on video tomorrow."

"Nothing's going on between Violet and me. She's my best friend's sister. She and I are just friends. You know that."

"Right. You keep telling yourself that. But for the record, from the way I've seen her look at you, the woman definitely wants you, brother be damned."

Since nothing I say will make him believe otherwise, I ask, "And how exactly do you plan to distract Camilla? Throw yourself at her? Take one for the team like I'm doing with this dumbass show?"

He smirks the infuriating smile of his that always leaves me grinding my unlucky teeth. "You wanted to breed horses. I wanted to keep breeding cattle. So suck it up, Buttercup."

Grind. Grind. Grind.

Forty minutes later, Violet breaks away from her conversation with Aubrey and Sophie. She's been talking to them since we left the dance floor. Noah is teaching Camilla the fine art of line dancing.

Violet walks over to where I'm standing with Jake. "I'm heading back to Granny's now."

Jake checks his phone. "Already? But it's not even ten."

"Welcome to being a mother."

"In that case, remind me to never become one." He winks at her and she laughs.

"Let me walk you to your car." My tone is casual. Or at least it sounds casual in my head. Although from the way Jake is clearly snickering in *his* head, I'm not so sure I pulled it off. "My parents raised me to be a gentleman," I say to her, "and that involves walking a woman to her vehicle. You wouldn't want to disappoint them after they worked so hard to instill those values in me, would you?"

Jake laughs out loud this time—mostly because he knows everything I just said is bullshit.

He grabs my arm as we walk past. "Do I need to distract Camilla?" he asks under his breath. "Or are you really planning to be back in a few minutes?"

I just shrug—because I have no idea which one is true. "I might go for a walk to clear my mind."

Outside, the night air has cooled a few degrees since we entered the bar. I scan the parking lot. No one's here, but it doesn't mean someone won't exit the bar at any moment. And it doesn't mean Austin won't drive past in his squad car while I'm making out with his sister.

I wrap my hands around her hips and draw her close. Then I trace my lips along her jaw to her earlobe, relishing the feel of her silky skin. "Do you have to leave right away?" My voice is husky with need and pent-up desire. Desire for this woman and only this woman.

"What do you have in mind?"

"This." I gently grab her wrist and lead her across the parking lot.

Joe's is located near the edge of the forest that sweeps down in this section of town. We disappear into the tree line and walk along the winding trail, the light from my cell phone making it easy to see where we're going. The world around us is quiet other than the soft sounds of nature. The occasional chirping of an evening bird. The rustle of leaves. The muted crunch from the layer of dead pine needles and twigs under our feet.

Several minutes later, we step into a small grassy clearing far from prying eyes. A large boulder, perfect for what I wish to do, sits near the outskirts of the area.

Before Violet has a chance to say anything, I pull her against me, and my mouth takes hers in an all-consuming kiss. I don't have much time before I have to return to the bar, and I plan to give Violet something to remember me by while she sleeps.

As my tongue continues enjoying the minty taste of her mouth, my fingertips glide along the edge of her strapless sundress. I've been fantasizing for the better part of the evening about pulling down the top and revealing those gorgeous tits that I know are waiting for me.

I cupped one of her breasts and almost groan at the way it fills my hand. I move away from her lips, slightly swollen from my kisses, and watch her face as I brush the pad of my thumb against her nipple. Even with the dress and bra in the way, I feel it tighten.

I gaze into her eyes, dark with want. "I need to taste you. Can I do that?"

Her answer is a single nod.

I lower the fabric of her dress and bra and take a moment to worship the view. Then my lips are around one nipple and I suck on it hard.

Violet moans.

My hat disappears from my head, to be relocated onto hers. Her fingers knot in my hair, keeping my head in position.

While my mouth is busy, I skim my fingers along her silky inner thighs and under her skirt, the heat of her pussy beckoning me. I continue my exploration until my fingers graze the elastic of her panties.

Payday.

Violet releases a needy gasp that makes me even harder.

I give her nipple one final flick with my tongue and pull away. Gazing at her through half-closed eyes, I trace my finger against her cotton-covered pussy.

She groans a sound of sweet satisfaction.

"Are you as wet for me as I think you are?" I ask.

"Maybe." Her voice is raspy with desire—just the way I imagined it would be if fantasy ever became reality.

"Sounds like a challenge to me."

Her lips curve into a teasing smile. "Maybe."

Taking that as permission for what I long to do next, I slide my finger under the fabric and run it along the promised land. It's slippery and feels just as I dreamed it would.

"Christ, Violet, I need to taste you so badly." I hook my thumbs on the waistband of her panties and slowly drag them down her legs. Her breath comes in ragged pants.

Once the fabric rests on the top of her cowgirl boots, I lift one ankle and remove her footwear, guide her panties off, and replace the boot. I repeat this with the other leg.

I shove the small scrap of material into my jeans pocket and smirk at her. "I'll just keep that for now. Sit on the boulder and spread your legs for me."

She does, lifting the hem of her skirt and giving me a tantalizing view. A tantalizing view of what I've fantasized about while jerking off in the shower.

It's just as I imagined, which says a lot.

My cock presses painfully against the zipper of my jeans, desperate to burst free, like the shirt-ripping Hulk.

I ignore it for now and crouch between her legs. I lift one then the other onto my shoulders.

"Shouldn't we be getting back now?" Violet asks, though her tone suggests the opposite. "They might start wondering what happened to you. Or more likely, Camilla will question where you vanished to."

"I'm sure Jake's doing a great job distracting her." I owe him big time—and I can guarantee he won't let me forget.

But whatever he has me do to make up for it will be worth it.

I lower my head between her legs and give her clit a single lick. Her answering moan leaves me grinning. "Like that, do you?"

"Very much."

"Then I guess I should do it again." My tongue teases her core, and I'm rewarded with a moan that gets my cock even more excited—a feat I didn't think was possible.

The faint snap of a twig registers somewhere in the back of my mind. I ignore it. It's just an animal passing through the forest.

I continue giving Violet's clit the lavish attention it deserves, then I press a finger against her entrance. Violet writhes at my touch. I plunge the finger in, letting her soft heat engulf me.

My cock demands some of that for itself; it's out of luck for now.

I push in another finger and scissor them, stretching her, driving her crazy.

"Oh, God, TJ," she says on a groan. The words are low, not much more than a whisper, but it's clear she's struggling to keep the entire town from knowing what we're up to.

Needing to taste her pussy, I remove my fingers from inside

her and replace them with my tongue. I shift my hand, and my thumb takes over the fun that my tongue enjoyed with her clit.

It doesn't take much more before her muscles clamp down on me and she comes hard against my face. Luckily, we're too far away for anyone to overhear us; only the wildlife in the vicinity get to appreciate the free entertainment.

I lower Violet's legs to the ground and straighten to my feet. "I guess by now everyone is wondering where I disappeared to. We should go back," I say after giving her a moment to recover.

Violet's gaze drops to my package, and a sensual smile stretches on her lips. She reaches for my zipper. "You can't go back to the bar like that. Let me help you."

Yes! screams my cock.

I ignore it because I meant what I said about getting Violet back to her car. I don't want Camilla to become suspicious. For one, if Violet's job finds out she was screwing with a contestant during the filming of the show, she might get in trouble. That's the last thing she needs, especially being a single mother.

And neither of us needs for what we did to hit the tabloids, which is always a possibility if word of it leaks out. If that should occur, Copper Creek will witness its first showdown since the town was founded—only I'll be the man toting a water pistol.

Austin will be the one with the real gun.

"I can wait until tomorrow night." I pull her to her feet and kiss her long and hard. It doesn't do much to solve the dilemma between my legs, but hopefully things will die down while we walk back to the parking lot.

"Are you sure?" she asks. "Because I'm not so sure I can wait that long before I have my mouth on your cock." Her eyes hold an impish gleam that matches the curve of her lips.

My cock cheers at her suggestion—clearly not understanding the seriousness of the situation if Violet and I are caught. "I'm sure."

And maybe after I've fucked her, things will be like my usual one-night stands. I'll be able to move past my lust for her.

The know-it-all voice in my head wishes me luck with that delusion—because a one-night stand and Violet aren't the same thing.

Not even close.

We traipse through the dark woods to the parking lot. The light from my phone leads the way. Violet stumbles a few times, but otherwise we make it back looking pretty much the same as when we entered. Maybe a little more disheveled than before, but nothing too noteworthy.

Before we step into the parking lot, I check to make sure no one is there. Then I escort Violet to her car. I ignore the urge to kiss her once more, and I watch her drive away before heading into the bar.

Camilla is on the dance floor again, except this time with Chase Scottsdale. She's laughing as he effortlessly guides her around the semi-crowded space.

"So, how long's that been going on?" I indicate at the pair.

"For three songs now," Jake replies. "And where the hell have you been? I wasn't expecting you to fly to the moon and back."

"It's not like I've been gone that long."

What are the odds of lightning striking me inside the building?

"Does she suspect anything?" I nod at the "she" I'm referring to.

"What—that you're screwing around with your best friend's sister when you're supposed to remain single until the final episode is aired?"

Yep, we're definitely talking you're-royally-fucked fodder for the tabloids if anyone else figures things out.

"That's only if I make it past the first round," I say.

The skeptical, bullshit bat signal? It's back on his face.

"All right, it counts now, too," I say. "But if I don't get picked to continue, then I won't have to worry about it. I can fuck whomever I want."

Except Violet will no longer be here.

"You're playing with fire, bro."

"You only get burned if you touch the flames."

I just have to make sure that I don't.

Or at least have a fire extinguisher handy.

13

The next morning, Noah parks the bowl of scrambled eggs in the middle of the kitchen table. "Can't believe today's your last day here," he says to Wilson and Craig. Violet hasn't arrived yet, and Camilla is still in her room.

"What are you talking about?" I ask Noah, then turn to the two men in question. "I thought you're here two more days."

And why didn't anyone tell me about the change of plans?

"We were, but now we have to return to LA tomorrow." Wilson helps himself to the eggs. "Our flight's in the morning.... Bet you'll be happy to get us out of your hair. For a few weeks, anyway."

Before I can point out that there's—hopefully—no guarantee they'll be back, Craig waves a slice of bacon at me. "You better have some more of this great stuff when we return. I swear you guys serve the best bacon I've ever tasted."

"When did this all go down?" I ask, ignoring the part about the food.

"Last night. When we were at Joe's. I'm surprised Camilla didn't tell you."

Or Violet.

She must have known.

Unless…

"Is Violet returning to LA tomorrow, too?"

Craig bites into his bacon. "That would be my guess," he says around the mouthful.

Shit.

"Deacon's grandmother will be disappointed." I somehow manage to sound nonchalant, as if I don't give a damn one way or another about her leaving tomorrow.

Which, of course, is a lie.

"I can imagine," Craig says. "He's a cute kid."

"He is." And surprisingly I'm going to miss him, even if he's only been in my life for a few days.

Camilla enters the kitchen and heads straight for the coffeemaker. She fills her mug and draws a long, fortifying sip. "So, cowboy, since it's our last day here, what are our plans for today?" In other words, what else can I do to pimp myself for the show and the viewers' benefit?

"One of the mares is ready to be bred."

"What does that mean?"

"It means today's the day Thor attempts to impregnate her."

Craig throws his head back in laughter. "You mean we're shooting horse porn?"

Camilla gives him a pointed look. I'll give it to her; she's unflappable when it comes to some of the things that motor from his mouth. "I can guarantee the network will thankfully not go for that."

The front doorbell chimes. Unfortunately, Noah is already bailing to get to his morning chores, which means he'll be at the front door before me. I could sprint there, but that might raise suspicion.

Violet enters the kitchen. I grip the edge of the table, gluing myself to my seat. It's that or give in to the urge to pull her into my arms.

"Violet, did you get the email my administrative assistant sent you last night?" Camilla asks.

"The one with the flight information?"

"Yes, that's the one. She really is a miracle worker, especially since she was able to get a plane ticket for your son, too." A miracle worker who works late at night, it would seem.

"You're right—she is a miracle worker. Especially since she was able to change the date he's flying back to LA."

Camilla's pale eyebrows pinch together in confusion. "Why would you want to change his return date? Isn't he going home with you?"

"Yes, but not this time. I emailed my boss last night and put in for vacation time. I'll be returning to LA tomorrow for a few days, just to finish off work I need to do. Then I'll fly back here for the week."

I can't help the upward tug on my mouth at her news. Not only will Violet be returning for a week, there will be no TV crew with her this time.

Which means as long as Austin and the town gossips don't figure things out, I can hang out with her like I want to...as well as delve deeper and discover Violet's dirty side.

"But you're still joining us when we go to the different ranches with Natalie, right?" Camilla asks her.

Violet nods. "Definitely. That's when the social media campaign will be going full force. Plus I'll still be working on it while I'm here, to help further build hype for the show."

I take the remaining piece of bacon from the plate, ignoring the puppy dog eyes I can feel Asgard directing my way. "Even though you'll be on vacation?"

"Yes, even though I'll be on vacation. But that part doesn't take long to do at this point in the season. Nothing like it will be once the cowboys have been selected for the next round. And I can easily schedule a lot of the posts and tweets ahead of time.

"And since I'm staying for the week. I can help you with your website and shoot photos of the ranch and the horses."

Then we can christen those locations with incredible, the-ground-is-trembling-under-us sex.

Works for me.

"Thanks. That would be great." I give her a brief nod. "Now, I've got a mare to get knocked up. But before I can do that, I need to finish my morning chores."

"Can we watch?" Craig's voice is a little too enthusiastic to be referring to my regular chores. Although if you ask me, it's also a little too enthusiastic for watching Thor go at it with Freida. But to each his own, I guess.

"Sure, if you want," I say to the two guys. "Are you ladies going to watch, too?"

Violet and I don't have a chance to talk while I do my morning chores. At least not the way I want to talk to her.

Teasing.

Flirting.

Dirty.

Thank Christ for the hard, physical labor required when running a ranch. It's enough to distract me from my thoughts of what my tongue and fingers were doing to Violet last night.

The same thoughts that visited me in the shower after I returned home from Joe's.

When it was only me and my hand.

"Why don't you just let the horses have a good fuck in the pasture?" Craig asks as we stride toward the paddock where Thor is waiting. Because Camilla doesn't wish Thor's mating to be caught on camera, all the equipment is stowed back at the house.

Since Violet is walking next to me—with only an inch or two separating us—I briefly stroke the back of her hand with my index finger. "You can do that. It's called pasture breeding. But you don't want to do it with a stallion who's considered valuable."

Everyone is looking ahead. No one notices what I'm doing to Violet.

From my periphery, I catch Craig turning his head toward me. I drop my hand away.

"Why's that?" he asks.

"Because if the mare freaks out, she can cause him serious damage."

"You mean like kick him in the nuts?" There's a wince to his tone, like someone just gave him a wedgie.

"Yeah, something like that. If we weren't looking to breed high-caliber rodeo horses, we could use pasture breeding. Our other options would be artificial insemination or sending our mares to be impregnated at another ranch. We breed quarter horses, but if we were breeding thoroughbreds, the mares would have to be bred the old-fashioned way."

"What's that?" Wilson asks.

Craig snorts a laugh. "Has it really been that long since you last got laid?" He demonstrates with hand actions exactly what I mean.

Wilson rolls his eyes. "My cousin had to use artificial insemination to get his wife pregnant. So how does it work with horses? You show them the horse's version of Playboy and give them a plastic cup to jack off in?"

"Yep, exactly like that," I say.

The men laugh but neither pushes further for details.

At the paddock, I open the wide metal gate far enough so Violet and I can easily slip past. We enter the grassy enclosure as I shut the gate behind us.

Because Violet's experienced around horses, I use that as my excuse for why she can join me. Camilla and the guys wait for us on the other side of the fence.

"You remember the old swing by the river?" I ask once we're out of the crew's hearing range.

She smiles in the way that always gets my heart thumping a little faster. "Of course."

"I thought maybe we could go there this evening...and reminisce about old times."

Minus those involving her brother.

"I'd like that. But I need to go to Granny's first to spend time with Deacon since I'm leaving tomorrow morning."

"Will he be okay with you leaving him in Copper Creek?"

Thor recognizes the halter I'm holding: his breeding halter. The halter that signals he's about to be one very happy stallion.

He approaches us, nickers, and nudges my arm with his head.

Violet strokes his nose. "He should be fine. He really likes Granny."

I chuckle. "As if it's possible for anyone to *not* like her? I bet she's got him wrapped around her fingers." Her chocolate chip cookies will do that to you.

Thor nudges my arm again.

"All right. I get it. You want to get laid. Who doesn't?" Especially since it's been a lot longer for me than it's been for him.

Violet giggles. I fake a frown. "Hey, don't laugh. I haven't had sex in a while. I miss it."

Those gorgeous brown eyes of hers travel up my body, rest on my package for a second, and continue northward to meet my gaze. "I guess we'll have to do something about that. God knows I'm more than ready to have someone fuck me."

She says the last two syllables in a voice that's equally low and equivalent to eight-packs-a-day husky. I'm surprised I didn't come hard in my jeans just at the sound of it.

"If it's me we're talking about thrusting deep inside you," I say in an equally sex-deprived voice, "then I'm all for it."

A whimper slips from her lips at "thrusting," and I can't help but inwardly grin.

I fasten Thor's halter on him and lead him to the gate. Not that I really have to lead him. He'll drag me there if he must.

I open the gate, and we walk to the teasing chute, where Jake is waiting with Frieda. It's nothing fancy, just two parallel fences set a little more than a horse-width apart.

Camilla looks back and forth from Frieda, who is standing between the fences, to Thor. "So what happens now?"

"Now we double check Frieda is in heat. She and Thor will let us know."

"How do they do that?"

The two men don't say anything—and I have a feeling Camilla is the reason behind that.

But while I would love to know what she said to them while Violet and I were in the paddock, I've got a more important job to do.

"Basically, if Thor flirts with her, she's ready to breed."

"That's it?" Camilla says.

I nod. "That's it."

"Thank God it doesn't work that way with humans. I'd hate to think that a man will only flirt with me when I'm primed to get knocked up. And what happens if you're on the pill? Does that mean no men will be interested in you?"

I'm not sure if I'm supposed to answer or laugh.

Violet doesn't have the same qualms. She laughs again. "That's one way to look at it."

I let Thor do his thing to confirm Frieda is ready.

"They're not going to do it in there, are they?" Camilla waves at the chute. " 'Cause I'm thinking that's not very romantic."

Wilson and Craig's best behavior ends with that comment. Both burst out laughing.

"Horses don't care about romance," Craig says, still chuckling. "They're just in it for a good time."

With his back to us, Jake strokes Frieda's neck and soothes the mare. "Au contraire." He turns to us. "Horses are very romantic. Just not the kind of romantic that involves candlelight dinners, moonlit strolls, and roses."

"In answer to your question," I say to Camilla, "now we have to clean Freida's and Thor's genitals to avoid the risk of infection."

The best way to get rid of two city men when you work on a ranch? Exactly what I just did.

Wilson and Craig choke out different excuses as to why they have to leave. I've never seen anyone move so fast.

The women laugh.

I'll admit I don't blame those guys one bit. Of all the tasks that go with breeding horses, this is the part neither my brothers nor I enjoy.

Humans have it so much easier when it comes to getting laid.

We just have to cover our dicks and we're ready to go.

"What happens if Freida doesn't want to do it with Thor?" Violet asks. Jake and I have just finished preparing the horses. "Maybe he doesn't meet her standards of what she's looking for in a stallion."

I gasp a mock-horrified sound. "How could she not want to be with Thor? He's the perfect specimen of a male horse."

Thor whinnies.

"You see?" I say. "He agrees with me."

Camilla glances at her phone.

Violet smirks. "Sorry, Thor. Hope I didn't offend your male ego. And you're right. He is the perfect male specimen." Her heated eyes are locked on mine when she says it, and I have a feeling we're no longer talking about my horse.

My cock twitches in full agreement.

"He accepts your apology." I wink at her. Like Violet's heated expression, Camilla also misses the wink.

"I'm curious too." Camilla looks up from her phone. "What if she doesn't wish to have sex with him?"

"First, you have to ensure she really is ready to breed. That might be why the mare is so reluctant. She isn't in her ovulation window."

"You mean horses are only interested in sex when they're ovulating?" Camilla says. "Remind me not to come back as a horse in my next life. 'Cause right now, I'm thinking they have the fucked-up end of the deal."

Violet laughs. "I'm with you there. Between that and the stallions only flirting with you when you're primed to get pregnant, where's the fun in being a horse?"

Jake looks between the two women, no doubt mentally rolling his eyes. "So come back as a stallion. They get to have plenty of sex during breeding season. Assuming they have access to more than a few mares."

Camilla's eyebrows shoot halfway up her forehead. "There's a breeding season? You mean they can't even have sex anytime they're in the mood?"

"Depending on where you live," I say, "it's pretty much during the summer. Or at least that's the prime time for them to conceive."

Camilla's expression is the one you have when someone you know has been given only five days to live. "You poor creature," she says to Frieda.

The mare whinnies, possibly agreeing with her.

"I really don't think she cares all that much," I say. "It's not like when humans go through a long dry spell without sex, then we crave it even more."

Or maybe I'm just speaking for myself.

Because right now, I want nothing more than to finish getting Frieda knocked up, so I can get dirty with Violet.

And it has nothing to do with getting horny after witnessing the horses go at it. Like Jake and Noah, I've learned to compartmentalize all of this. None of us gets off on watching Thor perform for the mares.

"What happens if she's ready to have sex but doesn't wish to have sex with Thor?" Camilla asks, repeating Violet's earlier question. "Does she have a choice?"

"Usually if they don't want to mate, it's because they're nervous. They don't know what to expect. It's not like they're gossiping while in the pasture, sharing secrets on how to please your stallion or fifty positions to increase sexual pleasure. There are no Cosmo magazines for horses."

Violet cocks her head to the side as she studies Frieda. "So how do you calm them so they're not so nervous?"

"Well, the goal is more to keep the mare from kicking the stallion and injuring him." Jake taps on his phone and hands it to Camilla. "Some breeders use this device."

She and Violet study the screen.

"It resembles something from *Fifty Shades of Grey*." Camilla tilts the phone, examining it from a different angle. "I didn't realize horses were into BDSM."

Violet snorts a snicker, then smacks her hand against her mouth. Adorable crinkles form at the corner of her eyes as she fights back another laugh.

And all I can focus on is how I crave to peel the lucky hand away from her mouth and kiss her.

Kiss her until she's moaning my name.

Kiss her until I'm all she can think about for the next few days.

14

An hour later, the deed is done.

When I say deed, I'm referring to Thor's gallant go at becoming a father. Again.

All the other tasks to be completed are wrapped up. Frieda is in her stall. Thor is back in his pasture for now. And Jake is heading back to the house.

"And that, ladies, is how a foal is conceived." Well, hopefully conceived. Like with humans, there's no guarantee it was successful this time. "Any questions?"

Camilla decides she's good on the Q&A. "Time for me return to the house and begin packing. Plus I need to respond to a few emails." She gives me her patented all-business smile and walks off, her designer heels clicking against the path.

Finally alone with Violet, I lead her away from the house, to a spot where no one there can see us. My pace is fast and purposeful, with Violet matching it stride-for-stride. And with each step, the need to possess her becomes stronger.

But that's not what this is about.

I miss the feel of her in my arms. I miss talking to her when it's just the two of us alone.

And I miss kissing her.

As soon as we get behind the barn, I push her against the wood, gaze into her eyes for a heartbeat, then crash my lips against hers.

I can't get enough of this woman. Can't get enough of how I feel when I'm with her. She's not a drug that burns addictive in the blood. She's something much brighter, safer.

If you ignore the part how her brother is an ex-SEAL and the town sheriff.

Her arms go around my neck; mine go around her waist. She tilts her head back, allowing me to deepen the kiss.

My cock stirs, its impatience to sink into Violet palpable.

I remind it that we'll have plenty of time for that tonight—assuming she's still game for it after witnessing Thor get it on a short while ago.

And I hope she is because after we've fucked, I'll finally get her out of my system. My fantasies and I can move on.

I pull back slightly. Our rapid breaths collide and comfort and copulate.

"God, I want you so badly." Violet's tone is that of someone who hasn't eaten in a while—or been eaten.

My favorite kind of tone.

"Glad to see none of that with Thor and Frieda turned you against ever having sex again."

Raw pain flickers in her eyes, and she releases a soft huff. But the emotion is so fleeting, I can't be sure if I read it correctly.

I trace the pad of my thumb along her lower lip. "What's wrong?"

She turns her face up to mine and a smile spreads across it. "Nothing's wrong." She reaches up and tenderly touches her mouth to mine. "What time do you want to meet tonight?"

"Are you sure you still want to?"

"Hmm, let me think on that for a second." She taps her index finger against her lips, her eyes a shade of I-want-you-to-do-me-now heated. "I haven't had sex in forever, and a hot man who I happen to know is capable of giving me orgasms is asking if I'm sure I want to have sex tonight. Hmm. Tough decision."

I chuckle, doing my best not to dwell on the part where she thinks I'm hot. Sure, I've had plenty of girls tell me that. But those girls weren't Violet. "Let me make the decision a little easier for you." I capture her mouth in another breath-stealing kiss.

A voice in my head points out that what's happening between us is only temporary. Her life is in LA, and mine is here on the ranch. And then there's the part where Austin will never approve of me being with his sister. Although if he had his way, Violet would never be with another man again. Period.

Which is fine with me. If I can't be with her, then no other man should be allowed to touch her.

Fair is fair.

And no—even if I can touch her, no other man gets that honor.

Maybe I should talk to Austin about putting her in a nunnery.

Problem solved.

"I'll see you tonight," Violet whispers and steps back, ending the kiss sooner than I would like.

She returns to the house, and I take a detour to my workshop. Once there, I check my wood supply to ensure I have enough for a rocking horse. The rocking horse that Camilla plans to video-tape when I give it to a sick kid...if I make it to the next round.

My gut twists into a not-so-neat bow and I let out a Christ-this-is-ridiculous grunt. I don't create the horses for publicity. I give them to cancer patients because I love seeing the kids smile, especially when the cancer hasn't given them anything to smile about.

Ignoring my gut, I calculate how much wood I'll need.

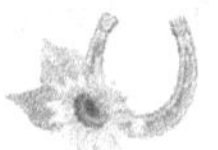

WILSON AND CRAIG ARE WATCHING TV WHEN I EVENTUALLY SLIP away from the house. Camilla is in her room. My brothers are off doing their own things.

I follow the dirt path, through the trees, and eventually end up at the grassy river bank where I'm meeting Violet. The sun is shining on the private alcove from low in the sky.

The tire swing still dangles over the water where it's been since I was a kid. Many a happy summer was spent in this spot when my brothers, our friends, and I were growing up.

The crisp snap of a stepped-on stick disrupts the quiet air. I turn and catch sight of Violet entering the clearing. She's no longer wearing the jeans she had on earlier.

What she has on gets me hard in record time.

The hem of her denim shorts barely brushes the tops of her thighs. The edges are frayed, carefree. My gaze travels from her cowboy boots, up her long, toned legs. After watching her chase after her son, it comes as no surprise that she still has runner's legs.

And it also comes as no surprise that my cock imagines said legs wrapped around my hips as I plunge inside her.

This time I don't tell my cock to cut it out. I'm too distracted.

It chalks this up as a score in its favor.

My gaze continues up and lands on my second favorite feature that is all Violet. No, I'm not referring to her tits, although I'll be the first to admit they are spectacular.

I'm referring to her face—her sweet, laughing face. Her smiles are enough to cause even the most hardened man to soften. And her impish brown eyes are always rich with compassion.

I stride toward her. "You made it."

She grins at me, turning my knees a little weak. "As if staying away was ever an option."

She steps farther into the clearing and her gaze drops to the water behind me. "What's the temperature like?"

"No idea. I haven't been in it yet." I set the folded towels on the ground.

Two more strides and I'm standing in front of her. But instead of kissing her like I had first planned, I scoop her up in my arms.

She squeals a laugh, and her arms go around my neck.

I chuckle. "I guess there's one way to find out."

She narrows her eyes at me, but it's far from convincing. "Don't you dare, TJ Christopher Daniels." Her lips form an adorable pout.

I take a step toward the slow-moving river. My mouth curls up to one side. "And what will happen if I do dare?"

"No blowjobs for you."

"Will I still get to go down on you?" Because right now, that's exactly what I want to do.

Plus, I'm not looking for blowjobs tonight. I'm one hundred percent in favor of being inside her.

Not that I have anything against them. I'm their number one fan, thank you very much. But not tonight.

Tonight is about my plan to move past my thing for Austin's sister.

She slowly runs the tip of her tongue along her lower lip as she considers my question. "As much as it pains me to say it, I must put my foot down. So no orgasms for either of us if you dunk me in the water."

She flashes me an I-win smirk.

Like most men, I enjoy winning. I wouldn't have gotten as far as I did in my rodeo career if not for my competitive nature. But there's a time when you have to walk away and let the other person win.

And when orgasms are at stake, that's definitely the right time.

I lower Violet to her feet.

Then I unzip my jeans and remove them. I'm not naked. Not even close. I still have on my T-shirt and swim trunks.

"Well, if you're not going in," I say, "I'll have to be the one who takes the first plunge."

She laughs. "You're crazy. You know that?"

Before I can respond, she whips her T-shirt over her head, revealing her black bikini top.

And everything I was just thinking about vanishes in a puff of smoke. *Poof!*

She unbuttons the top of her shorts and pulls the zipper down, tooth by slow tooth. I inwardly groan at what the action is doing to me. She then shimmies the denim down her legs and nudges them aside with her foot to join her T-shirt.

"Love your bikini," I say. "But I seem to remember the last time you wore one on the tire swing, the top came off."

And I can easily say that's up there on my list of favorite teenage memories.

Just don't mention it to Austin.

The poor guy was horrified when it happened and told every boy there that if he caught them looking at her, he would rip out their eyes.

Not wishing to go blind, everyone shut their eyes.

But despite his threat, there's a chance—a very strong chance —I might have peeked.

"Then I guess I'll have to make sure I don't lose this top." She reaches behind her and a second later, I understand why. The two black triangles release the world's most goddamn perfect breasts.

Violet lifts the scraps of fabric over her head.

With her arms up, her breasts are like peace offerings, waiting for me to delight in their taut nipples.

I stalk toward her in two easy strides and fill my large palms with her pale globes. She inhales a sharp soft breath but doesn't say anything. She just looks at me with vulnerability and challenge in her eyes.

"Let me warm them up for you." My voice is heavy with need. The need to worship her. The need to keep her safe. The need for her to give me permission to do all of that.

She gives a slight nod, her lips parted, her breaths coming in as wispy gasps. Unable to wait any longer, I lower my head to hers and tug her plump lower lip between my teeth.

I shift my hands and pinch her nipples. That is met with a moan...which I swallow as my mouth drops to hers.

Always the impatient one, my cock hardens in my swim trunks. I release her breasts and slide my hands down her sides until they rest on her ass cheeks. I squeeze them lightly and pull her against me, pressing my near-painful cock against her stomach.

Thank the Almighty Christ that we're not horses. Because if I have to wait until she's ovulating to fuck her, I'll die of the worst case of blue balls known to man.

And knowing Noah's sick sense of humor, he'll have that engraved on my tombstone.

My plans to swim first quickly take a nose dive.

And apparently I'm not the only one to feel that way. Violet cups my package, then strokes her palm along my length, clearly with plans to kill me.

Two can play at that game...

I slip a hand between her legs and run two fingers against her pussy. "Christ, you're so goddam hot and wet for me, Vi. Do you still want to do this or jump in the river?"

Please pick fucking. Please pick fucking. Please pick fucking...

"I think I'll go with option A," she says on a breath. "I need you to bend me over and fuck me. Fuck me hard, TJ. That's all I want. For you to fuck me and show me that I matter."

I'd be lying if I say I didn't almost come in my swim trunks right there.

Her hands move to my waistband, and she releases my cock. It springs free, happy to finally see some action that doesn't just involve my hand. Happy to finally find out if reality lives up to fantasy.

Violet peels the fabric down my legs. I kick them to the side, not caring where they land. Violet's bikini bottoms don't fare much better.

I guide her to a nearby cottonwood tree, solid as it is tall. "Bend over and place your hands on the trunk."

She does as I ask without a single word. I nudge her feet farther apart and reverently drop to my knees. I plant a gentle kiss on one ass cheek and then the other. This is followed by a light nip with my teeth and my tongue soothing the delicate flesh. Violet shudders slightly.

"Are you okay?" My voice is a rough sound—more than a whisper but quieter than a groan.

She makes a small affirmative whimper that has me smiling. "Oh, God. Yes."

"That's good." I push to my feet and kiss the curve of her lower back.

"So about that fucking..."

I stroke two fingers against her clit. "What about it?" I ask, working to keep my voice casual.

"I really need it now—more than you can ever imagine. Think drought and you're my oasis."

I chuckle at her impatience. She and my cock could be very good friends.

"Don't worry, I'm getting there. Just stay like that while I get the condom." Because brilliant me left it in my jeans pocket.

"Trust me, I'm not going anywhere."

Less than a minute later, my cock is covered and ready for action. I align the tip against Violet's entrance and inch my way in so only the head is burrowed inside her. There are no words to describe how it feels to have her heat hug me, even if I'm not all the way in yet.

I take a deep breath, fighting to keep the sensation from overwhelming me.

"You know, it's not nice to tease a woman who hasn't had sex in a while," Violet says in a sweetly mocking tone.

I chuckle again. "Good point. I wouldn't want you to die from sex starvation. I've heard it's not a pleasant way to go."

But since I don't plan for her to suffer a moment longer—because I'm just that giving—I plunge all the way inside her, burying myself to the hilt.

The groan is one hundred percent me.

The moan when I touch Violet's clit and trace my fingers around it? That's all her.

It's loud enough to stir the crow in a nearby tree. It squawks and flies away.

I have no idea where it goes after that, and nor do I care. My brain is too fuzzy right now to drum up a coherent thought—and I haven't even come yet.

I grab hold of Violet's hips, and a new rhythm takes over my body. The only sounds now filling the air are the slapping of skin against naked skin and our ragged breaths.

A tingling starts low in my back, warning me I won't last much longer.

Fortunately, I *don't* have to hold back another second. Violet's muscles clench hard on my cock, and she cries out my name.

My balls tighten, and the familiar sensation in my gut explodes with a mind-numbing heat. I can't remember the last time I came this hard, this completely—like my soul has been wrung inside out and will never be the same again.

In a good way.

Correction—in a fan-fucking-tastic way.

Only I have no idea what to do with this...or if I should do anything about it at all.

But I do know one thing: my goal of finally getting Violet out of my system has failed.

Damn.

15

The warm breeze flutters the leaves of the cottonwood tree. I lean down and kiss Violet's back once more. I'm not ready to leave her heat, but there's a condom to deal with, so I don't have a choice.

I remove myself and dispose of it. But as soon as I rejoin Violet, an unexpected awkwardness settles on my shoulders.

The problem? It's been a while since I've been in a relationship. With my ex-girlfriend, I would return to bed once I'd dealt with the condom. With one-night stands, I'd bail as soon as the woman and I were finished—no postcoital cuddling allowed.

But this feels different. Uncharted.

Right. We aren't in a real relationship. We're just screwing around. But since I haven't gotten rid of my craving for her yet, I only hope there will be another chance to get her out of my system soon.

Except...

Maybe Violet doesn't want to do it again. Maybe now that she's had her fill, she's ready to weather the next drought.

The possibility that she doesn't want to be with me anymore feels like a blow dart to the heart...and I can't understand why.

Violet collects her bikini bottoms from the ground and steps into them.

I retrieve my swim trunks and pull them on. "Do you need to get back to Grandma Meg's yet?"

"No, not yet. I tucked Deacon into bed before coming here." She smiles softly at her son's name.

"He's a good kid. I bet Grandma Meg is happy he's staying here while you're gone."

Violet walks to the water's edge and tests the temperature with her toes. "I swear she was close to doing backward handsprings down the hallway when I discussed it with her. She hasn't seen much of him since he was born."

I join her by the water but don't bother testing it. I'm the type of man who rips off the Band-Aid. "How come?"

"She doesn't like LA."

I laugh because I know exactly her opinion of that city.

Violet shrugs. "I guess she has a point when it comes to her reasons. But it makes it tougher for her to see her great-grandson."

"So why didn't you just bring him here to visit?"

She doesn't answer. Instead, she glances over at the tire swing and sprints toward it.

Because the last one in is a rotten egg.

Clearly we haven't matured all that much since she was eight years old.

And like back then, my longer legs easily devour the distance to the cottonwood tree.

As soon as I reach the tree, I grab hold of the old tire, pull it back to gain maximum trajectory, and jump on.

Swinging from a tire takes skill, strength, and timing...but most of all it takes an unshakeable fearlessness.

Years of practice doesn't hurt either.

As the tire approaches optimal height, I release the rope.

Back in the days, my brothers and I would judge each other

when it came to our jumps. Unlike with diving, where a barely there splash is preferred, here, the bigger the splash, the more points scored.

And on the scale of one to ten, this splashdown is a twenty. The advantage of being a one-hundred-and-eighty-pound man versus a kid.

That's my first thought. My second is: *Fuck, it's cold!*

I break free of the surface and wipe the water from my eyes.

Violet's still on land, holding on to the tire, grinning. Even though the smile on her face might be less than angelic, the sun low in the horizon forms a halo around her head, claiming the opposite. "How's the temperature?"

"It's great," I tell her.

If you're a goddam polar bear.

The smirk on her face says she believes that as much as she believes Santa is running for president in the next election.

"Hurry up, Mister. Let me show you how the pros do it." She gestures for me to move aside.

"Nice try, Vi. We both know *I'm* the pro. You'll never steal my championship title." I swim to the side, then tread water as I watch her.

Violet pulls the swing back, jumps onto it, then lets go, executing an impressive arc. The splash is also impressive, but she's smaller than me, so it costs her in the end.

Her head pops out of the water, wet hair slicked back like a swimsuit model's.

She grins at me. "What do you think? A definite ten, right?"

"Nine-point-three. You lost points on the splash."

At her adorably sexy pout, my cock groans. I'm not sure if that's because it was fantasizing about those lips wrapped around it—or because it figures the judge's score puts my cock out of contention for more mind-numbing sex with Violet.

"But I know a way to make the judge change his mind," I say.

Naturally my cock, being the helpful cock that it is, whispers a few of its own suggestions.

She swims over and stops within arm's distance of me. The outline of her naked breasts is barely visible in the murky water. "And what's that?" she asks.

I reach for her arm and drag her closer.

"If you kiss him, he'll give you bonus points for your dazzling end to the routine."

She doesn't resist as I continue pulling her to me. "Oh, he will, will he?" Her voice is sweet and sexy and down-right dirty.

I nod, the movement small.

"And what if I don't accept those terms?"

Before I can reply, she skims her arm in a wide arc across the water.

And a mini-tsunami hits me square in the face.

I wipe the water from my eyes. Violet is already halfway to shore by the time I can see clearly again. Luckily, all my years of living near the river mean I can swim like a shark in pursuit of its next meal.

Once I reach shallower water, I stand and race after her.

I lunge at her and wrap my arms around her waist from behind. She lets out a giggled shriek but doesn't resist.

My hand drifts up from her waist and cups her breast, the nipple hard from the cold water. And I see it as my personal duty to warm the bud.

Right after I pinch it.

Violet gasps and arches back, her ass pressing against my now hard cock.

"I want to be inside you again," I say against her ear, my voice gravelly and deep. "And I want you to ride me like the cowgirl I know you are." I pinch her nipple again, this time a little harder.

She moans, her head falling back against my shoulder.

"Is that a yes?"

"Definitely a yes." Her words come out on a whimper.

"Unless you want to walk through the woods practically naked—not that I would complain if you did—you might want to put your clothes back on." I roll her nipple between my thumb and index finger—just because I can.

"Woods? Where are we going? Because I assume you're not thinking of sneaking me into your house."

"Definitely not at the risk of Camilla finding out I'm screwing around with a woman who isn't my intended bride."

Right—this isn't like some cultures where they have arranged marriages. But at times, it sure as hell feels like this show is the same thing.

As for the sneaking part, I'm all for having her in my bed once she returns to town. I'm all for Austin not learning about any of this. And I'm all for the same when it comes to Grandma Meg and Tilly and everyone else in Copper Creek. None of them need to learn the truth.

"Then where are we going?" Violet asks.

"My workshop...or we can fuck in the back seat of your car." Where she is parked isn't visible from the road. And since most of the land is private property, few people have a reason to come out here.

"My car is out. Deacon's car seat is in the back. Between that and his stuff, there's no room. Not to mention it's a rental. I'm sure the rental agency doesn't want people screwing in it."

I smirk. "*Au contraire.* I'm sure they're jealous you get to screw in it and they don't."

We return to shore and quickly towel off and put our tops back on. Because we don't want the clothing to get wet from our swimsuits, we carry our jeans and shorts.

Then we walk the way I came earlier until we arrive at the edge of the woods. Since my workshop is not easily seen from the house, there's not much risk of being caught by Camilla or the crew. You can only see it from certain rooms, and they have no reason to be in them.

I unlock the door and flip the lights on as I enter, mentally thanking my grandfather for adding this building on the property.

Violet enters behind me. The door is barely closed before I have her pushed up against it, my lips exploring her neck.

My heart hammers in my chest and my cock does a victory dance at what's coming soon.

I slip my fingers between her legs and run them along the still-damp fabric of her bikini bottoms and pussy. Violet groans against my lips. I smile, then peel the fabric down her legs.

And because I have to see her perfect tits again, I remove the rest of her clothes in record time.

That's not to say Violet isn't an active participant during all of this. She's practically ripping the clothes off my body.

And because we're *that* talented, our mouths barely separate. The only time they do is when we yank our tops over our heads.

I take a step back and eye her the way a man fresh from the desert would eye a tall glass of water.

Water drips from her still-wet hair and forms tantalizing paths down her skin. I watch a drop travel down her chest, aiming for the nipple I teased not so long ago. *Lucky bastard.*

The pad of my thumb brushes against it, ending its hopeful journey.

I lean in and the day-old scruff on my face scrapes against Violet's cheek. She gasps, and damned if that doesn't get my cock more excited.

"Touch yourself," I murmur in her ear. "I want to watch you make yourself come." My tone is the same one I use when working with the colts. Firm. Unbending.

Only this time it contains the heat that burns in my veins. The same heat that, according to Violet's gaze, smolders in hers, too.

Violet lifts her hand to her breast and traces a path across one tit. The finger circles the nipple...once.

Twice.

Holy shit. I swallow back a groan.

Then she pinches the taut bud the same way I did earlier, rolling it between her fingers, tugging it. This time I barely hold back my groan.

Her smug, heated expression tells me she knows. She knows what her teasing is doing to me. Although it wouldn't take much to figure that out, what with the excited stance my cock has assumed. It stands to attention, ready for Violet to ride it.

Her hand leaves her breasts and traces its way down her stomach, with the same languid speed of the water drop only a moment ago. It disappears into the landing strip of fine, dark hair, and I run the tip of my tongue along my lip, craving the taste of her.

As her fingers circle her clit, her head falls back against the wall with a moan. Her eyes are closed, her breath coming in short pants. Just the mere sight of her like this sends my cock into a new painful territory.

I wrap my hand around it and give it a firm stroke, doing what I can to ease my neediness while I wait for Violet to come.

And come she does—long and hard—if her cry is any indication.

Even though I'm not directly responsible for her orgasm, I can't help the pride marching through me, which rivals Macy's Thanksgiving Day parade.

Violet sags against the wall. I catch her in my arms before she can tumble to the ground. Just the feel of her—naked and alive—in my arms, is almost enough to cause me to coat her with my cum.

"You ready to ride me, cowgirl?"

Her mouth tugs into a sweet, lasso-me-up-and-fuck-me smile. My favorite kind of smile. "Anytime, cowboy."

I walk to the wooden chair by the wall. It's the only piece of furniture in the room. I hurriedly slip on a condom and sit on the chair. The smooth wood nips my bare ass with its cool touch.

But I don't give two rattlesnakes about that—and neither does my cock.

I flash Violet a devilish grin and indicate for her to mount me.

With a smile to match my own, she straddles my legs and takes my cock in her hand. "How do you want this?" She strokes her thumb over the rubber-covered tip in the same way I imagine she just did with her clit.

And for the first time, the need to be ridden bare burns inside me. Not once in all the years I've had sex have I gone without a condom. Not once during that time have I ever wished to fuck without one.

But this time is different.

This time it feels like going without a condom is the equivalent of being branded. To belong to Violet and no one else.

And that's a feeling I can't afford to let in.

"Hard and rough," is my answer.

The grin on her face widens, and she slowly lowers herself onto me until I'm fully seated inside her.

She groans as my width fills her, stretches her, worships her. Never before has it ever felt this powerful, this intense.

Gazing into her dark, mesmerizing eyes, I slip my fingers between her legs and smooth the wetness on her core.

"Oh God," she calls out on another groan. Her voice and her erotic sounds make me harder.

With my hands on her hips, I encourage her to rock them. Her tight heat moving along my cock pushes me to dizzying new heights. I can't get enough of her, of this. And for the first time since becoming a horse rancher, I see how right Camilla is. Because even if you're a stallion whose job is to impregnate as many mares as possible during the breeding season, horses have the raw end of the deal.

While Violet maintains the pace, my thumb returns to her clit, applying the right amount of pressure. The room is warm, even though the nearby trees shelter the hut from the summer sun. Sweat covers our bodies with a heavy sheen.

Just when I think I can't last any longer, Violet's muscles clench around me. I pull her head down to mine and swallow her moan. Then I take control of her hips, for those final rough movements, as the tingling in my lower back intensifies. My balls tighten—and the much-anticipated orgasm rockets through me.

I groan out loud, the sound deep and guttural. It's a good thing they can't hear me from the house. There's no mistaking that the noise has nothing to do with woodwork.

Fighting to catch my breath, I drop my head to Violet's shoulder.

The countdown for her return to Copper Creek? It's now on.

16

It's been three days since Violet returned to LA. I walk to the training paddock while giving Deacon a piggyback ride; Asgard strolls alongside me.

Grandma Meg had a medical appointment today and asked if I could look after her great-grandson for a couple of hours.

Yesterday it was a dentist appointment.

The day before that, it was her weekly Zumba lessons at the senior center.

And let's not forget the lawn bowling tournament.

And snake charming lessons.

Yes, the last one finally triggered my bullshit alert. Which was when she decided to switch to the more realistic excuses.

Despite my initial reservations—because what the heck do I know about babysitting a twenty-five-month-old?—it's been kind of fun.

But, shit, for a little kid, he sure has a lot of energy.

What in the hell has Grandma Meg been feeding him?

"Deacon, you wanna learn how to rope a cow?" I ask.

Sophie is in the center of the paddock, holding one end of the lunge line, while the colt trots in a large circle around her, kicking up dust. Jake and Noah are leaning against the upper railing of the fence, their focus on the horse. Although in Jake's case, it's more likely Sophie's ass that has his attention.

At the sound of gravel crunching beneath my boots, they turn around. Deacon's currently sporting the finest in toddler cowboy hats. A present from Sophie and Aubrey. He's also wearing toddler-sized cowboy boots, Levi jeans, and a checkered shirt that resembles mine.

Noah's mouth twitches. "Hey, look, Uncle Jake. They're twinsies. Deacon, did you call your Uncle TJ this morning and ask him what he's wearing today?"

Both men crack up laughing.

Inwardly I flip them a double bird. "Very funny, guys. Deacon, how about we pretend Uncle Noah is a cow and practice tying his arms and legs together?" And his mouth, if I have my way. "Doesn't that sound like an awesome idea?"

Giggling, Deacon bounces on my shoulders. "Cow."

Jake laughs again, only this time it's directed at our brother.

"I think Uncle Jake would make a much better cow." Noah parks his hand on Jake's upper back and tries to push him forward.

Jake doesn't budge. "It's a rule that the younger brother always has to be the cow."

Noah snorts. "You made that up."

"Don't believe me? Check the rule book."

"There is no rule book."

"Then I guess you can't prove me wrong." Jake places *his* hand on Noah's back and gives him a shove.

Noah might be tall and muscular like rest of us, but he's no match for Jake. Hell, I'm no match for Jake. The guy could be a wrestler.

Noah stumbles forward.

"Don't worry," I say as Jake removes the two-year-old from my shoulders. "Deacon and I will go easy on you."

"I doubt it." Noah's tone is grumpy, but his expression is a supersized smirk. "Besides, won't it be dangerous? He might think that strangling people is a good idea."

He has a point there. Lassoing a person isn't the same as lassoing a calf.

"How about using Loki?" he suggests. Asgard barks in agreement.

"Hey, no hating on my cat." Noah and Loki have never seen eye-to-eye on anything.

Still in Jake's arms, Deacon reaches toward Asgard. Jake lowers him onto the gravel path, and the little boy toddles over to the Aussie shepherd. The dog remains seated, tongue lolling to the side. If he could adopt Deacon, I'm sure he would.

"Want doggie." Deacon flings his arms around Asgard's neck and giggles.

Asgard regards me with his satisfied, at-least-someone-around-here-worships-me expression.

I roll my eyes.

Gravel crunches behind me. I turn around...and my heart squeezes like an accordion playing an Irish jig.

I blink. Great, now I'm hallucinating.

"Mommy!" Deacon rushes over to Violet.

So not a hallucination.

I want to sweep her up in my arms and kiss her senseless. I want to show her how much I've missed her.

But I rein in the intense craving—not because I have to worry about the camera crew or Camilla or what my brothers think. Deacon doesn't need to see me kissing his mother.

Violet scoops up her son and hugs him.

"I thought you weren't back until tomorrow," I say, walking over to them.

"Guess we should leave those two lovebirds alone." Noah's voice is low enough that I doubt Violet hears him.

Jake chuckles his reply.

I glare at them over my shoulder. Jake laughs louder and walks away.

"Wow, don't you look like a proper little cowboy?" Violet says to Deacon, a grin in her voice.

"Aubrey and Sophie played dress up with him," I tell her.

"Me cowboy." Deacon points at the back of Noah, who is watching Sophie and the colt. "Cow."

"That's not a cow," Violet says. "That's Uncle Noah."

"Not that I'm not glad to see you," I say, "but how come you're back a day early? Is everything all right?"

And when do I get to hold you in my arms again—naked?

She squeezes Deacon one more time, then puts the squirming toddler down.

The colt neighs. Deacon points at him. "Horsie."

He doesn't wait for confirmation from either of us. He walks over to Noah, whose booted foot rests on the lower wooden rail. The same wooden rail that Deacon settles his hands on as he watches the colt.

Unable to wait any longer to taste Violet, my lips send an *Are-you-going-to-kiss-her-or-what?* message to my body—and my body heeds their request.

Or that's my excuse for what happens next.

I wrap my arms around her waist and pull her against me. Then my lips find hers and all bets are off when it comes to the contract I signed.

No one from the show is here to witness this.

And Violet is definitely not complaining.

Her lips part, and she welcomes me in. My tongue glides against hers, savoring, reminiscing, teasing, doing all the things I've been fantasizing about since I last saw her.

Her hands travel up my body to my shoulders. The heat from her palms soaks through the fabric of my T-shirt, adding fire to what already smolders deep inside me.

A moment later, the giggle of a little boy yanks me back to the here and now. A here and now that could, at any moment, include Austin if he stops by for an impromptu visit.

But despite knowing this, I don't release Violet like I should. Instead, my lips trace a path from her mouth to her earlobe. "I want you in my bed tonight," I murmur against her ear.

I'm aware I'm playing a dangerous game, especially since I value my life. But the risk is worth it. Neither of us is looking for something more. We're just looking for great sex for now.

What could be more perfect?

My heart mutters words I choose to ignore. Ridiculous words that include how I'm possibly falling for her. But what does my heart know? It has steered me wrong before.

"God, I want that more than anything," Violet says on a soft groan. "But first there's something I need to do. Something both you and I need to do."

"What's that?" I ask—because I can't imagine there's anything we have to do first that's more important than me fucking Violet into the next century.

"That" turns out to be an antique store.

"Why are we here?" I ask, following Violet into the brick building on Main Street. Dangling from her neck is her camera.

Only this time it has nothing to do with me—and everything to do with the Violet I knew in high school. Even back then, she always had her camera with her.

The store is crammed full of antiques: from the tiny wooden box to large pieces of furniture. It's a mishmash of different styles and different eras, but mostly western themed.

Because so much stuff has been stockpiled in the store, you have to weave between oversized decorative items, furniture, and shelving units with trinkets for sale. Even the walls are covered with paraphernalia.

Violet walks to an antique wooden desk and searches through the small items on it. "I'm looking for a birthday present for Deacon's nanny. She loves the unusual."

"What kind of unusual are you looking for?" I pick up a rusty horseshoe that looks nothing like the modern version. No idea what one would do with it. All I know is that you can't shoe a horse with it.

"I don't exactly know. I'll just know when I see it."

"Fair enough." I return the horseshoe to the desk.

"Howdy, you two," Mavis says next to me, surprising me. She wasn't there a second ago. "Is there anything I can help you find?"

Mavis is the store owner, and I swear she's older than most of the pieces here. She wasn't around when the dinosaurs were roaming the planet, but close enough.

"I'm looking for a gift for someone, but do you mind if I take a photo of you, Mavis? The lighting in this store is perfect for what I want to do." Violet indicates to the large windows. "As is the setting."

"Oh, I'm not so sure about that, dear. I'm not like the youth these days and their love of...what do you call those photos you take of yourself?"

"Selfies," Violet says.

"Right, selfies. I'm not young, and I'm a mess." She looks down at her jeans and long purple top.

"You look beautiful," Violet reassures her.

A few minutes later, Violet shows us the photos on her camera's LCD screen that she took of Mavis. These photos are nothing like the ones she's taken of me. These pictures look time-less, like something from a magazine. The kind of photos that give you a glimpse into who that person is, partly because of the setting.

"That's incredible," Mavis says, studying the last photo Violet showed us. "I'm still old." She shrugs. "But there's just something about this photo that's compelling. Do you think I can have a copy?"

Before Violet can answer, the bell over the door jingles. Mayor Wineberg enters, along with Cora Lee Giffin, the queen of cupcakes.

The mayor's gaze falls on us and she beams. She walks toward us. "Just the cowboy I wanted to see."

Cora Lee follows close behind.

Diane Wineberg is in her sixties and has been the mayor for the past fifteen years. She's wearing her typical jeans and cowboy boots and a red western shirt, with white embroidered roses and lots of sequins.

Mayor Wineberg loves her sequins.

Cora Lee is the complete opposite, in a summer dress and sandals. Her long, blonde hair is pulled back in two loose braids.

I dip the rim of my hat in greeting. "What can I do for you, ma'am?"

"I wanted to tell you how excited we all are—and by we, I mean the citizens of Copper Creek—that you're on the reality show. It's going to do great things for increasing awareness of our fine town. Lord knows we could benefit from the increased tourism."

Increased? We don't get tourists. Period.

"I'll do what I can." Which is pretty much a big fat zero. I've done my part. Now hopefully my part doesn't include being a contestant for the rest of the season.

She nods. "The town council and I met the other day to discuss how we can capitalize on the show's publicity for the town. For example, Jennifer Goodwin is thinking about starting a bed and breakfast. Her great-aunt died two months ago and willed her the old Mathews house."

"Isn't that place haunted?" Violet exaggerates a shudder.

The mayor laughs. "That's just a rumor her great-aunt started because she thought it would be entertaining—especially at Halloween."

"Did she die in the house?" Violet asks.

"Nah," I say, "she died in a car accident. Old Bert Saunders claims Bigfoot caused it. Bert was in the car at the time but was drunker than a skunk found in a beer keg." According to Tilly.

What actually caused the accident? A deer.

"So her spirit isn't haunting the house?"

"That's right. It's one hundred percent ghost-free," Cora Lee reports. "And the perfect location for a bed and breakfast."

"And it's just one of the many businesses that will benefit from the show," Mayor Wineberg says. "And from our plans to revitalize the town."

"It would be nice to have more customers come into the store," Mavis says on a sigh. "The way it is now, business is not all that great. An influx of tourists would be wonderful."

"Have you thought of starting an online business?" Violet asks. "Then you won't be as impacted by the lack of tourists."

Mavis's eyes widened as if she's just seen the Grim Reaper himself. "Online business? I wouldn't even know how to start one. It's a miracle that I figured out how to turn on a computer."

Violet smiles softly. "How about I drop by tomorrow afternoon and we can talk?"

The panic on Mavis's face fades a bit. "That would be wonderful, dear."

Mayor Wineberg turns back to me. "When the TV crew comes back to town, it will be a great reminder that Copper Creek exists. We'll have to do more than that to help make this town great, but it'll be a start."

"You do realize I might not make it that far in the show? If not enough viewers vote for me, then I'm out." And I'll be one very happy cowboy.

"Oh, don't you go worrying yourself there, young man. We've already got that covered." She pats me on the back. "This time next year, you and the missus will be working on your contribution to increasing the town's population."

"From what I've heard," I say, "Natalie isn't interested in kids." Which is why I was picked as a contestant—thanks to Noah's answers on the application form.

The mayor's shoulders droop before perking up again. "Oh, that's a shame."

"It's not like TJ's looking to have kids either," Cora Lee says, stating what I didn't realize was public knowledge. "Which is why on paper they would be a perfect match."

Mayor Wineberg goes from looking disappointed to horrified. "After seeing you with Violet's son around town, I pegged you as a family man. Oh, well, just as long as you're marrying Natalie because you love her and she loves you, that's all that matters. Now, I should get back to check how the campaign is going."

"Campaign?" As far as I know, the next town election isn't for another two years.

The mayor's smile when she entered the store is nothing like it is now. "As I said before, you've got nothing to worry about, TJ, when it comes to the next part of the show."

Am I the only one who finds that far from reassuring?

VIOLET AND I RETURN TO THE RANCH HOUSE AFTER THE ANTIQUE store. Neither of us mentions what the mayor said. Right now, I don't even want to think of the show.

There's only one thing on my mind—the first position I plan to fuck Violet in.

My brothers are on the couch, watching an action movie.

Jake raises his beer bottle at us. "Hey, Violet, what are you doing here?" Somehow, he keeps the knowing smirk off his face that is buried in his tone.

She crouches and gives Asgard all the attention he's been starving for since we entered the room. "I came to help you guys with your website and social media accounts."

A loud explosion from the movie pulls Jake's attention back to the screen. "Well, have fun with that," is all he has to say. Noah doesn't even acknowledge our existence, too focused on the TV to notice us.

I slip my fingers between Violet's and lead her down the hall to the office.

The room is dark when we enter.

"Wait a second," she says as I reach to turn on the light. "I want to see the view when it's dark." She smoothly navigates her way to the large window.

I join her there. The nearly black sky is filled with billions of tiny dots of light. Some are faint. Others form the constellations.

Can I name them?

Not at all. Jake tried to teach me them when we were kids. I was too busy to pay attention, my head always in one comic book or another.

"It's so beautiful," Violet says, face turned skyward. Her voice is soft, awed. "I forgot just how beautiful it is here." A long, slow breath releases from between her lips. "I've always wanted to make love under the stars." This time the words are said in almost a whisper, and for a second I wonder if I misheard her.

It's the increased *da boom, da boom, da boom* of my heart that tells me I heard her correctly. And with each beat, my chest feels like it's filling with helium, making me lighter, making it easier to breathe.

Why? I have no idea. Biology wasn't really my thing in high school.

I wrap my arms around her, her back pressed against me. I tenderly kiss her neck, inhaling the sweet scent that is all Violet. She trembles at my touch. With a level of reverence I've never experienced before, my mouth slowly travels up her skin. At her earlobe, I nibble and tease and enjoy the sweet erotic noises she makes.

"Want to go to my room?" Then we won't have to worry about Jake or Noah accidentally barging in on us.

"That might be a good idea," she murmurs back.

My fingers threaded with hers, I lead her upstairs, where the view from my room matches the one from the office.

As she gazes out at the starry night, I brush my thumb across her nipple, hidden under the fabric of her dress and bra. But it's not enough. I need to feel her naked against me.

I let my hand drop to her hips and turn her around to face me. It's too dark to see her expression, but her soft pants tell me all I need to know. I unbutton the front of her dress, then help it slide down her body—revealing her lacy pink panties and matching bra.

I nudge back the urgent need to turn on the light, so I can memorize what she looks like standing in front of me this way.

But this isn't about what I want. It's about Violet wanting to make love under the stars.

Or close enough, given it's chilly outside at this time of night.

I reach behind her and unhook her bra. With my fingertips blazing a path along her skin, I slip the straps down her shoulders.

Once her bra joins the dress on the floor, I cup her full breasts in my hands. They fit perfectly...like this is where they belong.

My hands keep exploring her body, slowly stroking her smooth, silky skin. Tasting it with my lips and my tongue. Memorizing the sweet sounds she makes every time I hit the right spots.

I'm not the only one exploring. Violet's mouth and hands are equally adventurous. Although in my case, the noises I make are hardly sweet. I do, though, keep them down so my brothers won't hear them unless they walk past my bedroom.

Violet's fingers move to unbutton my jeans. One moment I'm fully dressed, and the next I'm standing in front of her, naked. My cock is hard and ready to plunge deep inside her. To claim her for its own in a way it hasn't with any other woman.

Violet traces the pad of her thumb across my swollen head, spreading the pre-cum. My balls tighten, and I have to remind them to be a little more patient. I'm not looking to shoot my load just yet.

Violet turns her face up to me. Desire shines in her eyes. My cock hardens some more.

I lead her to the bed, grab a foil package from my bedside drawer, and pull her onto my lap. "Straddle me but don't go on me yet."

She does as I ask, opening herself to me. My fingers take advantage of the position, finding her pussy. Her breathing climbs a notch—matching my own.

I tease her, alternating between the lips of her pussy and her clit. She whimpers and bucks against my hand, but I don't give in. I keep pushing her to the edge.

"I want you in me." Her voice is raspy with need.

I chuckle—which sounds kind of funny given that I moan at the same time. "Are you sure you're ready?"

The woman is dripping wet. I have no doubt that she's ready, but teasing her is so much fun.

She groans loudly, fully turned-on but also ready to curse me a thousand times. I laugh again, roll the condom on, and guide her onto my cock.

She lowers herself inch by inch, taking me in deep, pushing me further toward exquisite, mind-numbing pain. Once I'm fully seated inside her, I settle my hands on her hips. Her arms go around my neck, and I show her the slow pace I need.

She doesn't fight it. Nor does she beg me to go faster and harder and faster. If anything, she seems to crave this pace as much as I do. Her heated gaze remains locked on mine as we move closer, closer, closer to the edge. The intensity of what we're doing is nothing like anything I've experienced before.

We keep going, wrapped up in the moment. I never want it to end—but at the same time, I'm hungry for the much sought-after release.

I don't know how long we've been moving like this before

Violet's inner muscles tighten around me. It feels like forever, and it feels like it's not long enough. The tingling in my lower back becomes more intense, and the grip of Violet's heat is sweet torment.

"Oh. God. TJ." Her words shudder on a groan.

"I'm right with you." That's the last thing I manage to say before an orgasm barrels through me, sending me to the constellations that I wish I knew the names for.

Not a bad way to go, if you ask me.

But as I return to the woman in my arms, a startling revelation burrows itself into my heart.

I'm falling for the one woman who is off-limits to me.

Falling for the woman who has no interest in staying in Copper Creek. Falling for the woman who doesn't feel the same way about me that I feel for her.

Well, isn't that just fucking fantastic?

18

There's nothing like having a revelation knock you on your ass. Especially when said revelation is in the magnitude of "I'm falling for my best friend's sister" or "Austin is going to fucking kill me."

But either way, it's official—I'm in my new happy place, and I'm in no rush to leave just yet.

I inhale the soft perfume that is all Violet and lightly kiss her naked shoulder. The salty dampness is a welcome reminder of what we just did.

Violet makes a move to climb off me. I slip my arms around her and tighten my hold. "Sorry, you're not going anywhere. I'm quite comfortable like this."

She laughs. "What about the condom?"

"I'm sure it's comfortable, too." Because why wouldn't it be?

She laughs again and once more attempts to get off my lap. This time I let her go...only because I know what she's talking about. She already has one child who wasn't planned—a child without a father.

It's not like she's looking to be knocked up again.

And I'm not looking to become a dad.

I stand. "Don't go anywhere. I'll be right back."

She settles in the bed and pulls the covers to her waist. I quickly dispose of the condom and rejoin her.

She curls up against me and rests her head on my chest. "So what happened to your ex-girlfriend—the woman my grandmother was positive you were going to marry?" Her tone is soft, almost hesitant, her breath warm against my skin.

I'm about to brush off her question with a non-answer because Katherine is not something I wish to talk about with Violet or anyone else.

So why don't I?

Because life is a give and take. If you want something, be prepared to give something else in return. And I want to know about the asshole who knocked Violet up and left her to raise their child alone.

"The last I heard, my ex-girlfriend is married and living in Silicon Valley." I stroke her shoulder. "Turns out not everyone is suited for small-town life."

Violet finally glances up at me, her eyes wide with an emotion that I can only describe as sadness. "She broke up with you?"

"You seem surprised."

A light blush spreads from her neck and covers her cheeks. "That's not what I mean. I'm just surprised because you're a great guy, TJ. And I don't just mean it because you're hot."

My mouth tugs up to one side. "You think I'm hot?"

"Of course you're hot. You wouldn't have been selected for the show if you weren't."

"They didn't want me because of my intelligence? Wow. That's mighty shallow of them." I playfully pinch her ass.

She chuckles. "Well, if some of the contestants are any indication, the producers were definitely not interested in brainpower when it came to the selection process."

"That bad, huh?"

"From what I saw of the cowboys, yes, some were lacking in the intelligence department. Or they came off that way during the two days I spent with each of them. Maybe that's the producers' way of making it easier for the audience to narrow their choices down to eight."

"You only spent two days with the other cowboys?" That's news to me. I just assumed she had spent the same amount of time with them as she had with me.

"That's all I had time for. The camera crew stayed with each cowboy for the week. And there was more than one onsite team doing the filming, so several cowboys each week were videotaped."

I cup her face with my hand and run my thumb against her lower lip. "Well, for the record, I'm glad we got you for as long as we did. And also for the record, the show is a piss-poor way of finding a husband."

Violet grins. "Try telling that to the target audience. I guess it's different when you're not the one at risk of marrying the wrong person."

"I was dating a woman who claimed to love me but who was also willing to throw herself at Noah. You can't get much more in the 'wrong person' department than that."

Violet's eyes go as round as Thor's oat bucket. "She was cheating on you with your brother?"

"Not according to him. But the fact that I caught her kissing him didn't bode well for her."

"I can't believe your brother would do that to you." Her tone is soft and pained and I-want-to-kick-him-in-the-shin protective.

I move my shoulders with a barely there shrug. "He claims he did it to prove that she wasn't right for me."

"He's got that right. But I can't believe you've given up on finding love just because of one woman. Not everyone is like her."

"What can I say? I'm a quick learner."

She looks down at the bedding and plucks an invisible thread from it. "Did you love her?"

"I thought I did at the time. But after what happened, I realized I never really did."

Violet's gaze meets mine again. The kickass attitude might have vanished, but the pain in her eyes is still there. "You're not the only one who has screwed up when it comes to falling in love with the wrong person or believing you're in love with them. Only in my case, I ended up with a baby in exchange for services rendered."

I thread our fingers together on my stomach. "What happened?"

"I met Mark at a photo exhibit I was participating in. He was really impressed with my work and invited me out for coffee. He was a few years older than me, but he seemed nice, so I went out with him."

"Even though he could've been a serial killer?"

She smiles her *Do-you-really-believe-that?* smile. It's the one normally accompanied by some serious eye rolling. "I wasn't that much of an idiot. An idiot for falling for his lies? Yes. An idiot for putting myself in a dangerous position with a man I didn't know? Not so much. We always met in public places in the beginning. I Googled him, and he didn't show up on any Wanted posters of serial killers."

"Well, that's good to know." Austin would've run a background check on the man if he had known. And probably would've scared the crap out of him just to be certain.

"We started spending more and more time together as friends," she says. "Then things progressed, and eventually we became romantically involved. Which I now realize wasn't really romance. It was just two people fucking, and one of them was too stupid to see the truth in front of her."

"What truth?"

"Turns out the asshole was married." Her mouth twists into a half smile. It's a sad smirk, a wish-I'd-known-better smirk. "And I only found this out by accident, when I saw him and his wife together at the mall. And for someone who had a dirty little secret on the side, he sure looked cozy with her."

"And then you dumped his sorry ass?" I ask as I contemplate the likelihood of getting caught dumping horse manure in his vehicle. Let's see him explain *that* to his wife.

Violet nods. "Yes, faster than he could come up with another lie." This time the smirk isn't so sad. It's filled with satisfaction.

"Was this before or after you found out you were pregnant with Deacon?"

"Before."

"What did he say when you told him?"

She sits up, letting the sheet pool around her hips, possibly to distract me from my question. "I never told him."

I frown. "Even though he should be paying child support?"

"It doesn't matter. What is done is done." And then, as if to shift the topic, she says, "You asked me the other day why I didn't bring Deacon home to visit. It was because I was ashamed. Not of Deacon, but of what happened. Because I was an idiot and fell for the wrong man. Austin and Granny understood. They didn't like it, but they understood. I think they were just hoping that eventually I'd change my mind."

I push myself up to sit. "Well, at least there's one good thing to me being on this ridiculous show. Now you know you don't have to be ashamed. Everyone loves having Deacon around. And for the record, you're not an idiot, Violet. You're sweet and amazing. You just trusted the wrong guy. And yes, it matters about the child support. It was his sperm—that makes Deacon his responsibility."

"Yes, but what if he tries to take Deacon away from me? I couldn't risk it. Besides, the man is a liar. I didn't trust him after what he did to me. How can I know for sure that he won't hurt Deacon? I can't. My son deserves better than that."

I've got no answer for that. "So what are you planning to tell Deacon when he asks about his father? Because at some point, you'll no longer be able to tell him that a stork delivered him in the barn while you slept."

Yes—that's exactly how my grandmother explained it to me when Jake was born. Even when I was sixteen and knew better, she stuck with that story.

Violet bursts out laughing, and her cheeks turn adorably flushed. She was there the day my grandfather overheard Granny tell me that. She was also there a few minutes later when he quite graphically explained how babies came to be. But instead of explaining it in human terms, he explained how cattle fucked.

I'm not sure which of us was more traumatized: Violet or me.

"I don't know," she says. "That might buy me time. It's probably better than believing his father never wanted him." A wide grin takes over her face, and she giggles. "Or I could tell him Santa's reindeer ran over his father because his father was on the naughty list. I'll never have to worry about Deacon misbehaving after that."

I grin back at her. "Sounds like a plan. Or maybe you'll marry a man one day who loves Deacon as his own and it won't matter."

"Ha! As if that will ever happen."

I open my mouth to ask her why not but don't get that far. Austin's and Jake's voices can be heard coming toward my room.

Shit.

Jake's voice is the louder of the two, as if warning me that my best friend is about to kick my ass. My stomach quickly drops like a *Cirque du Soleil* acrobat who missed the trapeze bar.

I survey my room for a good hiding spot. "Quick, in my closet." The words are a hurried whisper.

"Why?" she whispers back, her gaze on me and not on the doorway to impending doom.

With my eyes, I show exactly why. My gaze settles on her

spectacular tits. Fortunately, my cock has the good sense not to get excited by the view.

She yanks the blanket up to cover herself.

If only it were that easy.

"Austin can't find you in here. Especially not naked in my bed —unless you wish to witness my murder."

The frown deepens. "What difference does it make if I'm naked in bed with you? It's not like *your* brothers care. They're not going to murder you because we were having sex."

I want to roll my eyes, but I don't think she'll appreciate it.

She raises her chin in stubborn defiance. "I'm a grown woman, TJ. I get to decide who I sleep with, not my brother."

Since she's not cooperating, and I prefer my package to remain where it is, I have no other choice. I pull the blanket over her head to muffle her protest.

"You know what? I think TJ might be sleeping." Jake says it loud enough to wake up a hibernating bear.

"This is important," Austin says.

Praying Violet won't harm me more than her brother most definitely will, I hoist her off the bed.

A small yelp slips from her lips, the blanket already yanked off her head.

"Shh," I whisper and carry her to my closet. This time she does exactly as I asked.

I lower her feet to the floor.

"I just need you to stay in here until he's gone," I say, a man-sized amount of pleading in my voice.

She makes a move toward the door. I block her with my arm.

"Violet, just trust me when I say he's not going to be happy about me being with you this way. I don't want to hurt my best friend by betraying his trust in me...."

I place my finger against her lips to stop what I have a feeling she's about to say. "But I also can't keep away from you even though I know I should. God knows I've tried." I replace my finger with my lips for a brief kiss. "So please stay in here until he's gone, and I'll satisfy you in bed any way you want. Whatever it takes. For the rest of your time in Copper Creek."

She pretends to think about it for a second. I can hear the two men draw closer to the room, but I can't hear what they're saying. The closet door is muffling the sound.

"You've got yourself a deal, cowboy. But you do realize my clothes are still out there, right?"

Not good. Not good at all. Especially if Austin recognizes her dress. "Stay right here. I'll get them."

I give her a quick yet thorough kiss, then step from the closet, pulling the door shut behind me.

But before I can close it all the way, my bedroom door swings open. *Fuck-a-rific.*

"Any reason why you didn't knock?" I grunt out the words caveman-style.

As if pulled by a magnetic force, my gaze drops to Violet's clothes on the floor.

"Am I interrupting?" Austin asks.

I look up in time to see Austin's gaze jump from the clothes on the floor to the bed and then back to me.

Yeah, about that...

"Why? Are you gonna arrest me for having sex?" My tone is amused and easygoing—the opposite of how I feel.

He surveys the room. "Where is she?"

"Who?"

Austin steps across the carpet to the pile of clothes and nudges Violet's panties with his shoe. "Unless these are yours, I'll venture a professional guess and say they belong to the woman you just had sex with."

"And what if they are mine?" Yes, because that was such a brilliant response.

Unseen by Austin, Jake gives me the thumbs up sign for "Man, you're royally fucked now."

Static crackles from the radio on Austin's shoulder and I hold my breath, willing for him to be called away on an urgent call. His deputy alerts him to a herd of sheep wandering through downtown Copper Creek.

Close enough.

Austin confirms he's on his way and ends the call. "That's the third time in a month," he says to Jake and me. "Jeffery keeps forgetting to shut the gate to his pasture."

Old Man Jeffery has been forgetting a lot of things lately. "Hopefully he remembers to put on his pants this time," I say. "He gave Gertrude quite the shock last time he had to round up his sheep."

Jake laughs. "She didn't stop talking about it for weeks after that. Nor did she let poor Jeffery forget about it."

Austin moves away from the clothes. "You don't by any chance know where Violet is, do you?" he asks me.

"At Grandma Meg's is my guess."

He shakes his head. "Already tried that. Granny figured she's out with a man." And from the way his hands tighten into fists, he's imagining them around said man's neck. *Lucky me.*

"Or she could be with Aubrey and Sophie."

"I'll swing past their places after I deal with the sheep situation."

"Sounds like a good idea." And I'll make sure Violet is at Aubrey's when he shows up. Because the last thing I need is for Austin to believe his sister is seeing someone while she's here for the week. That will only make him more determined to track down who the man is.

Austin walks out of my room. Jake throws me a shit-you-were-lucky smirk over his shoulder and follows him.

Don't I know it? Old Man Jeffery is about to get a bottle of Jack for saving both me and my package.

I shut the door behind them and slouch against it for a second.

Right, I need to get Violet out of here in case Austin decides to come back. And then I'm installing a lock on my bedroom door.

Violet pokes her head around the closet door. "I guess I should be getting back to Granny's now."

"Why does she think you're seeing a man while you're in town?" I ask as she walks out of the closet, the sheet wrapped around her like a toga.

She reaches for her panties on the floor. "It's probably just wishful thinking. She's no doubt hoping I'll fall in love with someone in Copper Creek and stay here. She loves having Deacon around."

She gathers the rest of her clothes and dresses while I do the same. Then she kisses me on the goddamn cheek. "I'm taking Deacon to the county fair on Saturday. Did you want to join us? Aubrey and Sophie are also coming."

I grab her around the waist and haul her against me.

"And tomorrow afternoon," she says, "he and I are watching the movie *Frozen* if you're interested."

"I can be convinced." I proceed to show her exactly how to convince me. Convince me in a way that puts the kiss she just gave me to shame.

19

"Where to now, Deacon?" I ask the two-year-old sitting on my shoulders. We walk past a group of kids playing Whac-A-Mole. The smell of grilling meat and barbecue sauce from the annual cook-off beckons to my stomach. "You want to see animals or do you want to sample some amazing ribs?"

He bounces on my shoulders. I take it that's a yes—except I have no idea which he's agreeing to.

Violet beams at her son, my cowboy hat in her hand. She's looking especially hot this afternoon, in her denim shorts, black tank top, cowboy boots, and the belt I gave her.

"Why don't we see how Uncle Austin is doing," she says, "then we can go see the animals?"

We're not the only ones who've heeded the cook-off's call. There's a mob of people hanging around the tables that are offering a variety of foods: casseroles, grilled meat, potato salads, baked goods. Each dish is vying to win the fair's most prestigious awards.

Well, prestigious around these parts.

Austin is at a grill, brushing on a generous helping of his infamous barbecue sauce. It's the secret recipe he wins with year after year.

A group of women in their twenties is swarming around his table. All look hungry. Only it's not his beef ribs I suspect they're hungry for. I recognize their expressions. They're the same ones the girls who hung around the rodeo events wore. Not the girls genuinely interested in watching the events. But the girls who were interested in hooking up with the contestants. "That's a first."

"What's a first?" Violet asks.

"You know what a buckle bunny is, right?"

"I do. You used to hook up with them all the time." At what is no doubt a surprised look on my face, she says, "Austin told me."

Of course he did—because she wasn't around when I started hooking up with them. Austin telling her is the only way she would have known about those women.

"Plus I overheard some girls at the rodeos I attended talking about you and comparing notes," she adds.

Ouch.

Only an idiot would ask what they said about him.

I'm no idiot.

"I haven't been with those kinds of women since the accident," I point out in my defense...and then attempt to put the train back on the track. "The way those women are eyeing up your brother, I'm starting to wonder if cook-offs have their own breed of bunny." Or if those women are badge bunnies who have sniffed him out, even though he's not currently wearing his uniform.

We walk around them, only to be brought up short by the sight of Miss H, my old high school teacher. Grandma Meg, Gertrude, and Tilly are also with her.

Or rather, Gertrude is talking to her and showing her a piece of paper. Grandma Meg hands a couple of girls each a sheet of paper with what looks like a photo of someone on it.

"The reality show *Cowboy Most Wanted* is coming soon to a TV near you," Tilly shouts, gaining the attention of people passing by. She hands them a piece of paper, similar to the ones her friends are handing out. "Vote for Copper Creek's very own hot cowboy, TJ Daniels."

She practically shoves a piece of paper at the chest of an elderly man. His cowboy hat prevents me from seeing who it is.

He must have said something she didn't agree with because she then says, loudly, "Don't you be giving me any trouble, Gary Umbridge. Or else I'll make sure there's no more of Cora Lee's cupcakes for you. Now, you make sure you vote for TJ."

Whatever he grumbled must have made Tilly happy. She grins and turns to the next person.

"What's going on?" I ask, even though I have a pretty good idea. I take the flyer from her hand and read it.

Violet giggles next to me.

On it is a picture of me shirtless. I recognize it from the show's website. "You're seriously going around telling people to vote for me?"

"Damn right," Tilly says. "It's called marketing."

I shoot Violet a dark look. "Did you know about this?"

She giggles harder, presses her hand against her mouth in an attempt to muffle the sound, and shakes her head.

She removes her hand. "Granny asked me a few questions the other day about marketing, but I had no idea she meant this. I thought she was talking about her knitting club."

"Well, don't the three of you make a handsome family?" Miss H says, eyeing Deacon, Violet, and me. Because her hearing isn't what it used to be, she says it loud enough for Austin to overhear.

He stops brushing the sauce on the ribs, and his expression hardens as he watches us.

Christ, you don't have issues with your grandmother pimping me when it comes to that show, but you have issues with Miss H's comment?

"We're not together. I mean we're friends, and we're here together," I say, stumbling over the words.

"Are you forgetting that TJ is betrothed to the woman on *Cowboy Most Wanted*?" Gertrude says.

"Betrothed?" I look at Violet to see if she knows what Gertrude is talking about. She just smiles back at me, her expression part naughty, part nice, and clearly entertained by all of this.

"They haven't even met yet," Miss H says. "How can they be engaged if they haven't met?"

"That's neither here nor there," Gertrude says. "I'm sure it will happen. That's why the girls and I are out here promoting TJ."

"What's going on?" Austin asks, brush in hand. "Am I going to have to break up a fight?" He winks at Miss H.

Deacon wiggles his butt on my shoulders. "Go. Go." He says it with a near-urgent tone, like a bank robber after a heist while climbing into the getaway vehicle.

Violet helps him down as Austin looks at the seven of us in turn, waiting for a reply.

It's Miss H who puts him out of his misery. "I was just saying that TJ, Violet, and your nephew make a beautiful family."

Austin chuckles. "Except they're not a family. TJ's not the kind of man to settle down with one woman, never mind have a kid with her."

Gertrude's gaze shoots to mine. "But...but what about the reality show? Aren't you planning to marry the star if she picks you during the final episode?"

Impatient to get going, Deacon makes a break for it.

Before he has a chance to get far, I scoop him up. "Hey, little cowboy. Where you going?"

He giggles. "Horsie."

"You wanna see the animals, do you?" I ask. Then to the women, I say, "There are fifteen other cowboys on the show. And there's a good chance I won't be voted to the next round." *If I'm lucky.* "Plus Austin's right. Violet, Deacon, and I aren't a family.

Hell, they don't even live in the same state as me, never mind the same town." I turn to Austin. "We'll be back in a bit. Save us some ribs."

Without giving him and the older women a chance to respond, I walk off with Deacon still in my arms. Violet quickly catches up to us.

"Here's your hat, cowboy." Her mouth twitches, but it doesn't quite turn into a full smile.

I stop walking, bow my head so she can place the hat on it, and straighten. "Thanks."

My gaze drops to her lips, and for once I wish I could kiss her in public. Kiss her and not pretend that she's just a friend to me.

Kiss her and show the world that I'm falling for this woman, hard, even though I shouldn't. Especially since we can't be together. Not now. Not ever.

At the petting zoo, we enter the enclosure where three little kids are stroking the piglets. Deacon and I walk over to a pink piglet with black spots. The pig's busy snorting and sniffing the dirt.

Kneeling, I gently pick him up and cradle him against my body. He squeals but doesn't fuss beyond that. Deacon squats in front of me, and at my encouragement, strokes the small pig.

Violet's camera clicks repeatedly in the background. Ignoring it, I smile at Deacon as he inspects the animal in my arms, a grin on his cute face.

A surge of a raw emotion I can't explain almost knocks me back into the dirt. An emotion I have no right to feel when it comes to Deacon or Violet.

Doesn't that just fuck all?

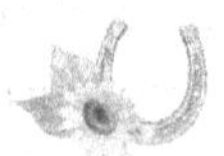

By the time we return to Austin almost two hours later, Deacon is asleep in my arms, his head on my shoulder. Which comes as no surprise when you think of all the things he did this afternoon: Meeting the piglets, the lambs, the chicks, the baby goats. Going on the hayride. Winning the small stuffed horse. Well, technically, I won the horse, but he was extremely excited about it.

I kiss Deacon on the top of his head. All around us, laughter, loud country music, the mayor declaring the winner of the Best Chili category, and applause fill the air. Deacon sleeps through it.

"Looks like they're about to announce the winner of the best barbecued ribs." I indicate with my head where we can get a better view without the risk of being accidentally bumped.

We move to the side, Violet carrying Deacon's floppy horse.

Her hand shifts to rest on my lower back. Her thumb lightly strokes against my T-shirt. The heat from her palm seeps through the fabric, and a dizzying need to kiss her and to claim her surges through me like a tsunami.

Her hand is only on my back for a moment before it moves away, and I'm left with an empty coldness in its place.

Aubrey and Sophie approach us, smiling and laughing. Neither of my brothers is with them.

"What did you do to the poor kid?" Aubrey grins at Violet and then at me. "Well, aren't you just adorable with Deacon asleep in your arms like that?"

"She's right," Sophie says. "If the fair had a contest for the hottest man with a child, you'd win it for sure."

Aubrey lifts her phone and shoots what I guess to be photos of Deacon and me. She shows Violet the screen.

A sweet smile spreads on Violet's lips, but it only lasts a handful of seconds. My chest suddenly feels two sizes too small, and I would do almost anything to bring that smile back.

"And now for the winners of the best damn ribs in all of

Beaver Ridge County." Mayor Diane Wineberg's friendly voice rings loud and clear through the nearby speakers.

And still Deacon doesn't stir.

She announces the two runners-up. "And the winner is...our very own Sheriff Brooks."

An excited, heartfelt applause breaks out among the crowd. A few girls nudge their way closer to the table that separates the contestants from the eager audience.

And for a brief moment, I wonder if this would be a good time to announce to Austin that I'm falling in love with his sister. That my goal of getting her out of my system has been a complete and utter fail.

But what's the point of destroying my friendship with him when Violet doesn't feel the same way about me? She's just passing through town. Tomorrow, she and her son will be returning to LA. Returning to the job she enjoys.

Returning to a life that doesn't include me.

20

A week after Violet returns to work, I'm about to head out to do repairs on the pasture fence when the front doorbell rings. Noah and Jake are off doing their afternoon chores.

Which means none of us are expecting visitors.

I open the door. Cora Lee is standing on the porch, a white cardboard box perched on her hand.

She smiles. "I come bearing a gift. May I come in? I need to talk to you for a moment."

I open the door wider. "Sure. But I can't talk for long. I've still got lots to do before I can call it a day."

She enters the house and heads for the kitchen.

Oookay.

I follow her with Asgard trotting beside me.

In the kitchen, Cora Lee parks the box on the table and opens it. Three cupcakes sit inside. Two are plain—each with a big swirl of blue icing. The other one is green, with a marzipan rabbit on top.

"You dropped by to deliver cupcakes?" That would be a first.

"No, I came to talk to you about *Cowboy Most Wanted.*"

I mentally groan at the name. "What about the show?"

"Well, it's not so much about the show. It's about how I have something you don't want the producers to hear."

"What the hell are you talking about?" Because I really have no clue.

She removes the marzipan rabbit from the cupcake. "I know you and Violet have been screwing like bunnies since she came back to town. And from what I've learned, that's against the show's contract you signed."

At her last words, unease starts pumping through my veins. A small amount. At first. Growing with each subsequent word. *Thump. Thump. Thump.*

"I have no idea what you're talking about, Cora Lee. There's nothing going on between Violet and me."

"Didn't look that way the day I saw you with your head between Violet's legs, not far from Joe's. If memory serves me correct—and it does—the producer and some of the camera crew were also in the bar that night."

Busted.

"I must admit, that was extremely hot." She fans herself. "I even made a recording of it. You know...just in case." She taps on her phone and a distinctive "Oh, God, TJ. Yes. Yes. *Yes.*" comes from the speaker. I probably could have claimed it was someone else if I hadn't said Violet's name right after that.

Which means I can't even say it happened before the show started taping. Everyone in town knows Violet hasn't been in Copper Creek in over three years.

"What is it you want?"

And why do I have a feeling it's going to be expensive?

"As you know, my cupcakes are popular. Right now, I'm baking and decorating them in my kitchen. It's not the ideal situation, especially since I want to expand the business. To do that, I need to rent some space and install professional-grade ovens and equipment."

"And you want hush money from me?"

"No. I'm not a villain from one of your comic books. But I need you to help me with the bank. I'm not in the position to take out a business loan. I don't make enough money waitressing at Joe's for the bank to do anything beyond laugh at me. So I need you to cosign the loan."

Shit.

"And what happens if you default on your payments? I could be in a worse position than if the show just sues me."

"That's not going to happen. For one, I don't need to borrow that much. Twenty grand should do it. And I plan to pay it all off myself. It's my business. You're just cosigning the bank loan."

I cross my arms. "And what if I say no?" Because despite what she says, twenty grand is a lot of money. The last thing I need is to be stuck paying her payments if she defaults on them.

"I'll let the producers know how you violated the contract. And given that Violet is one of their employees, I'm sure the producers won't be impressed with either of you."

My breath stops, my mouth goes dry, and my heart goes, *Oh shit, oh shit, oh shit.*

All Violet's hard work, all her sacrifices, will be for nothing.

"Or I could just sell the story to the tabloids. Just think of the scandal that would cause." Cora Lee bites off the rabbit's head. I inwardly cringe on behalf of the poor fellow.

Despite the seriousness of the situation, my mouth slides into a smirk. The number one rule when dealing with the villain? Don't let them see you sweat. "Is that supposed to be your version of the boiling bunny?"

She shrugs. "Melting a marzipan rabbit in boiling water doesn't have the same effect as biting off its head." Her mouth moves into its own smirk. "Besides, I love marzipan—so no way in hell am I wasting it in boiling water. But don't think for a second that I'm not serious about my promise."

"You mean your threat."

She shrugs again. "To-ma-to. To-mah-toe."

"Who else knows about Violet and me?"

Austin clearly hasn't heard about it yet. He would have said something to me by now.

Or maybe he's on his way—ready to defend his sister's honor.

"No one. And I'll keep it that way as long as you help me out." She flashes me a bright smile. The smile of someone who got the Christmas present they've been hoping for.

"I'll give you twenty-four hours to get back to me. Then I can book an appointment with the bank." With that, she walks out of the kitchen, her heels clicking against the tile floor.

And I'm left wondering what the hell I'm supposed to do now.

"Remember, you're doing this for the sake of the ranch," Jake says for what has to be the fifth time in two days.

That's right—the odds were not in my favor when it came to the reality show.

I can blame Mayor Wineberg for that.

What happened? After the show opened the phone lines for people to vote for their favorite cowboy, she took it upon herself to campaign on my behalf. With Grandma Meg, Gertrude, and Tilly as her assistants, I never stood a chance.

Too bad "my behalf" wants nothing to do with the show.

I just want my life to return to normal. Well, a normal involving Violet and Deacon physically in my life and not just via Skype.

And there might have also been a few texts to Violet while she was away.

Dirty, forbidden texts.

The last time I saw her was six weeks ago.

Six weeks of missing her.

Six weeks of not kissing or touching her.

Six weeks of not being with her as her friend, as her lover.

But I can't be too mad at the mayor and her cohorts. Because of them, I get to spend the next five days with Violet. Except this time, we have to be extremely careful. If I look at her the wrong way, betraying how I feel about her, her brother will be the least of my problems. For now.

What happens if I do look at Violet the wrong way?

Go ask Roger Mathews from Texas. Turns out the guy had a girlfriend he'd failed to mention.

Now he's facing a lawsuit. A lawsuit for a lot more than Cora Lee requested on a loan from the bank.

And worse yet?

Because of the contract, I have to be intimate with Natalie—if that's what she wants. She gets to call the shots...even if *I* don't want to be intimate with her.

Luckily, "calling the shots" excludes sex.

The gravel crunches underfoot as Jake and I walk down the path to the driveway. A bird chirps behind me. I turn around and spot a chubby chickadee sitting on a wooden post.

I raise my smartphone and aim it at him. Several clicks later, I have a good picture to post on our social media sites. Yes, the ranch is now on social media...thanks to Violet.

Jake laughs. "She's really got you trained, hasn't she?"

"Who?" I ask even though I know who he's talking about. I just don't want to admit it.

Because he's right. Violet has me trained. Do I believe the dramatic increase in Facebook page likes following the episode I was on is due to people wanting to buy a horse from us?

No—if the number of requests for shirtless pictures on the page are any indication.

But it's a start.

"I don't suppose you could marry Violet," he says. "Then she can do all the social media for us?" He might not be laughing this time, but it's definitely in his tone.

"Yes, maybe we could include that in our wedding vows." I shove him on the arm.

He chuckles. "Hey, it was just a thought. But at least Cora Lee's blackmail didn't involve you marrying Natalie. Be grateful for that."

I admitted to Jake and Noah what happened after Cora Lee blackmailed me. They decided not to kill me when I told them, although I'm sure the thought has crossed their minds a few times since then.

The good news is, Cora Lee did delete the audio recording once I cosigned the loan and it was approved.

The other good news? Jake got a lawyer friend from college involved. If she has another copy and it's released, she'll be in legal hot water.

I post the picture on Instagram with a bunch of hashtags, including one for our ranch. Like with Facebook, our Instagram followers grew exponentially after the episode I was on aired.

A limo pulls up in front of the house as Jake and I approach the driveway.

"They sent her in a freaking limo?" A white limo with big-ass steer horns tied to the grate. There would be less disbelief in my tone if Santa had landed on the driveway with his flying reindeer. "Please tell me she's not one of those city girls who can't handle getting a fleck of dirt on them."

What do I know about Natalie? Not a helluva lot. I didn't bother watching the episode when she was introduced to the viewers.

Noah filled me in on the highlights. But I have no idea what they are. I was fantasizing about Violet at the time.

Violet's rental car and two white vans park farther back from the limo. From where Jake and I are standing, we can't see much of anything. But a moment later, a tan cowboy hat covering long, wavy blonde hair pops into view from the other side of the limo.

The owner turns around, giving us a better view of her face.

Jake lets out a low, appreciative whistle, heard only by me. "Shit, she's a fucking Victoria's Secret model. Or she could be. No wonder Noah's had a boner for her ever since he saw her on TV."

"*Now* are you sorry you didn't volunteer to take my place?"

He laughs...because we both know the answer. "Not at all. I'm still sticking with better you than me."

"Speaking of Noah, where is he?" You would think he'd be falling over himself to meet Natalie in person—even if he's not a contestant.

"No idea. But look who did show up...." His gaze shifts to the small, bright green car driving up the driveway.

Now imagine a clown car at the circus. The door opens and a never-ending stream of clowns pour out of the vehicle.

Welcome to Gertrude's car. She climbs out of it, along with Grandma Meg, Tilly, and three other old ladies from the senior center. I have no idea how she even fit them all in the car.

And what's worse? They're outfitted with binoculars and cameras.

"What the heck are they up to?" I ask. "They look like spy-wannabes."

Jake bursts out laughing.

Did I mention they're also wearing trench coats? Bright, colorful trench coats.

"To them," Jake says, "this show is the best thing that has happened since Pastor O'Reilly's granddaughter ran off to Vegas to marry Barry the Bug Exterminator."

The six elderly women spot us looking at them and wave wildly at us.

I give them a halfhearted wave. "At least someone is excited about this."

"I bet if you're real nice, they might even ask you for your autograph." He chuckles.

I scowl at him. "You know, you're enjoying this way too much for your own good."

He laughs again. "I know. But it's worth it."

I backhand him in the chest.

We walk around to the other side of the limo. Grandma Meg and her cohorts move closer, their faces alive with mischief. They lift their cameras to take some photos.

Unlike Camilla, Natalie is dressed like a cowgirl. A sexy, pin-up poster version of a cowgirl. Her boots match the color of her hat. She's wearing jeans that appear molded to her legs. Her denim shirt, rolled up to just below her elbows, skims over her body and tits, and is unbuttoned low enough to catch a glimpse of her cleavage.

But despite all of that, there's something about her that doesn't scream city slicker. It screams, "I'm comfortable around horses and don't mind getting dirty."

"Makes you wonder, though," I say, "why she agreed to be on the show."

Despite the urge boiling inside me, I avoid glancing, even for a second, at Violet. The consequences are too great.

Camilla introduces everyone—including the spy wannabes. "And here comes TJ's youngest brother, Noah." Her gaze is directed over Jake's shoulder.

Jake and I turn to see our brother coming from the stables, my old lasso hanging from his shoulder. The lasso that I purpose-fully stored away to keep the competitive craving at bay.

The old desire at seeing the familiar rope is like puppies clambering over each other for a much sought-after bone.

I tear my gaze from it and focus on his face. The face that I'm imagining covered with huge warts, like a witch.

He gives Grandma Meg and her cohorts an amused grin. I can't tell if he knew they were coming. He doesn't give anything away.

Camilla introduces Natalie to him.

He shakes her hand. "So, what do you think of Montana so far? Not quite North Dakota, is it?"

He's definitely done his homework—unlike me. I had no idea where she's from.

Or maybe that's not where she's from. Maybe she spent last week in North Dakota with the cowboy of the week.

She smiles at him. "No, it isn't." She turns back to me and her smile widens. "I didn't realize how beautiful this part of Montana was until I saw the video footage and the gorgeous photos of the area."

"So you're familiar with brutal winters then?" I'm hoping she's a southern girl, whose idea of cold doesn't involve a thick winter coat, boots, and enough snow to build an army of Olafs.

Natalie smiles again. "Very familiar. Granted, I prefer warm days...but not the sweltering southern heat. That's why I'd never make a very good Southern girl." She lowers her voice for the last part, as if to keep it a secret from the TV crew, and winks at me.

Shit.

"What did she say?" Gertrude says a little too loudly.

"Shh," Tilly says, equally loud. "I can't hear them if you're jabbering."

Grandma Meg says something to Gertrude, who then gives me a double thumbs-up.

Note to self: find out just how many cowboys from the north made it to this round of the show.

I turn to Noah and clench my fingers into a fist, fighting the urge to stroke the lasso he's holding. Stroke the rope like it's my favorite pet. "What's the lasso for?"

Noah shifts on his feet, his expression one I recognize from when we were kids. Only I have a feeling it's not because he was caught sneaking cookies before dinner.

"Camilla requested that you demonstrate your calf roping skills." He rubs his hand against the back of his neck, then leans in close so only I can hear him. "I did explain to her about your knee. Maybe you can talk some sense into her."

I shake my head. "Don't worry....I'll do it. This show was

supposed to help us gain exposure for the ranch, so Jake could stop regretting our decision to switch to horses. I'm sure it'll be fine. It's just this one time." It's not like it will be a real competition.

Camilla rejoins us. The crew is now scurrying around, setting up the lighting and the sound equipment. "All right, now that TJ and Natalie have had a chance to get acquainted, we will do that again, with Natalie climbing out of the limo. But Jake and Noah, you won't be in the shot. It will just be TJ and Natalie. And TJ, once Natalie is out of the limo, you'll present her with this rose."

A short girl in her midtwenties hands me a single red rose. Then the pair walks away, with Camilla dolling out instructions to everyone nearby who works for the show.

"Doesn't the director usually do that?" Jake nods at Camilla, who is too busy to notice. She's talking to Grandma Meg and her fellow spies and pointing to where the white vans are parked.

The elderly women nod and scurry off to where she was pointing.

"She's both the director and producer this time," Natalie says.

"What happened to the director who was here last time?"

"I have no idea. He was with us for the first ranch, but I don't think Camilla was happy with him. He didn't share her vision for this part of the show. Rumor has it she got him fired." Natalie glances briefly over her shoulder to where the crew is working. "Welcome to what the show is really like. It's not as spontaneous as you might believe. If she's not happy with a shot, she'll force us to do it again. And again. And again."

Noah chuckles. "You sound like you speak from experience."

"More than I care to admit," Natalie says on a sigh.

Camilla strides toward us with a determined look on her face...and my brothers leave. Which is a nice way of saying they wish us luck and bail while laughing their heads off.

Fortunately, Noah takes the lasso with him.

Camilla shoos Natalie back into the limo and tells me where to stand. "Okay, places everyone....Action!"

The driver opens the vehicle door and helps Natalie out of the limo. I can feel Violet watching as the scene unfolds. The burning need from earlier, to turn around and smile at her, comes back with the intensity of a grade five hurricane.

I glue on my I'm-happy-to-meet-you smile. I didn't need it when I first met Natalie, but that was when there were no cameras recording my every move, my every expression, my every word.

In contrast to my smile, Natalie's appears genuine. But this is week number three for her. She's had a lot of practice.

"Hi, Natalie. Welcome to Pine Meadow Ranch." I hand her the rose.

Right—that doesn't feel phony at all.

She takes the flower and sniffs it. "It's nice to finally be here. It's a gorgeous place."

I offer my arm—as Camilla instructed me to do. Natalie accepts it, and we walk toward the ranch house.

We reach the bottom step.

"Cut!"

We both turn to see what Camilla wants us to do next.

Violet is watching us, her face an expressionless mask. My heart clenches and drops like an elevator after its cables fail. *Heart, meet gut.*

Camilla has us wait by the stairs while the cameramen videotape the limo driving toward the house.

"Is it going to be like this all week?" I ask Natalie.

"Pretty much."

"And you've still got two more weeks of this after you're finished here?"

"Plus the four weeks after that, when the six of us converge on the ranch resort they've lined up for the remainder of the season." She places her hand on my arm, either in support or condolence. "Don't worry, TJ. You'll get used to it."

I'm not so sure about that.

I peek at Violet to check her reaction to Natalie touching me. She's busying herself with her camera.

Remember, dumbass, Violet and you were only having sex. Nothing more. At the end of all of this, she will return to her life in LA.

That was the deal.

End of story.

Too bad that's not how I want the story to end.

But unfortunately, this is real life—not an episode on a reality show.

All right—my life *is* currently a reality show. But it's not like I can ask Camilla to give me a happy ending...with Violet as my forever.

22

A few hours later, I'm standing outside the stable, saddling up Thor. Everyone else is next to the training ring, waiting for us.

"Why don't you just tell Camilla you can't do it?" Jake says from behind me. I didn't even hear him approach.

"Won't make a difference. Noah already tried. Besides, the video footage of me roping the calf might go a long way in helping the ranch. I'm no longer on the rodeo circuit. People don't know my name—other than as a contestant on the show. This way they can see me in action. It might help get the ranch's name out there to the correct target market. It's worth a try."

"Except we can't afford for you to get injured over something as stupid as this." Jake doesn't say it in his concerned brotherly voice. The words also hold his typical business-minded tone.

I tighten Thor's cinch. "I'm not going to get injured. It's just this one time. I rope the calf, they capture it on video, and everyone is happy. Isn't that right, Thor?"

Thor whinnies his reply.

"Remind me to kill the Masons for loaning the calf to Camilla." Jake smacks me on the back. "Just be careful, okay?"

I have a feeling he's not only talking about the calf roping and my knee. "Make sure you videotape this, in case the network won't let us use their footage on our website."

"Will do."

He walks away, leaving me alone so I can focus on my pre-race ritual.

I pat Thor on his shoulder. "All right, boy. You haven't failed me yet." It was my knee that fucked it up for both of us.

Although I'm sure Thor has no complaints about that. He got to become the ranch stud. One of us definitely got the better end of the deal.

Once I'm finished with my ritual, I lead Thor to the training ring. Because this isn't a real event, we have to improvise. There is no chute or starting gate.

Plus the ground is muddy from yesterday's rain, making for less than ideal calf roping conditions.

I dare a glance in Violet's direction. She's holding her camera up, the strap looped around her neck.

I double-check the cinch and mount Thor. I adjust my seat, pick up my lasso from the saddle horn, and nod for Jake to open the gate.

I exhale slowly to bring my heart rate under control, then kick Thor at the same time Noah gets the calf to race away from me.

And as we have done thousands of times in the past, horse and rider move as one. Seconds later, the calf is on the ground, tied up.

Cheers break out from the other side of the fence.

My knee is not so impressed. I bury the pain deep, so no one is aware of what this stupid stunt cost me. It's nothing painkillers and a dip in the cold river won't cure.

An image pops to mind. Of me. Naked. In the river. With Violet.

Naturally, she's also naked.

Maybe realizing things didn't go as smoothly as I had hoped, Jake jogs over and unties the calf.

"How did it look?" I ask. The animal scrambles away free. "Think the video will impress anyone?"

By anyone, I'm referring to potential buyers who are looking for quality, future rodeo horses.

"You and Thor looked good out there."

"But?"

"Anyone who is seriously considering one of our horses, and sees that footage on the show, will hardly be impressed."

My mouth jerks up to one side. "Maybe I can break into their rooms tonight and delete it."

"Then they'll make you do it again."

Good point.

Natalie steps between us, oblivious to what Jake and I just said. "Oh God, that was the hottest thing I've seen so far on the show." She flings her arms around my neck and kisses me.

I stiffen—and I'm not referring to my cock.

When I don't kiss back, she pulls away and smiles. It's the twin to the smile she wore when we met for the first time in front of the camera.

The one I assumed was genuine.

"Sorry," I say. "I don't usually kiss right after I race. Adrenaline high."

Although if Violet had just tried to kiss me, I wouldn't have stiffened. I would've gone along for the ride and thoroughly enjoyed it.

"I'm sorry," Natalie says. "I just got caught up in the moment. It was really exciting watching you ride."

"Thanks...and it's okay." It's part of what the show expects of us—the role we have to play.

But at least Natalie wants to be here.

I just want to be in bed with Violet.

My head begins to turn to where I last saw her. *Don't look at Violet. Don't look at Violet. Don't...*

"How come you don't compete anymore?"

...look at Violet.

It doesn't help that my body isn't listening to my brain.

Violet is still holding her camera up, the lens aimed at Natalie and me. My gut ties itself into a sloppy bow at how bad this looks. But it's not like I'm cheating on Violet. Besides, Natalie and I are just talking...if you ignore the part where she kissed me.

"Sorry," I tell Natalie, "What did you say?"

"Why did you stop competing in rodeos?"

"I got injured. My orthopedic surgeon told me to stop competing, or I'd regret it later. So I listened to him."

Natalie's hand rests on my arm again and she strokes her thumb along my biceps. "Good choice. There's nothing worse than an athlete who would rather risk his body than end his pro career. I've seen it happen all too often in my clinic."

"Clinic?" If I had done my homework, I would know what she's talking about—and her slightly taken aback expression confirms this.

"My physical therapy clinic. I'm a physical therapist."

She doesn't resemble the physical therapists I've ever dealt with. My last one would have left Marines cowering in fear. He was that much of a hard-ass.

"Right," I say as if I already knew that.

I want to take a step back, to remove her hand from my arm, but there's probably some fine print in the contract I'd rather not violate. Some rule that says I can't rebuff any of her advances.

Thor comes to my rescue. He shoves his head between Natalie and me, nudging me back.

And an extra helping of oats for you, buddy.

Not deterred by Thor's actions, Natalie strokes his nose and talks to him in a flirting tone.

And just like that, she has him under her spell.

"I can't remember the last time I rode a horse," she says, and I almost expect the traitor of a stallion to offer to let her ride him.

I glance at Camilla, hoping they have enough material for now so that she can call it a wrap.

She gestures for me to keep going and mouths, "offer to take her horseback riding."

Or I think that's what she said.

"If you'd like, I can take you now," I tell Natalie.

She smiles and gives me flirty eyes. "I'd love that."

"And cut," Camilla yells.

Thank the fucking lord.

23

———

The sun is an hour from setting when I enter the office, a slight limp to my gait. Natalie and I returned hours ago from our ride, and now all I'm capable of is pacing. Asgard fell asleep watching me in my bedroom, hypnotized by my back and forth motion across the carpet.

"How's the knee?" Jake doesn't bother to turn around, his attention on the computer screen.

"Sore." Before he has a chance to say it, I add, "Yeah, I know, I screwed up." And it didn't help that I went riding after roping the calf. "I need to get out of here for a bit before I go crazy. Can you cover for me?"

Jake groans. "You can't, TJ. You know what will happen if you go see her. There's too much at stake."

It takes me a second to get on the same train as him. "That's not what I meant. I'm just going to the river. The cold water will help clear my head and soothe my knee." And it will also help with the semi hard-on, thanks to my thoughts constantly drifting to Violet.

Naked.

Riding my cock.

182

And *Christ*, now it's even harder.

I inwardly groan—and not in the same way I would if Violet really were riding my cock.

"Okay, I'll figure something out if anyone's looking for you." He gestures at the computer screen. "I see our social media campaign about the ranch is going well."

Even though Jake's smiling, something in his voice causes me to check the screen. He's looking at the latest Facebook post. The post I certainly didn't put up on our page. The post that has been shared over a hundred times.

It's of me shirtless in front of the barn. I'm staring at the camera with a bend-over-the-bale-of-hay-and-I'll-fuck-you-from-behind, half-dazed expression.

It captures perfectly what I was thinking when Violet took the photo—except *she* was the one I was focused on at the time.

"Violet must have posted it." I know she didn't want to. She's trying to help us promote the ranch after all. So why did she? That damn contract. According to it, I gave them permission to post any photo on the page that benefits the show or promotes it. Except this image looks more like it's promoting *me*...as a male model.

Which is further confirmed when I read the comments.

Yummy. He's even hotter than a Calvin Klein underwear model.

He should be a male model with a body and face like that.

I'm an agent with a modeling agency. Message me and we can set up a meeting.

Right—as if I believe the last one. Especially since the bio mentions the person is a data entry clerk at an insurance company.

I'd ride his horse anytime. A winky-face emoji completes the comment.

I scrub my hand over my face, as if it will magically solve the problem. "*Shit*. This is the last thing we need."

Jake shakes his head, gaze still on the screen. "Based on these comments, maybe Mayor Wineberg isn't too far off with her suggestion to turn the ranch into a destination vacation. We can promote it to young single women who want to ride horses and ogle their shirtless, cover-model guide." He laughs, but the sound is halfhearted at best.

"Welcome to our new reality," he says. "And it's not just this photo. Violet has uploaded at least twenty others, and the comments are all the same. No one is taking the ranch seriously."

"Are those comments just on *my* photos?"

He nods. "The ones you modeled for. Anything to do with the ranch and horses barely gets any views. The posts have a few likes but that's about it."

My stomach clenches into a tight rubber ball. "Now I really need to go to the river to clear my head."

Thanks to my teen years, I've grown quite skilled at being stealthy. The CIA could learn a trick or two from me. The early evening air is silent, other than the soft tread of my feet against the dirt ground and the breeze playing with the leaves in the trees. The same leaves that will be turning to fall colors in another month.

I enter the clearing where Violet and I had first fucked over a month ago. I kick off my boots and unzip my jeans. A minute later, my clothing is dumped on the fallen tree trunk near the river edge, and I stride butt-naked into the water.

The cold water laps against my ankles. My knee twinges in anticipation. My cock isn't quite as delighted at what's coming soon.

I keep going until the water is waist-high, then dive under the surface.

Fuck, it's cold!

By the time my head emerges, my body is happily numb. My cock and nuts, on the other hand, aren't anywhere near as pleased.

Deal with it, boys.

With two problems solved, I work on number three: clearing my head.

My knee isn't one hundred percent onboard with the plan, but we do come to an acceptable compromise. And by the time I'm too exhausted to take another stroke, my head is clearer than when I entered the river.

It's too bad the water doesn't solve my problems when it comes to the reality show, the ranch's reputation, and my feelings for Violet.

I'm fucked. Plain and simple.

I wade through the water to where I left my clothes.

Except my stuff is no longer alone—I'm no longer alone.

Natalie is standing at the water's edge...wearing only a bikini bottom. Her arms are by her sides, leaving her heavy breasts on display. She's not even attempting to cover them to keep warm.

She unties one side of her bikini bottom. And then the other. I will my legs to move, but they aren't interested in listening to me.

"What the hell are you doing?" I ask.

She smiles at me. "Same thing you are. Skinny dipping. It's so beautiful out here. I couldn't resist."

She steps into the water, not at all fazed by the temperature. I scan the area for the TV crew. But then remember the contract specified that nudity is not permitted on the show.

"Camilla's concerned at how tense you came off on camera every time I kissed you today." That's right—she attempted to kiss me at least four other times during the day.

She takes another step forward. "I have an idea that will help you be less awkward when it comes to kissing in front of the camera." She keeps moving, coming closer and closer and closer. The theme music for *Jaws* plays in my head.

"What's your idea?" My legs finally get the hint from my brain to move. I back away, keeping pace with each of her steps.

If I keep going in this direction, I'll soon be at the point where the current is faster, more dangerous. I pivot toward the shore and take a few more steps back. The ground starts to change from silt to rocky—rocky with a covering of something slimy.

Natalie doesn't answer. She lunges at me.

Like with her kisses today, I wasn't expecting it. Nor was I expecting her to wrap her arms around my neck. Her body's forward trajectory combined with the slimy rocks cause my feet to slip from under me.

My back hits the water first, then my head goes under the surface. And since Natalie's arms are still round my neck, she goes down with me.

Her thigh hits my package. A groan bursts from my lungs, forming bubbles in the water.

Shit.

I regain my footing and push myself upright. I surge up from the water and gulp down the cool evening air.

Natalie is attached to me like a piece of soggy weed. I reach back and unhook her arms.

"Whatever you had in mind to make my kisses appear less awkward...it didn't work." My tone isn't pissed. It's sitting between annoyed and mildly amused.

I turned to head back to shore and freeze.

Standing at the water's edge, her face pale, is Violet.

Fuck.

And her brother.

Double fuck.

24

As if frozen, Violet continues standing on the spot. The backpack with her camera gear stowed inside is on her back, and she's holding her tripod. I have no idea what she saw, but I have a feeling whatever it was is a strike against me. Austin is also standing there, in his uniform, appearing unconcerned by the current situation.

Needing to explain things to Violet, I surge forward. It's only as I reach shallower water—and thanks to the cooler air—that I'm reminded that I'm naked.

Faster than a cop car chasing a speeding Ferrari, Austin's hand covers Violet's eyes.

She grabs his wrist and tries to pull his hand away. "For God's sake, Austin. I'm not five years old. I've seen a naked man before."

"Yes, but this is TJ we're talking about."

She attempts once more to pry his hand away. "What does that have to do with anything? Are you seriously trying to protect his virtue?"

A bubble of laughter threatens to escape my lungs. He's a little late when it comes to Violet.

But no way in hell am I admitting that.

"Wow, this is awkward." Nothing about Natalie's tone agrees with any of that. If anything, she sounds happy to be caught in this compromising situation.

That makes only one of us.

And to further prove this, she walks forward, making it clear she's also naked—at the same time Violet pulls away from her brother.

Her gaze falls on Natalie and her eyes go wide with hurt.

"It's not what you think," I say.

Austin steps in front of Violet. "You're two consenting adults and this is private property. *Your* private property, TJ. You can do what you want. Mind you, if you were naked at the public beach, I would have to write you up for indecent exposure."

Natalie lowers herself into the water, covering her tits and everything south of them. "Could you do us a favor and not tell anyone about this? If the network or the producers find out, TJ and I could get in trouble."

A little late for that.

"Sure. Okay, we'll just leave you two alone." Austin turns to his sister, his body shielding her from seeing me, and steers her away from us.

Fuckity-fuck-fuck.

Needing to explain things to her, I start running toward the shore, except the rocks and water are not in favor of my plan. I'm vaguely aware of Natalie saying something but ignore her.

When it comes to my clothes, I have two choices. One is to yank on my boots and chase after Violet, with my package waving in the breeze like a white flag.

But while I'm more than willing to surrender to her as long as she gives me a chance to explain, my exposed cock and nuts won't do me any favors—especially when it comes to Austin.

So, plan B it is.

Ignoring Natalie's questions, I grab my jeans and drag the

denim onto my wet legs. I shove my feet into my boots, and race in the direction Violet and Austin disappeared.

Unlike when I was sneaking to the river, there's nothing quiet about my movements. A male bear lumbering through the forest, chasing a girl bear in heat, would make less noise.

My breath comes in fast. My knee screams, "Fuck you."

I arrive at the small clearing where Violet's rental car is parked. Austin's marked vehicle is parked next to it. She reaches for the driver's door.

"Violet," I gasp. "Please...listen...to me." I press my hand against the window, preventing her from opening the door.

Austin is standing near his vehicle, talking on his police radio.

"You don't owe me any explanations, TJ," she says, "if that's what this is about. You and I were just a fling. Nothing more. I knew that going in." From her expression, you'd think I just slapped her face.

The pain in my knee is nothing compared to the one in my heart.

"You know I'm not interested in Natalie," I say, "nor am I interested in being part of the show." *It's you I want, not her.*

"That's because you aren't interested in settling down. She's actually really nice if you give her a chance." The pain in her tone is still there.

She has a point...or does she? In the past, I wasn't interested in settling down. I'm still not. I don't have a bucket list that states I plan to get married and have a family before I die. The ranch is my life.

It doesn't mean I'm not interested in a life with Violet—assuming her brother doesn't kill me first. But I also can't expect her to give up her life for me. She's worked hard for it. She's earned it.

"Jeffery's sheep are on the loose again," Austin says, walking over to us. "But instead of going downtown, they're blocking the road into town. You think you and Asgard can help me round them up, TJ?"

"Sure, we'll meet you there." I throw Violet a glance that says we're not done yet with our conversation.

She doesn't see it. It's Austin who intercepts the message. And his reply can be loosely translated to "What the fuck is going on?"

Time to get out of here.

I return to the clearing where I left the rest of my clothing, to find Natalie dressed and guarding my shirt and hat.

By guarding, I mean she has them on, the shirt left unbuttoned.

Seeing her like this is a fist to the gut. Not because she's wearing my shirt and hat, but because it's not Violet who has them on.

I remove my hat from her head and set it on my own. I leave her with my shirt since the air is chilly.

"We should head back now." I begin walking.

"What's wrong with your leg?"

I turn back to her.

She's still standing where I left her. "You're limping."

"It's no big deal. It's dark and I didn't see a branch until it was too late." I mentally kick myself for the pathetic excuse. It's not *that* dark.

"Maybe I should check it out."

"Like I said, it's not a big deal." I resume walking. If she wants to stay here, that's her choice.

We walk along the trail back to the house. "Do you think we have to worry about Rose?" Natalie asks.

"Rose?" It takes me a second to figure out who the heck she's talking about. "You mean Violet? The photographer?"

"Yes, that's her. I didn't see her camera but..." She leaves the sentence dangling.

It isn't so much what she said as how she says it that causes me to stop abruptly. "Violet is an award-winning photographer.

She's not going to risk damaging her reputation just to sell topless photos of you to the tabloids."

Natalie studies me for a moment, as if she's seeing me in a new light. And it's not the kind of light shining down from the heavens. "Fair enough. Camilla said you and Violet have known each other since you were kids. Do you think she'll tell Camilla about what we were doing back there?"

A snorted laugh pushes against my squeezed-shut lips. Camilla finding out about what just happened is the least of my problems. "I doubt she'll say anything." Especially since Violet won't care if Natalie fucks up when it comes to the rules.

It's her own reputation and career at stake.

We approach the garden that was Granny's pride and joy when she was alive. Back then, it looked a little less wild than it does now.

"Why don't we go to the gazebo and I can check your knee," Natalie says.

Do I say no and keep on walking...or just get it over with? I have a feeling because she's a physical therapist, she won't let it go so easily. "Okay, but make it quick. Asgard and I have to go into town."

Natalie and I step into the gazebo. She grabs my hand. That's when I realize it's lighter in here than it should be at this time of the evening. Various pieces of lighting equipment for the show have been set up and turned on. Craig is waiting for us, a video camera perched on his shoulder.

Natalie leans into me and presses her lips to mine. As much as I want to push her away, I can't...for the sake of the show.

In the past, kissing a woman wasn't hard to do. I've kissed plenty of them. I enjoy kissing and I'm good at it. But for the first time ever, it doesn't feel right. I'm not saying that kissing Natalie is like kissing a frog—not that I've had any experience kissing amphibians. It just feels off.

The kiss ends, and I pray to all the Norse gods that it's good enough for Camilla, so I don't have to do it again.

WITH THE TV CREW HANGING AROUND THE GAZEBO, NATALIE wasn't able to examine my knee. Which was probably a good thing. I have no idea how she was planning to examine it when I had my jeans on...unless she expected me to remove them, leaving me in only my boxer briefs.

"You ready for this?" I ask Asgard, who is sitting in the passenger seat of my truck. Behind us, in the white van, is the TV crew.

That's right—they couldn't resist joining us on the sheep-herding mission.

Woof.

"I'm with you. I wish they weren't coming with us." I have no idea if that's what Asgard said, but the sentiment is still the same.

How am I supposed to talk to Violet with the tagalongs joining me? And that includes Natalie. Somewhere in the span of three minutes, Camilla got the idea that having Natalie help me with the sheep would make for entertaining television.

I park my truck behind the sheriff's car on the side of the main road into Copper Creek. The sheep are happily chewing the grass, not at all concerned with Austin waving at them to get moving.

Violet's also here, leaning against a fence post and laughing at her brother's antics. Asgard and I approach the pair.

"You could help me here, sis," Austin says.

"And miss the fun of seeing our town sheriff play herder boy? Never."

"I love you too, Vi." There's definitely eye rolling in his tone.

She laughs again.

Her gaze turns to me and the familiar heat in her eyes from the last time she was in town is back.

A van door slides shut from somewhere behind me. Violet's gaze shifts to over my shoulder. Then the heat in her eyes vanishes faster than a box of chocolates left with Grandma Meg and her friends.

And I don't have to turn around to figure out why. For someone who was telling me to give Natalie a chance, she's not acting like she's one hundred percent onboard with the idea.

Warm satisfaction fills my chest. She's not as indifferent as she pretended to be earlier.

A desire to pull her into my arms and admit that I love her nudges at me. Fortunately, common sense has a different take on the matter.

With his tongue lolling to the side, Asgard waits for me to give him the signal to herd the sheep. I give him the command and he's off. He's not trained for sheep herding, but his natural instincts don't care about that.

I weave through the herd of sheep. Other than moving out of my path, they don't exactly make an effort to stroll back to their farm. Asgard commands a greater power, like the Norse gods who live in the location he is named after. The sheep trot forward as he walks past them.

Only they aren't trotting in the direction we need them to go. They're just moving to the side of the road. Some are moving north...when we need them to go south.

Austin waves his arms at them, encouraging them to turn around and head the other direction. Gone is his intimidating ex-SEAL stance. It's now replaced by something more comical.

"You're doing a great job there, Sheriff." I wink at Violet.

She giggles, the tension from earlier faded...for now. Maybe after we're finished here, Asgard can herd everyone else away so it's just Violet and me. So I can talk to her, touch her, kiss her.

The upside of the TV crew joining us...well, there is no upside. They're busy setting up the lighting. Which means they're preventing the animals from moving in the direction we need them to go.

The sheep decide that between Asgard and the TV crew, my dog is the least threatening. Which says something right there, given that the sheep think of him as a hungry wolf and not a dog doing his job. They lunge northward, with Violet in their path.

Violet attempts to dart out of the way, but the heavy rain from yesterday made the ground wet and muddy here. Her foot slips from under her and she goes down with a shriek.

Before Austin has a chance to rescue her, I race over, drop beside her, and shield her with my body. Luckily, we're dealing with sheep and not cattle. They veer around us.

The feel of her soft body against mine is almost my undoing. I've missed her more than words can say. And if we weren't in this awkward situation with her brother and the camera crew looking on, I would show her just how much I miss her, how much I love her.

Even if it isn't the smartest thing to do.

Once the risk of Violet being hurt has passed, I move off her.

"Are you okay?" I ask, body tingling from head to toe. Tingling from having her in my arms. Tingling from having her against me.

She flashes me a sweet smile. "All good."

Austin finally makes his way to us and we both help her up. He fusses over her like a crazed mother hen—in a uniform.

Violet rolls her eyes. "Seriously, I'm fine." She glances down at herself and attempts to wipe away the mud clinging to her clothes. "Maybe a little dirty, but it's no big deal."

I push aside the need to check for myself just how fine she is...since it involves my hands on her body.

"As long as they're here"—I gesture with my head at the

camera crew and all their gear—"the sheep won't move in the direction we need them to go."

"Let me deal with this." Austin strides over to the group, the intimidation factor back on.

"Christ, I can't wait for this week to be over," I grumble to myself, Violet, and the sheep. "You're the only thing that makes putting up with this week worth it, but I can't touch you or risk looking at you the wrong way." I say it while my gaze is directed at a nearby grazing sheep.

Violet laughs. "Are you referring to me or the sheep? Because unless you're staring at them like you're imagining them as roast lamb, I don't think they're too concerned."

I flash her a grin. "I guess not."

She smiles back and nods at the crew. "Looks like my brother convinced them to leave."

She's right. And about ten minutes later, their gear is stowed back in the van and they're driving away.

Except for Natalie and Craig. The pair approaches us, with Austin appearing smug behind them.

What the hell?

"Sheriff Brooks asked for a few volunteers to help you, TJ, since Violet needs to get back to her son," Craig says. "He said we can drive back to the ranch with you."

Of course he did.

"It's okay," Violet says. "I can stay a few minutes to help out. Granny won't mind. Deacon's asleep by now."

Except now that I'm expected to drive Natalie and Craig back to the ranch, it will be impossible for me to talk to Violet.

Oh, who am I kidding? With Austin here, it would be impossible anyway.

And what would I say?

Maybe if you let her know that you love her, a voice in my head says, *that you've always loved her and will always love her, things might be different.*

My heart rate speeds up for several rapid beats, seconding the suggestion.

I ignore them both.

Now that the TV crew is gone, the herding of Old Man Jeffery's sheep back to his farm goes a little smoother.

As Violet, Natalie, and Craig encourage the flock to pass through the open gate to the pasture, Austin joins me. "Whatever you're thinking of doing with my sister, don't even go there." His tone is what I've always imagined it would be if he ever discovered the truth: Calm and lethal.

There's only one thing you can do in a situation like this. I wouldn't call it lying. I prefer to call it creatively twisting reality to make the other person happy. "I have no idea what you're talking about. Violet and I are friends."

Before Violet, I'd never done the friends-with-benefits thing. And Austin knows this. Other than Katherine and a few short-term girlfriends in high school, I've only had one-night stands.

"Just make sure you remember that," he says. "The last thing she needs is to get messed up with someone like you. She deserves more than that. Deacon deserves more than that."

I do my best not to be offended. I fail.

What I don't fail at is keeping it out of my tone. "Message received. And you're right. They both deserve someone better than me." But try telling that to my heart.

Once the five of us have finished getting the sheep back to their pasture, I drive Natalie and Craig to the ranch. Then I excuse myself and go to my bedroom and shower.

But I'm not as tired as I should be. I sit at the window and send Violet a text, even though I know I shouldn't.

> Me: I've missed you.

She responds a few seconds later.

Violet: I've missed you, too.

And then...

Violet: What are you doing?

Me: Lying in bed, thinking about you.

Violet: What are you thinking about?

Me: You, in your purple and black lace bra and panties.

I wasn't thinking about them before, but I am now.

My phone rings and I answer it. Violet. I move to my bed.

And so begins the most incredible phone sex I've ever had.

But as the post-euphoria fades, I realize that what we just did isn't enough. Once she returns home to LA, phone sex and sexts won't be enough to fill the empty space in my chest. The empty space I hadn't realized was there until now.

The empty space that I have no idea how to fill.

Well, doesn't that fuck all?

25

"Natalie can go with you," Camilla says over her coffee after I tell her my plans for the morning. The plans involving the text Aubrey sent me earlier. The plans that have nothing to do with Loki, Asgard, or the horses—Loki is just my excuse for going to the clinic. The plans that don't involve Natalie or any of the TV crew.

"And then we can get some great footage of you two together," Camilla adds, "bonding over this sick cat while at the vet's. It will be perfect."

Loki, who is currently doing a great job looking limp and lifeless in my arms, peers up at me as if to say, *What now, human? Clearly you didn't think this one through as well as you thought you had.*

"That will only stress Loki out more," I say. "He's a very sensitive cat."

Someone snorts. Most likely Jake or Noah. I choose not to dignify it with a response.

Violet looks at Loki as though his sudden "illness" is breaking her heart. As far as I can tell, she has no idea her best friend texted me this morning, which means she also has no idea why Aubrey wants to talk to me.

I want to comfort her and tell her he's fine. He's just adding to his résumé, which currently includes "couch warmer" and "tormentor of Asgard."

"Plus the waiting room is really small and the exam rooms even smaller," I explain. "There's not enough space for everyone to join me. But I promise, as soon as I'm done there, I'll be right back, and we can resume filming."

Camilla appears to contemplate this for a moment before nodding. "All right. And don't forget, we're visiting the little girl's home this afternoon, so you and Natalie can present her with the rocking horse."

I shake my head. "Sorry, but her parents changed their minds last night. They don't want their little girl on TV."

That was mostly true. They were against her being a pawn on the reality show, but they were all for my suggestion that I give the horse to their daughter next week. Just as long as no one from the show comes with me.

Loki releases a pitiful meow—and I almost laugh at his brilliant performance. *Wow.* Who knew my cat had it in him?

After I finish cleaning out the stable and grabbing a quick shower, Loki and I drive to town in my truck. The cat meows at me from the passenger seat. It's not a ticked-off meow, so that's a good thing.

"Do you think Austin suspects something is going on between Violet and me? Or was he just threatening me in case the idea crossed my mind?"

Loki meows again, but I have no clue if he's answering my question or telling me that I'm an idiot.

I park the truck behind the brick building and carry him into the vet clinic. He looks nothing like the cat who pulled off the performance of a lifetime back at the house. Now he's watching everyone as though they are his servants.

So, back to his typical self.

I approach the receptionist, but before I can say anything, Brianna, the vet assistant, rushes over. "Loki! I can't believe you've grown even more adorable since the last time I saw you."

Loki purrs at her and willingly goes into her arms.

"Aubrey will be out in a minute," she tells me. "She's just finishing up with Mr. Clydesdale's cocker spaniel."

While I wait, Brianna asks me questions about the reality show. "Is it really as awful as it sounds?"

"More so. I'll be glad once the week is finished."

"And then what happens?" She scratches Loki behind the ear. He leans into her hand and continues purring like a jackhammer.

Then they go away, and I never have to be involved with the show again.

That's the fantasy version of the answer.

"Then they have just over three weeks left of filming Natalie with the final three contestants. After that, she picks her top five choices, and they spend four weeks filming the second part of the season."

"When does it start?"

"In the new year."

Her eyes go as wide as Loki's chubby head. "How many weeks is the second part before they announce the winner?"

"Four."

"And if you make it to the next round, you can't reveal the winner until the final episode is aired?"

Which is why I have to figure a way to avoid the next round. Unfortunately, my brain's suggestion box when it comes to this topic is empty.

"That's about right," I say.

Aubrey enters the waiting room. She's skilled at hiding her emotions. It's why she's a great vet. Which means I can't tell what she knows about last night and about Violet's and my current relationship.

And right now, a little foresight would be nice.

I tell Loki to be good, then Aubrey and I walk down the block to The Coffee Nut. The café isn't too busy when we enter.

"Morning," Maddie, the owner, says. "What can I get you two? And just so you know, Aubrey. I have a fresh batch of blueberry scones waiting to be devoured."

Aubrey moans an I'm-going-to-die-if-I-don't-eat-one noise. "I'll have a vanilla coconut latte and a blueberry scone please."

I place my order and pay for them both, then we sit at a table next to the window. Aubrey starts with the usual small talk we typically skip whenever we see each other. Once our order is delivered to the table, she drops all pretenses and gets to business. "So what's going on between you and the star of *Cowboy Most Wanted*?"

Definitely not what I was expecting. "You asked me here to discuss that?"

She takes a sip of her coffee. "Among other things. Are you hoping she picks you in the end?" She watches me with an appraising eye.

"I think you already know the answer. If I had my way, the show would end today, with me not being the man expected to propose to Natalie."

"Of course if it ended today, that means Violet would be returning to LA. And who knows when we'll see her again."

My heart and my lungs squeeze in my chest, tighter and tighter, until I can no longer suck in any air.

Breathe. She's not going yet.

"Did Violet tell you what happened yesterday...before Austin recruited us to round up the sheep?" I ask.

"You mean how she found you and Natalie in a compromising position?"

Given that "compromising position" can mean anything, I

clarify. "No, I mean how Natalie joined me in the river. She was topless and jumped at me, causing us both to slip into the water. And for the record, it's not how it sounds." Natalie being topless was bad enough. No point mentioning to Aubrey that the rest of Natalie's bikini was missing, too.

"If it's not how it sounds, then how is it?" Aubrey's tone is free of judgment.

"I hurt my knee yesterday. I thought a swim in the cold river would help it feel better."

"And Natalie decided to join you?" Again, no judgment.

"No. I snuck out of the house because I wanted to be alone. I either did a crappy job sneaking or it was a fluke she ended up at the same spot as me." Violet has probably filled Aubrey in on the part where I was naked, so I skip that detail. "I tried to explain things to Violet, but Austin was there."

"Yes, I did hear about that part. God, what I would have done to see his face when he realized you were naked. In front of his baby sister." She chuckles, then her face goes cardiac-arrest serious. "You do realize he'll kill you if he figures out what's been going on between you and Violet, right?"

"I'm aware of that." I take a long sip of my coffee and wait for Aubrey to explain why she wanted to meet with me this morning. But instead of saying anything, she butters her goddamn scone.

"I love her." The words slip out, unrestrained. *Shit.* I hadn't meant to blurt it.

I expected to see any number of emotions on Aubrey's face from my revelation. But while smugness wasn't part of the list, it's the number one and two and three emotion stamped there. "And when are you planning to tell Violet this?"

"My vote is never. What's the point? She doesn't live here. She has a great new job in LA. And as you've pointed out, her brother will kill me if he finds out she and I have been having sex." I doubt the last part comes as a surprise to Aubrey. Women talk.

"So in other words, you're being a coward."

I cross my arms and lean back in my chair. "Not a coward. Smart."

Aubrey laughs again. "Definitely not smart. Both you and Violet are cowards. Your ex-girlfriend made you a relationship cynic. Violet fell for a man who was married. You're both afraid to fall in love and admit it."

"This why you texted me this morning? To insult me?"

"No, that's just the added bonus." She winks at me.

"It doesn't matter if I love her. She deserves better than me." She deserves the world.

"She deserves a lot better than what Deacon's father gave her. Both she and Deacon deserve a lot better. The question is, do you want Violet and Deacon in your life? Or are you going to be that much of a coward and let her walk away?"

"Are you telling me that she loves me?" Because things would be simpler if I knew how Violet feels about me.

Aubrey peers into her coffee cup and swirls the contents, as if she's about to tell me my fortune. "To be honest, I'm not sure if she has even admitted it to herself yet. After what her ex did, she's afraid to let anyone in that way again."

"So you want me to throw myself out there and tell her, even though she might not feel the same way about me?" That doesn't seem quite right.

That gets an exaggerated eye roll from Aubrey. "God, you really are an idiot, TJ. That's what love is all about. It's about taking risks with your heart."

I smirk. "Says the woman who's sworn off falling in love."

She returns my smirk with her own. "My sentiments on falling in love have nothing to do with my best friend."

"You're forgetting about her great job in LA."

"Have you even talked to her about it?" Aubrey pops a piece of scone into her mouth.

"You're also forgetting the reality show and Austin. Austin will never let me be with his sister. And if I even look at Violet the wrong way and the producer suspects something is going on between us, I could be slapped with a lawsuit."

Aubrey leans forward in her chair, elbows on the table. "I think it's time you discuss all of this with Violet. And do it *before* she leaves Copper Creek."

"But if the show's producer finds out, it could damage Violet's career." And she and Austin will never forgive me if that happens.

"Then you need to figure a way to tell her the truth, without anyone discovering what you're up to."

Fuck. And how the hell am I supposed to do that?

26

When was the last time I sneaked into a girl's room late at night? Try sometime in never. It's suicidal to do it and assume you won't get caught.

Yet here I am—doing exactly that.

"Why are you in the tree?" Violet asks in a loud whisper from Aubrey's open guest room window.

And my heart almost leaps from my chest. Not because I'm afraid of falling from the tree and not because she spooked me. It's from the need to have Violet in my arms and to tell her how much I love her. It's from the need to bare my soul to the woman currently leaning out of the window.

"Why do you think I'm in it?" I pull myself up with the next branch. Now I just have to hope the neighbors don't see me and call the cops—and more specifically, Austin.

Yes, this is my great plan to talk to the woman I love. Only I hadn't anticipated the tree to be so damn tough to climb...especially with my sore knee. Whoever lived in this house before Aubrey never had to worry about their teenagers escaping at night by way of this tree.

"I don't know. Maybe to hang out with the squirrels?" she

205

says. "Are you sure you should be doing that? It's not like you're seventeen anymore."

"Are you insinuating I'm old?" I might not exactly be old, but damn, right now I feel as though I am. Tree climbing is a lot easier when you're younger.

And in a different tree.

"Why didn't you just come in the back door?" Violet asks.

"Because Aubrey told me to climb the tree," I huff. That, and because I had no idea if the back door was unlocked.

Violet laughs. "I don't know about you, but I'd rather you didn't die. So get out of the tree and come in through the door like a normal person."

I gauge the distance between me and the ground versus between me and the window. And then factor in the difficulty rating when it comes to climbing into the window from the tree.

Apparently, Aubrey isn't helping me talk to Violet; she's hoping to kill me off.

If I were the same seventeen-year-old who frequently scaled the tree outside his bedroom window, I would have scoffed at the odds of falling and breaking every bone in my body.

But somewhere between then and my thirtieth birthday, common sense kicked in. I start my slow descent.

I climb down until there are only a few feet between the ground and me, and then I jump. My knee doesn't even bitch about the rough landing. It's just relieved I'm finally out of the tree.

I try the back door. The handle twists easily in my hand, and I make a mental note to get revenge on Aubrey for my near demise.

Except, if I'm being fair, without Aubrey, I wouldn't have this chance to tell Violet that I love her.

Yes, I know that telling her how I feel about her won't change anything. She's leaving Copper Creek in two days either way. But at least I will have told her the truth. And once she leaves, we can go back to our neat little lives of denial, where we pretend I never said those three words.

Violet isn't downstairs waiting for me. I head upstairs to the guest room where I had planned for my dramatic entrance. That had been Aubrey's suggestion.

The grand romantic gesture.

If I hadn't died first.

A soft light glows from under the door at the end of the hallway. I push the door open and enter. Violet is pacing across the floor, wringing her hands.

"Hey," I say.

She startles but quickly recovers. "Aubrey said you need to talk to me. Alone."

Remind me to send Aubrey a big box of chocolates.

I walk farther into the room and my palms go sweaty, my chest tightens, and the fluttering sensation of a jar full of butterflies takes up residence in my stomach.

I lick my suddenly dry lips. "I didn't know Natalie was following me yesterday when I went to the river. My knee was sore from the calf roping. So I figured the cold water would ease the pain. I didn't realize Natalie had followed me, not until it was too late."

Now I have to just hope no one witnessed my great escape this time and track me down here.

"If that's true, why were her naked breasts pressed against *your* chest?"

"You've seen what happens every time she kisses me in front of the camera, right?"

The corners of Violet's mouth twitch up. "My advice? Don't give up your day job to become an actor. Your kissing skills need a lot of work."

I step toward her. "I don't remember you complaining about my kisses." My gaze drops to her luscious mouth. The memory of her kisses from a few weeks ago parades across my mind in all its HD glory.

The tip of her tongue traces along her lower lip. I close the gap between us.

"Maybe it's not my ability to kiss that's the problem. Maybe it's the woman." I lightly drag the pad of my thumb along the same path her tongue just took. Her lips are invitingly soft.

Violet releases a shuddering sigh.

"Because I know when I kiss Natalie, it feels nothing like when I kiss you. When I kiss her, it feels empty and fake. When I kiss you, it's like every part of my soul is buzzing with life. And when I'm not kissing you but you're in the same room as me, it's all I can do not to show everyone that you're the part of me I never want to give up."

I lightly press my lips to hers. "What were you and Austin doing there last night? You never did say."

"I was looking for you." She kisses me back. "Jake told me where I could find you."

"So how does Austin factor into this?"

"He saw me driving and followed me. I couldn't very well tell him I was hoping to see you there and do things to you that would freak him out. So I told him I was there to shoot photos of the river. I had my camera gear in my car, so he bought my excuse."

My lips brush hers again. The air swirling around us becomes electrically charged. "Do you believe me when I say nothing happened between Natalie and me?"

It takes a heartbeat, but Violet nods. It's not a fast nod, the nod that she's one hundred percent certain I'm telling the truth. It's a slow, hesitant nod—which will have to do for now.

"I love you, Violet. I hadn't planned on it. Hell, I hadn't planned on any of this. But I fell in love with you during these past few months. Oh, who am I kidding?" I caress her jaw with my knuckles. "I was in love with you even when we were teens.

But I knew your brother wouldn't approve...and then you went to college and never came back."

My breath clings to my lungs, unwilling to let go, as I wait for her reply. I don't need her to tell me that she loves me. But I do need for her to see how important she is to me.

She caresses my mouth with her lips. "Make love to me, TJ."

Her voice is a whisper, then her mouth is on mine again.

Our lips part and our tongues glide together. There's nothing rushed about it.

She might not have said the words I long to hear, but her actions tell me what her heart is not ready to say yet.

And that's all I need.

Her fingers work on unfastening my shirt. Mine are busy slipping the tiny buttons of her knit top through the holes. Our movements aren't hurried. They're slow and teasing and filled with longing.

Once her top is undone, I remove it and her bra. With our mouths still attached, I knead her beautiful, full breasts.

She moans, and I breathe it in. Forget chocolate—I owe Aubrey so much more.

Maybe a new house.

Preferably one with a tree designed for climbing.

My hands leave Violet's breasts and travel to the waistband of her jeans. I'm no longer kissing her. I want to see every one of her reactions, hear each of her sounds, touch every part of her.

I'm not the only one who's thinking the same way. Violet unzips her jeans.

Once free of our clothing, I guide her onto the bed and lie down beside her so we're facing each other. I kiss her again, shifting her onto her back.

I study her for a long moment, heat rolling throughout my body. My fingers move to between her legs. I brush her core with my thumb. She gasps. I grin.

"I could make love to you all night," I murmur against her lips.

"I wish we had all night," she whispers back and reaches for my cock. Her fingers wrap around it and she pumps her hand down its length. "Especially since we can't take any more risks like this again."

I grunt—because I know what she's thinking, and it pisses me off. "I can't do this anymore."

I'm not talking about the sex, because hello, there are no "I can'ts" when we're talking about Violet.

"You want me to go?" Disappointment and raw emotion drips from her tone. The same raw emotion I can't get a grip on but it feels like an echo to the one in my heart.

I circle my fingers around her clit, then run them along her dripping pussy. My length swells some more, almost painful in Violet's hand.

"I don't want you to go anywhere," I say. "I want the show to go away. I want Camilla and Natalie to go away." Far, *far* away. "Thank Christ, I only have to put up with this crap for two more days, and then it will be over."

Violet pumps her hand along my cock again. I groan.

"Except it won't be over. Natalie told Camilla she's picking you. You've still got months before you're free."

Free, but not with the only woman I want. She's returning to her life in LA.

"Not if I can help it. I'll tell them the truth. I'll tell them that I'm in love with you and can't keep doing this." I lightly press my finger against her mouth, stopping the words I'm aware are coming. "I know you're going back to LA and back to your career once this is all over. But it doesn't matter. I can't keep pretending I want to be with Natalie when she's not the woman I crave." It's not like I'm doing the show for fame or for the chance to do endorsements.

And it's not like Noah's plan has worked like he had hoped. It hasn't gained us visibility with the correct target audience.

I just want my life back to the way it used to be.

Violet scrapes her lower lip with her teeth. "If you quit pretending that you're hoping to win Natalie's love, you could face losing the ranch because of the potential lawsuit."

I can guarantee my grandfather is currently searching heaven for a lightning bolt to fry my ass with.

Hopefully he finds one with Noah's name on it, too, since he's the one who got me into this mess to begin with.

"So I just need to figure out how to avoid advancing to the next round," I say.

Violet caresses her thumb over the most sensitive part under the head of my cock. My dick sings a round of hallelujahs. I won't last much longer.

"Could you do that after we finish making love?" she says.

I'm all for that.

"Let me just get a condom from my wallet," I say.

"I'm on the pill now and I'm clean...so...if you want to go without one..." She leaves the rest of the sentence hanging.

"I'm clean too. And more than anything, I want to be bare inside you." I tenderly kiss her.

I shift to between her legs, my tip against her entrance. She wraps her legs around my hips and I ease my way in.

Her soft heat devours me, hugs me, begs for its release. And everything from the past few weeks is forgotten. We're in the here and now—with me repeating Violet's name again and again like a prayer.

I plunge deep inside her, twisting my hips in the way I know she enjoys. "Oh. God. *Yes*. TJ. Just like that."

Those are her last words before her inner muscles clench down on me. A mild tingling forms in my lower back, like the early beginnings of a storm. Just a few clouds that build into something bigger, something more intense, something mind-numbingly spectacular.

My balls tighten, and I call out my release.

Once I'm finished, I remove myself from Violet and collapse onto the bed. I pull her against me and hold her tight as our breaths return to normal.

Then I consult with the angel and the devil on my shoulders for the best way to get me out of the show.

Too bad neither of them is all that creative.

It's official.

I'm screwed.

27

___

There comes a time in a man's life when he just has to suck it up and get over his fears. It's the only way he can move forward. And if good fortune is shining on him, things won't be as bad as he expected.

"You said you needed to talk to me. Is now a good time?" Austin asks from the doorway to the tack room. "I've got a few minutes before my shift starts."

"Sure." I gesture for him to enter.

Well, here goes nothing. World, it's been nice knowing you.

He glances around the room, then his mouth slides into a one-sided grin. "Where's the TV crew and your future bride-to-be?"

"I'm assuming you're referring to Natalie? I have no idea. She's not here flirting with me. That's all I know."

His appraising gaze studies me for a second. "I take it you're hoping she doesn't pick you for her happily ever after."

"That obvious, huh?"

"It's hardly a surprise for anyone who knows you. You're not the marrying type." Austin was away on a mission when I found out about Katherine's wandering ways.

"It's not that I'm against marriage. I'm just against marrying someone who has no issues with cheating on me."

He frowns. "Katherine was having an affair?"

"It wasn't an affair. Noah wouldn't have let it get that far."

His frown twists into eyebrows-raised astonishment. "Wait, you're saying she cheated on you with your brother? Shit, man. I'm sorry. Why didn't you say anything?"

"Because by the time you returned, I was past it and didn't want to discuss it anymore. You were only on leave for a few days. You didn't need what happened to be dumped on you."

"Okay...so you're not against getting married, but you're not interested in marrying Natalie. That's what you wanted to see me about?"

"No." I start pacing. Not only because I'm still figuring out how to break this to him...I figure it's a lot harder to shoot a moving target. "You remember how I gave Violet the belt buckle for her seventeenth birthday?"

"Yeah...?" The word is drawn out in an *And-your-point-is?* question.

I stop, pivot, and walk toward the opposite wall. "And you interrogated me as to why I gave her the gift?"

"Yes, I remember that. You told me it was because you guys were friends, and you figured she'd like it."

I pause for a moment and look him straight in the eyes. "That much was true. But I was also in love with her." The pacing resumes. "Don't worry, nothing happened," I quickly add. "She had no idea of my feelings for her."

"Okay, so you had feelings for her back then." His nearly casual tone has only a hint of tightness, but I keep on pacing. "Can't say I like it, given you were nineteen and she was only seventeen. But that's in the past. Yes, I would have beat the crap out of you if you had told me the truth back then, but that was over ten years ago. So that's why you wanted to talk to me? To confess that once a upon a time you were in love with her?"

I stop pacing and turn to him. "I wanted to see you, so I can tell you that I'm still in love with Violet."

The frown returns to his brow. "That's impossible. And please don't tell me you've been having sex with my sister or I'll have to arrest you."

I chuckle—which is a dumbass thing to do given the circumstances. "On what grounds?"

"On the grounds that she's a minor and you're two years older than her."

I'd roll my eyes but I figure he won't appreciate it. "Violet is a twenty-eight-year-old woman with a toddler. I'm pretty sure she stopped being a minor a while ago. Look, I know you don't think I deserve her, that she's too good for me—"

"She's my sister. She too good for any man."

"All right, I'll give you that. But it doesn't change the fact that I love her. Always have. Always will."

He scowls at me. Not exactly a good sign. "Does she love you?"

"I have no idea." She didn't exactly say the words while we were making love—and I had no intention of pushing her just to hear them. "But I'm done keeping how I feel about her a secret from you. You're my best friend...although I'm guessing after this, you might not feel the same way."

He shoves his hand through his hair. The classic sign that he's thinking. Too bad it's not necessarily a sign that whatever he's thinking about is in my favor. It could go either way.

"If I wanted to," he says. "I could hide your body, and no one would know where to find it." He takes over my role of pacing.

I lean back against the workbench. "I don't doubt it."

"The last guy who she believed loved her ended up hurting her. What makes you so sure you won't do the same?"

"Because unlike the last guy, I do love her. I'd do anything to protect her and Deacon."

Austin stops pacing, his gaze a laser beam. "So you don't care that they're a package deal? Want one and you get them both. Together."

"I wouldn't have it any other way. I would love him like he's my own flesh and blood. But you're getting ahead of yourself. I'm just telling you that I love her. That's all. In case you've forgotten, Violet doesn't have a life here anymore. Her life is in LA."

"True. So what are you going to do about it? And what about the reality show? Are you going to tell them?"

"If there was a way I could without losing the ranch and without costing Violet her job, I would. But there isn't a way. So I just have to hope Natalie doesn't pick me in the end."

"And if she does?"

"If she does, well, there's no way in hell I'm going through with the marriage. At least the contract gives me that as an out." It's the only good thing about the contract. Whoever wrote it wasn't interested in doing the male contestants any favors.

"And Violet?"

"That's up to her. I just want her to be happy."

Austin exhales a long hard breath. "That's all I want, too. I wouldn't complain, though, if you can convince her to move back to Copper Creek." He smacks me on the back.

I smirk. "Does this mean you're not going to kill me?"

He smirks back. "For now."

Asgard barks. The signal that someone's coming.

"Oh, there you are, TJ," Natalie says a moment later from the doorway. Her tagalong crew is behind her. Unlike before, she doesn't look like your run of the mill, genuine cowgirl. She looks like she stepped out a sexy cowgirl calendar. "Violet was taking photos of me for the show's website, but now we need some of you and me together."

"It's actually for a women's fashion magazine," Camilla explains.

"Duty calls." Austin grins—and just like that, I'm partially forgiven for falling in love with his sister. "I'll let you get to work."

He nods at the two women and leaves, chuckling at the latest screwed up thing I have to do for the show.

Natalie and Camilla walk farther into the tack room. They aren't alone. Camilla's assistant and one of the cameramen enter behind them.

"The fashion layouts are mostly of Natalie," Camilla explains, "but they also want Violet to shoot photos of you and Natalie together. They sent the clothing they want you to wear for it."

It's only then that I notice the pair of jeans in Camilla's assistant's arms.

I eye the clothing like it's a rattlesnake poised to strike. "I'm really busy right now. I need to fix the barn door before the storm hits."

"Can't Noah or Jake do it?" Her tone is one I recognize. It's her *Do-I-need-to-show-you-the-contract?* tone.

"They've got their own jobs to do." As it is, if I'm selected for the show's final round, my brothers will have to pick up my slack for possibly up to four weeks.

"The photo shoot won't take long, and then you can fix the barn door." She indicates for her assistant to hand me the clothing.

"Fine." My tone is several steps below polite. But the sooner I get this over with, the quicker I can get back to work.

Violet tells me where to meet them since I have to return to the house first to change.

I stalk to the corral where Violet and Natalie are waiting for me. The lighting equipment has already been set up. "Where do you want me?" I ask Violet. I have a few suggestions—dirty suggestions—all which involve Violet and me. Alone.

Violet directs Natalie on how she wants her to pose. It doesn't take long for me to realize that modeling is no doubt listed on Natalie's résumé. She moves effortlessly into position.

Me? Not so effortlessly. It was one thing to pose when it was just Violet and me. All I had to do was glance at her, and it was enough for me to come off as swoony—Violet's word, not mine. It's a different story when you're posing with a woman who doesn't set your heart galloping, but you're expected to look like she does.

"Okay, I think I have enough photos to make the magazine happy," Violet says as a gust of wind picks up, whipping Natalie's hair in my face.

"If you'll excuse me," I say to Camilla and Natalie, "I have a barn door to fix."

I don't wait for a response. I jog back to the house, change into my work clothes, and head to the barn. Inside the tack room, I grab the toolbox from the workbench and the stepladder from against the wall.

I take them outside. The wind is now stronger and heavy with the promise of rain.

I open the ladder, locate the correct screwdriver head, and climb the steps. A few random raindrops splash against my sleeves.

With one hand, I push the door into the overhead track. The door is heavy and awkward and my muscles sing "Fuck you" as I work. I tighten the screw, one hand holding the door steady, the other gripping the cordless screwdriver.

I strain to focus on the task. Focus on the task and not on the image in my head of Violet. Bent over. Holding on to the ladder. Her fine ass in the air. And wearing nothing but my tool belt.

The raindrops start coming down heavier than before, soaking through my shirt. But since I've yet to witness a flash of lightning or rumble of thunder, I keep working.

"Do you need help?" Natalie asks. I look down to find her standing next to the ladder.

"No, I'm good." I keep working, my muscles threatening a revolt if I pause for even a second. The longer it takes to finish this, the longer I have to hold the door in place. "Why aren't you back at the house?"

Or wearing a rain jacket.

She still has on the same tank top from the fashion shoot.

"I thought you might need help. Then we can both get inside and stay warm until the storm passes." She nods at the barn and flashes me the same look from the other day at the river. The look she had right before going topless.

I return to tightening the screw. "That's all right. I think I have it now."

"You don't mind if I stay and watch, do you? I can keep you company."

"Wouldn't you prefer to be back at the house?"

"No, I'm fine. I enjoy watching you work." Her final words come out breathlessly.

"I'm returning to the house as soon as I'm done here."

Where the inspiration behind my dirty thoughts is waiting. I might not be able to hold Violet or kiss her, but at least I can be in the same room as her.

"I'll walk back with you," a persistent Natalie says over the rain.

"Your choice," I halfheartedly say and squeeze the screwdriver's trigger for the final time. *Perfect.* I release my grip on the door and shake out my hand to get the circulation moving again.

I push the door to the side several inches, testing it. It slides smoothly in the track.

I return the screwdriver to my tool belt and begin climbing down the ladder. A sudden gust of wind, stronger than before, catches me off guard.

That's not the only thing it catches.

I reach out, grabbing for my hat. Yes, I know—stupid, *stupid* idea. The steps are wet, and I'm not holding on as tightly as I should be—thanks to the fantasy of Violet in my tool belt and only my tool belt.

My foot slips on a rung. I loosen my grip on the ladder, prepared to jump the remaining distance. But I misjudge it and fall down, down, down. I attempt to land on my feet, but my bad knee has other ideas. It buckles, causing me to twist awkwardly, and I land on my outstretched arm.

And because my life isn't screwed up enough, my clavicle surrenders to its new fate. Pain cuts through my shoulder.

Fuck-fuckity-fuck.

I'm not sure which is more pissed at me right now: my shoulder or my knee.

Stand in line, guys. I'm not too impressed with myself either right now.

Groaning, I clutch my injured arm to my body with my left arm.

Natalie drops next to me on the wet ground. "Oh God, TJ. Where do you hurt?"

Where don't I hurt is more the question.

I fill her in on the injuries. My teeth chatter, and nothing I do will stop them. But it's the shudder rolling through me, stoking the pain, that has me gasping. My knee and my shoulder continue their argument as to who hurts worse.

"I need to get you out of the rain," Natalie says. "Can you make it to the barn with my help?"

I nod, then grimace as the pain in my shoulder intensifies.

She helps me into the barn and onto the cold concrete floor, so I'm partially leaning against the wall. Our soaked clothing clings to our bodies. The smell of horses and pine shavings and rain sits heavy in the air, grounding me against the intense pain.

As I focus on that, I hear Natalie talking to someone on the phone. I have no idea what she's saying. I'm preoccupied with thoughts of Violet...naked. Pounding into her. Kissing her. Telling her I love her.

Anything to distract me.

Another shudder wracks my body, making a seven-point-five earthquake seem like nothing more than a tiny tremble.

Violet's name pushes past my lips—a chatty parrot wanting to reveal all my secrets. Fortunately, it's not as loud as Tilly's parrot. There's a chance Natalie didn't hear it.

"Jake's on his way," she says. "Just hold on a little bit longer, TJ. Then we'll be able to warm you up. That should help lessen the pain for now."

"Tell him to bring me a bottle of Jack. That will help too." I'm joking, not joking.

"Nice try, but right now that's the worst thing you can have. You don't want to be drunk when we arrive at the hospital, do you?"

"I wouldn't complain." Except I might say something I shouldn't. On camera.

Like declaring my love for Violet.

Or better yet...I'll start singing cheesy country songs—karaoke-style—about how much I love her.

If the producers need more drama, I've just handed it to them. I can guarantee Camilla and the TV crew will show up at the hospital, eager to film me there.

Natalie keeps talking to me while we wait for Jake to arrive.

Don't quiz me on what she says. I'm back to my dirty thoughts about Violet—all to keep me from focusing on the pain.

After what feels like several days, Jake finally enters the stable. But it's not him I notice. It's the dark-haired angel with him wearing a flirty floral dress, cowboy boots, and a denim jacket who snares my attention.

"Violet," I murmur as she rushes over.

She drops to her knees and gently cups my cheek with her hand. I lean into the warmth. "It's going to be okay. Jake's taking you to the hospital."

"Come with me." The words slip out through the haze seeping into my mind. "I want you there with me."

I hear voices, but I can't make out what they're saying. It's like my head is underwater, pulse thundering in my ears.

"Okay, big guy," Jake says, "let's get you into the truck. Can you walk on your leg at all?"

I nod, the movement small.

He helps me to my feet. My knee yells out a victorious "I win!" in the game of who hurts worse. My shoulder grumbles, "I don't think so" and sets out to prove it.

An agonized groan stumbles from between my lips.

"Are you sure you can walk?" Jake asks.

"I'm a cowboy. I laugh at pain." I think I do a pretty good job proving that...even if my laugh is slightly off-kilter.

The progress to his truck doesn't have me hitting any Guinness Book records. And climbing into his vehicle is all kinds of hell.

I attempt to hoist myself up with my free arm. "You couldn't own a car that's easy to get in and out of, could you? Like a mini coupe?"

Jake gives me a boost from behind, helping me into the back seat. "We could have driven in Violet's car, but I doubt you'd fit in the back."

He might have a point.

I carefully shift onto the seat, doing my best to avoid igniting a new round of pain in my knee and shoulder.

"Violet," he says, "ride in the back with TJ. Natalie, you can ride up front with me."

I expect Natalie to protest, but she doesn't. She jogs around to the front passenger side and climbs in. She glances behind her and watches as Violet joins me in the back.

Her brow twists into a mask of confusion. "I'll let Camilla know that we're taking you to the hospital. She'll want the guys to get down there and videotape as much as they can...including me with you if the hospital permits it?"

"He's in no state for that." Violet reaches past me to fasten my seat belt. Even with the haze still hanging around my head, I notice her sweet scent of vanilla and roses. I inhale as deeply as my shoulder injury allows.

Natalie says something to Jake, but I can't hear what she says. He turns over the engine and the truck rumbles to life.

Violet rests her hand on my thigh—where it belongs and where I wish it would always be. I close my eyes and keep breathing through the pain.

By the time we drive up to the emergency entrance, the cold that had filled every inch of my body has lessened, thanks to the heat blasting from the truck's air vents. My clothes are still damp, but I'm no longer shivering. That's the advantage of the hospital being so far away—if you can call it an advantage.

Jake jumps down from the cab and disappears into the building, only to return a moment later with a wheelchair.

He helps me down and I ease myself onto the seat. I swear after this, I never want to see another truck again.

"I'll park while you two get him admitted," he tells Violet and Natalie as soon as they join me.

Natalie—now wearing Jake's jacket—pushes the wheelchair through the sliding hospital doors. Violet walks alongside.

Neither woman speaks. The tension between them is thicker than the Bitterroot River morning fog.

Yup—definitely not a good thing.

We join the triage line. Luckily, Jake arrives a few minutes later, easing the tension between the two women. We only have to wait a few minutes before it's my turn. Jake, Violet, and Natalie all join me, making for a very cozy space.

"Aren't you that really hot cowboy on *Cowboy Most Wanted*?" the triage nurse asks me. Before I have a chance to concoct some sort of response, she says to Natalie, "Does this mean you two will end up together? Please tell me you two end up together. Oh, who am I kidding? Of course you're together. That's why you're here. Together." She talks faster than Thor can gallop across the training ring.

Or maybe it just seems that way—a side effect of the pain.

Natalie does the talking. Which is a good thing. If I say anything, I'll either be begging for painkillers or blurting how much I love Violet.

Or a combination of the two.

Jake talks to the nurse, but I can't hear what he's saying. She's pretty, so maybe he's asking her what time she gets off work. Nice, I'm injured and he's trying to get laid.

Lucky bastard.

I'm wheeled back into the waiting room. As I wait for my name to be called, I keep glancing at the main entrance. What are the odds that Camilla and Co. got lost on their way here?

Or maybe Old Man Jeffery's flock is on the loose again, blocking the road out of Copper Creek.

If that's the case, forget the bottle of whiskey I owe him. I'll owe him a crate of the stuff.

Words from the TV show contract creep into my head. Words about what would happen if I'm injured prior to the final episode. Words that I've read a thousand times, looking for a loophole to get me out of the show.

I straighten a little too quickly and grimace.

Note to self: Don't do that again. *Holy fucking hell.*

"The contract," I say to no one in particular. My tone is a mix of agony and self-congratulations.

Jake frowns. "What contract?"

"The one for the show."

Natalie glances between Jake and me. "What about it?"

"If my memory is correct, this injury might be enough to get me booted from the show."

"If you have a broken clavicle like I suspect," Natalie says, "you should be fine by the time they shoot the second part of the season." Lines form between her eyebrows. Lines of confusion. Lines of hurt. "You want off the show, don't you? But why?"

My gaze falls on Violet—and my heart rate kicks up another notch. This time it has nothing to do with the pain in my shoulder and everything to do with the love reflected back at me. Reflected back from the woman who owns one hundred percent of my heart.

"I'm sorry...but I'm in love with Violet."

Natalie blinks, as if she misheard me and is now reviewing the conversation in her head.

"I never planned for it to happen," I say. "She's the sister of my best friend, which has always made her off-limits to me. But that didn't matter. I fell for her, and I fell for her hard." I look briefly at Violet. Her eyes are shiny. Is that a good thing? I have no idea.

I swallow back the pain and pray someone puts me out of my misery soon. "I know that I was supposed to stay single for the duration of the season—or at least for the portion of the show I'm involved with." I shift position and a new round of pain hammers my shoulder. I flinch. "But I can't keep hurting her this way."

Natalie glances back and forth between Violet and me. She nods, a soft smile playing on her lips. Then she checks her phone. "I should probably tell Camilla which hospital you're at." At our confused expressions, because there is only one hospital in the area, she explains. "There's a chance I might have told them the wrong hospital. There's a chance I might have told them to go to the hospital in the next town." There's no missing the smirk in her tone.

"You did?"

She nods. "There's a time and place for them to be video-taping us together, and this isn't it." She shrugs. "But I guess I should let them know the correct hospital." She looks at her phone screen. "Hmm. How about I give them another five minutes...just to be sure."

She pushes herself to stand. "Does anyone want a coffee while we wait?"

Jake places his request with her. Neither Violet nor I want anything.

As Natalie walks away, Jake pulls his phone from his back pocket. "I need to call Noah and give him an update."

After he calls our brother, he phones Grandma Meg.

And Aubrey.

And Sophie. That call results in a goofy grin on his face. I inwardly snicker.

He eventually puts his phone away.

Violet's hand is on my thigh the entire time he's updating everyone about the situation.

"He's in love with Sophie, isn't he?" Violet says. Her words have the *Isn't-that-adorable?* tone she usually reserves for cute animals.

This time I snicker out loud. "Possibly. Just don't mention that to Sophie. I'm waiting for those two to finally figure things out on their own." Although at the rate they're going, it might take a goddamn miracle before it happens. By miracle, I'm referring to Cupid shooting an arrow in my brother's stubborn ass.

Beyond that, Violet and I don't talk. At this point, there's not much we can say. I'll be free from the show soon—lawsuit or not —and Austin isn't going to kill me for being in love with his sister.

But at the end of the day, none of it matters. She's still leaving Copper Creek.

There is no Violet and me.

Maybe I'll get lucky—and the ER doc has something for broken hearts...along with broken bones.

"TJ Daniels," a woman in a white lab coat and holding a clipboard says. She scans the room.

"He's right here," Violet says, giving my thigh a light squeeze.

29

The next two hours at the hospital are spent with the ER physician examining my knee and my shoulder, getting X-rays, and learning that I sprained my knee and broke my clavicle.

The good news? I won't need surgery for either injury. But I will need time to recover.

I'm sitting on the ER bed when the camera crew enters the room. My knee is elevated with an icepack on it, my arm hangs in a sling, and my pain meds have finally kicked in. I'm just waiting to be discharged, and then I can return home.

The men don't say anything to me as they quickly arrange their equipment. Then the next thing I know, Camilla calls out "Action," and Natalie rushes into the room and over to my bed like I'm her long, lost love. The cameras watch her every move.

"How are you doing?" she asks. This is the first I've seen her since before I was admitted.

"I've had better days." Which is true. "Looks like I won't be riding for a while." Among other things.

The camera guys spend the next few minutes filming us talking and flirting with each other. Now that I know I'm going to be cut from the rest of the season, I make sure they get the performance they were hoping for while at the ranch.

At least I assume I'm going to be removed from the show. No one from it has confirmed this yet.

"Cut!"

At those magic words, the men start packing up the equipment.

Camilla joins Natalie by my bed. "Because your shoulder won't be fully recovered in time, the executive producers and I have decided to terminate your involvement with the show—as per stated in your contract. Natalie won't be selecting you as one of the final five contestants."

I feign a well-that-sucks expression, which I figure will be better received than one that exclaims, "Thank the ever-loving Christ."

"I understand." *So how soon before you leave and my life gets to return to normal?*

"Since you're physically unable to do anything for the next few days," she says, "I've determined that we have enough footage for the episode you're in. But before we head to our next location, we'll film your thoughts on how you felt the week went."

I can live with that.

NORMALLY THE DRIVE BETWEEN GOLDEN FALLS AND COPPER CREEK is just over an hour...when you're driving the speed limit.

"When did you turn into a little old granny?" I say to Jake after we've been driving for twenty minutes on the main route between the two towns.

"What do you mean?"

I can't tell if he's smiling or smirking. His eyes remain on the road.

"If you drive any slower, we'll be going backward."

He laughs but it doesn't change anything. He continues driving at a dragging-your-ass speed.

"At this rate, my painkillers will wear off before we get home. And then I'll be one cranky asshole."

"From the sounds of it, you're already there." His words hold a gruff edge, but his tone is one hundred percent smirk. He does get the hint, though, and increases our speed. Slightly.

After what feels like two lifetimes, because he drove under the speed limit the entire way, we finally arrive home. Not a single vehicle is in sight.

"No white vans? Does this mean everyone's gone? Permanently?" I ask.

"Yep. They're gone. Thank God."

My heart clenches at what this also means. *Don't go there*, I remind myself.

Jake helps me down from the truck as a car rumbles down the driveway. Cora Lee?

This can't be good.

"You want me to deal with her?" Jake asks.

"No, that's okay." I let out a hard breath.

Cora Lee parks her car and climbs out. With another box of cupcakes.

Her eyes take in my sling and widen. "What happened? Are you okay?"

"Broken clavicle. I'll be out of commission for a while."

"I'm sorry to hear that." Her tone sounds genuinely concerned, and she flashes me a sympathetic smile. She then hands the box to Jake. "It's a peace offering," she says as he opens the lid.

He peers inside the box. "I swear you could cause world peace if you delivered your cupcakes to the leaders during peace talks."

She smiles, the gesture more grateful than happy. "If only it were that simple. But I'm hoping it's enough to show you how sorry I am for the stupid way I acted," she says to me, then her eyes shift to Jake.

"He knows," I say, and her face flushes to a tomato red.

"I should never have threatened to expose you and Violet. You've done so much for Copper Creek, TJ. You don't deserve what I did."

Before I have a chance to respond, she powers on. "I was visiting Katie Higgins's mom the other day and saw how happy Katie was with the rocking horse you made her. I don't remember the last time I've seen her smile that much since the cancer diagnosis."

Cora Lee's gaze drops to the ground for a second before returning to me. "No matter what happens with the show, your secret is safe. Plus I have this for you." She hands me an envelope.

I take it from her and she grins like a giddy school girl. "What's this for?" I ask.

"It's a bank document, showing that I've paid off the bank loan in full."

Holy shit. "But how?" Because the last I heard, there haven't been any bank robberies lately.

"One of my great aunts died recently. She loved my cupcakes and willed me money—so I can follow my dreams, as she put it. My cupcake business is my dream. It wasn't a lot of money, but it was enough to pay off the loan and provide a little extra for the start-up costs. Anyway, I just wanted you to know so that you don't have to worry anymore about the loan. And I really hope things work out between you and Violet."

I don't have the energy to explain to yet another person that there is no Violet and me. There's just Violet and Deacon living in LA.

"I should go," Cora Lee says. "Tilly and her gang are waiting for a cupcake delivery. And when it comes to those women, it's never pretty if I'm even a few minutes late." She chuckles, wishes me a speedy recovery, and leaves.

Jake helps me into the house.

Inside, my gaze lands on the stairs that I'll have to walk up while my knee is still sore. "Shit." It was bad enough walking up the porch steps.

"I'll move your things into the downstairs guest room," Jake says, reading my thoughts.

"Thanks."

"You don't have to thank me. It was either that or I carry you up the stairs every time you need to go to your room. And that's just not happening." He smacks me on my good shoulder. "You might as well go rest up in the living room while I move your stuff. I'll bring you a new ice pack in a few minutes."

"Sounds good to me." It's not exactly how I want to spend the rest of my day, but thanks to my injuries, I don't have much choice.

I limp into the living room.

The lights from the iron chandelier have been dimmed. Near the couch, a forest of lit candles sits on every available surface.

And glowing in their soft light is Violet.

My heart races, my knees go weak, and the fine art of breathing is lost on me.

What the hell is in my meds? They're causing me to hallucinate.

Yes, that must be it.

"You're not real, are you?" I say more for my benefit than anyone else's.

She steps toward me, her gaze drinking me in the same way I'm drinking her in. "I'm *very* real." Her voice is soft and sweet and heavenly, like I imagine an angel's voice would be.

A sexy angel. Not a fallen, I'm-having-a-bad-millennium angel.

"You didn't have to go with the rest of the group?" With each word, hope that she's staying in Copper Creek—permanently—fills me.

"I'll be joining them tomorrow."

Hope crashes and burns somewhere near the rug, leaving no survivors.

"And then back to LA?" I ask.

She smiles. "Yes, once the show is finished, it's back to LA—but only long enough for me to give notice."

"Notice? But I thought you loved your new job."

"It wasn't the job I wanted. The company passed on me for the position I'd been working hard to get. Again."

"So after you give them notice, what then?"

She doesn't answer right away. She walks over to me, takes my hand, and leads me to the couch. She indicates for me to sit.

I do as I'm asked, even though I'd rather not. People typically tell you to sit right before they dump you with bad news. But since my knee is demanding that I listen to her, I lower myself onto the couch.

I'm not sure what I was expecting to happen next, but it sure as hell wasn't Violet straddling my legs. But that's exactly what she does while keeping her weight off them.

I shift my free hand to her hip. There's a chance my thumb might've slipped under the hem of her top. There's also a chance it might've caressed the soft skin there.

She cups my face with her hand. "I'm moving back to Copper Creek and starting my own photography business and online marketing company. I've spoken to Mayor Wineberg and a few businesses in town. They're interested in working with me to increase tourism and to help promote their businesses."

Please tell me the meds aren't causing me to mishear things. "Is this because I told you that I love you?"

"Partly because of that. And partly because I realized this is where I belong. Copper Creek is where Deacon and I belong." She slowly drags the pad of her thumb across my lower lip.

My breath catches.

My cock rejoices.

"And it's not just Copper Creek that I love," she says. "I love you, too, TJ. I have for as long as I can remember. But I have Deacon to consider. We're kind of a package deal. And I know you don't exactly want kids. So if you're not looking to have him in your life, now's the time to walk away." She chews on her lush lower lip—and just like that, she's even more adorable, more desirable.

Shaking my head slightly, I smile. "I can't walk away—and that has nothing to do with my knee being messed up. I want Deacon to be part of my life. I want you both to be part of it. I couldn't imagine it any other way. And if one day you want more kids, nothing would make me prouder than to be the one who gives them to you. Nothing would make me prouder than to be their father."

My hand moves from her hip to knot in the silky strands of her hair. I bring her head to mine and tenderly kiss her.

My lips move away from hers. "I would like that very much." She rests her forehead against mine. "Rumor has it my brother isn't planning to kill you for being in love with me?"

I chuckle. "I'll probably have to spend a lifetime proving to him that I'm worthy of you, but it's a lifetime I'm happy to spend. Just as long as I'm with you." I bring her back for another brief kiss. "Although I'll be a lot happier once I can make love to you again." According to the orthopedic surgeon I saw at the hospital, I'm looking at a few weeks...but hell if I'm waiting that long.

A sweet smile slips onto her face. "Me too. On all of that."

This time when we kiss, it's more heated, more passionate.

Just more.

EPILOGUE

Six Months Later

"**M**ommy, look!" Deacon points at the small herd of deer ahead of us on the trail. He's practically vibrating with excitement.

The deer take off, bounding deeper into the forest. The April sun lights up the ground, the new leaves on the trees barely obscuring the rays.

He watches the animals go. An adorable pout forms on his face.

I chuckle. "Do you know what they were?" I ask him.

He shakes his head.

"Those were deer."

"Sven?"

"No, Sven is a reindeer." A reindeer from the movie *Frozen*, which we've watched a gazillion times.

Truth? Sven is my favorite character from the movie...even more so than Olaf.

236

Just don't tell Violet and Deacon that. They're proud members of the Olaf fan club.

Deacon nods, then runs ahead of Violet and me on the dirt path. Asgard trots alongside, keeping an eye on the mischievous two-and-a-half-year-old.

It's Sunday afternoon. Most of the chores for the day have already been completed. Jake and Noah are finishing what I still need to do. They know this isn't just a hike through the forest for me.

It's the possible beginning of something new.

Ahead of us, Deacon stops at a wide puddle. He pauses for a moment, then jumps in, creating an epic splash with his bright yellow rubber boots.

Asgard barks.

Violet and I laugh.

Encouraged by our reaction, Deacon continues jumping and splashing in the muddy water.

With him currently distracted, I pull Violet against me and gently kiss her.

Then I kiss her again, only deeper this time. That's the benefit of having a dog who also doubles as a babysitter when we go for walks. We never have to worry about Deacon wandering off while I'm showing Violet how much I love her.

Asgard takes his job of herding sheep and little boys very seriously.

Woof.

Speaking of which.

I stop kissing Violet and look over at the puddle. Deacon has moved on, ready for a new adventure.

I thread my fingers with Violet's and we follow him.

A short while later, we break through the trees and enter the small meadow. The grass is green and a few eager bitterroot flowers have started to bloom. The fresh smell of spring floats in the air like a bright yellow balloon.

I hand Deacon Asgard's ball. The goofy dog eyes it eagerly, waiting for Deacon to throw it.

Deacon tosses it. It lands a few feet away.

I chuckle. "We definitely need to work on your throwing arm, Deacon."

Asgard retrieves the ball and drops it at my feet.

"You want me to throw it, huh?" I pick it up and hurl it. Asgard goes chasing after it. Deacon giggles.

"I can't believe I gave this all up for LA," Violet says, slowly turning around. Her face is full of wonder. "It's so beautiful here."

Can't disagree with her there.

"But at least you got wise and moved back." I wink at her.

She laughs.

"So does that mean you're planning to stay in Copper Creek for the rest of your life?" I already know her answer, but it doesn't hurt to double-check.

"I couldn't imagine being anywhere else. Especially now that my marketing company is starting to gain ground."

"I'm glad to hear that." With the beat of my heart rivaling the volume of the birds in the nearby trees, I shove my hand into my jeans pocket and pull out the ring. I fist it. Violet is watching her son and doesn't see what I'm doing. *Breathe in and out. That's all I have to do. Just keep breathing.*

I've participated in big stakes rodeo events—yet none of them ever felt like this. But what was the worst that could happen then? I fell on my ass, maybe hurt my knee. That's nothing compared to proposing to the woman who has your heart.

Keep breathing. Nice and easy. I can do this.

I stroke her cheek, regaining her full attention. I rest my hand on her face, and she leans into it.

Her beautiful brown eyes search mine, so trusting, so loving.

"A year ago," I say, "my world revolved around my horses, my family, my love of Norse mythology. I couldn't imagine wanting anything else. I mean other than sex." I smirk at the last part and she laughs. She knows how much I love sex.

With her.

"I guess deep down, I knew there was only one woman for me. But at the time you were both off-limits to me and weren't living here." I give her another light kiss. "And now you're living here, and you're my girlfriend." Another brush of the lips. "But I'm a greedy bastard. I want more. I want to wake up each morning with you curled around me. I want to go to bed each night knowing you're mine and that you'll always be mine.

"I want to spend each day with you as my wife." I open my palm, revealing the engagement ring. "Violet, will you marry me?"

Woof.

Her eyes widen, and she presses three fingers against her mouth.

But she doesn't say anything.

Which is never a good thing in a situation like this.

My heart groans.

Woof.

"Not now, Asgard, I'm trying to propose to Violet." And doing a crappy job at it.

Her eyes fill...also not a good thing.

Have we discussed one day becoming a family? Not at all. I mean, other than when I told her that if she wanted to have more kids, I would be thrilled to help her out there and proud to be their father.

I thought she wanted the same as I did.

Woof.

I pick up the ball and hurl it again. Asgard chases after it. Deacon cheers.

I turn back to Violet.

She lowers her hand and blinks. "Did you just ask me to marry you—or did I imagine that?" Her voice is clogged with emotion, yet at the same time it pours over me like hot fudge and melted raspberry ripple.

"That's right. I want you to marry me, and I want to officially adopt Deacon...if you're fine with it. I want to legally be his father."

She chokes out a sob and throws her arms around me. "Of course I'm fine with you adopting him." She kisses the nook of my neck. "And of course I want to be your wife." She kisses my jaw. "There's nothing I want more than either of those things."

And then her lips are on my lips.

I open my mouth and let her in. Our tongues glide and dance together. They worship each other, exchange our silent vows. If we were alone, I'd also make love to her.

But that will have to wait until tonight.

I pull slightly away from her, and we look over at Deacon. Both boy and dog are doing fine.

I slide the gold ring on her finger. The diamond sparkles in the sunlight. *Perfect.* Just like Violet.

"Please tell me you don't believe in long engagements," I say. "Because I'm not sure how much longer I can last before the two of you move in with me." As it is, I miss her every night when she has to slip away after I've made love to her.

"I'm fine with a short engagement," she says. "In fact, the shorter the better. Besides, this is Copper Creek, not LA. We don't have to book things a year in advance."

True.

"So how about June?" Because two months is about as long as I can last.

Violet laughs. "You really are impatient to get married, aren't you?"

"Can you blame me?"

Her bright smile is enough to melt what's left of the snow on the Bitterroot Mountains.

She presses her lips softly to mine. "Not at all. And yes, June will be perfect."

"I was hoping you'd say that." I sweep her up in my arms.

Her arms slip around my neck, and she giggles. "What are you doing?"

"Practicing carrying you over the threshold. What does it look like I'm doing? And just wait until tonight...when I practice for our honeymoon." I lower my mouth to her ear. "And I plan to do lots of practicing before the real deal." My tone emerges, gritty with lust and smooth like syrup.

"What would you say if I told you I want to save myself for our honeymoon?"

I trace my lips along her jaw. "I'd say I have no idea what that means." Something tells me I won't be doing cartwheels once she tells me what she has in mind.

"I want to wait until we're married before we have sex."

Yep, no cartwheels in my near future. "Then I'll have to change your mind. And trust me, future wife, I can be very persuasive." I nibble her lower lip.

She laughs and kisses me back. "That I don't doubt. But as you know, I can be very stubborn."

She's got that right.

I lean in, my breath brushing against her ear. "What do you say we have our picnic, then go home and begin planning our big day?"

She grins. "I would say that I love that idea."

And afterward, I'll convince her to let me make love to her.

One final time.

Before our wedding night.

Because as much as the thought of not making love to her during the next two months gives me hives, I'll do anything she wants.

All she has to do is ask.

**TURN THE PAGE FOR AN EXCERPT
FROM THE HOT AND HILARIOUS
ONCE UPON A COWBOY**

CHAPTER 1
JAKE

"What do you think?" Noah, my youngest brother, nods at Sophie—my best friend—and the brown mare in the outdoor training ring.

The sun is shining on her long, blonde ponytail. The Bitterroot Valley breeze, scented with the kick of manure, blows strands of loose hair about her face. Unlike my brother and me, Sophie doesn't have her cowboy hat on. Right now, it dangles in my hand.

She's holding the lunge line in her left hand, the training stick in her right, and slowly turning on the spot as the horse trots a large circle around her.

Instead of saying what I'm really thinking—how I'd like to shove her against the stable door and kiss her senseless—I simply answer with regard to the mare. "Looking good."

Noah laughs. "I was referring to the horse."

I scowl at him. "So was I."

He laughs harder. "If you say so."

I pretend not to understand what he's talking about.

Noah returns his attention to the training ring. "She definitely has a way with horses."

"Which is why I told you and TJ that we should hire her when you guys decided to switch from cattle to breeding horses," I say.

Our grandfather's life had revolved around cattle. There was a good reason for that. Cattle make money; breeding horses doesn't. But when he died and willed us the ranch, TJ and Noah itched to do something they were passionate about. And raising cattle wasn't it.

"I can't believe you weren't dating her in college," Noah says. "You should've dated Sophie instead of the thief you hooked up with."

No argument there.

This would be the same thief (aka ex-girlfriend) who was a business partner for the company I started with my roommate while we were in college. The same ex-girlfriend who did our accounting, who had all our company passwords, and who ended up stealing from us.

She was also the same ex-girlfriend who taught me that dating your co-workers is a bad idea.

Right, she wasn't the only one who taught me that. A friend of mine a year later dated one of the waitresses he worked with. It was all fun and games until he ended it. She got upset and... well, having a bull gouge your balls with his horns would've been less painful than what she put my friend through after that.

I shrug my shoulders in a *What-can-you-do?* move. "You know what they say about love being blind..."

"More like stupid."

The corner of my mouth twitches up. "That, too."

"So what's your excuse now? Why don't you just go out with her?"

Noah's idea of going out with a woman doesn't entail an actual date. It just means sex.

And until our older brother TJ fell in love with his best

friend's sister, he shared Noah's sentiment. Now he can't keep his eyes off his fiancée.

What about me? I'm no virgin when it comes to one-night stands. But my focus is more on running a business than on getting laid.

"You know why." I pretend not to be enthralled by the sight of Sophie's sexy ass in her slim-fitting jeans.

Noah snorts a laugh. "Because it's against a company policy you came up with. A policy TJ and I had no say in."

The infamous clause was written for Sophie's sake, not theirs. After I'd asked her if she was interested in working for us, she visited the ranch. And Noah had eyed her up in a way that told me exactly what he was thinking. Except Noah had no such policies when it came to women and was notorious for leaving behind trails of broken hearts.

Since I had no intention of watching him hurt Sophie, I added the "No dating and no sex with an employee" clause.

"First," I say, "Sophie and I are just friends. That's all. And even if I was interested in screwing around with her, I'd rather not risk our friendship over a short-term fling. Second, is this your way of saying you want to hook up with one of our employees? Which, when it comes down to it, is just me, TJ, and Sophie. And Violet—if you count the marketing she's doing to help the ranch's reputation after your dumbass plan with *Cowboy Most Wanted* backfired on us."

He lifts his hands, palms out. "Hey, I had no idea TJ would become the poster boy for sexy cowboys. And no, I'm not interested in hooking up with any of you."

"Smart answer, given that TJ won't take too kindly to you hitting on Violet."

Noah chuckles, the sound just short of devious. "So you don't have a problem with it if I hook up with Sophie? Or does the company policy still even exist, given that TJ ignored it with Violet?"

Maybe if I stopped eyeing Sophie's fine ass and the way she's handling the horse, I'd pay attention to the warning in my head. The warning telling me to say something...*anything.*

"That's what I thought." The low rumble of his voice gives away the barely suppressed laughter. "Don't worry. Sophie's more like a sister to me. I'm not interested in her that way."

The muted crunch of gravel approaches us from behind. "Which is a good thing," TJ says before I can turn around to see who it is.

Violet's two-year-old son is sitting on his shoulders, grinning. Deacon is wearing jeans, a cowboy shirt, and a toddler-sized black cowboy hat that matches the adult-sized one in TJ's hand. A small, floppy stuffed horse is gripped in Deacon's equally small hand and dangles in my brother's face.

TJ's Aussie shepherd, Asgard, walks alongside them.

"Hey, Deacon." I hold up my hand to fist-bump him, which he does like a pro.

"Hi, Uncle Jake." He reaches for me to help him down.

I haul him off TJ's shoulders and lower him to the dirt ground. He toddler-swaggers to the bottom wooden rung of the fence, folds his arms on it, and watches Sophie and the horse. Asgard sits next to him.

"Yes, the company policy is still in effect," I tell Noah. "TJ and Violet are exempt from the rule because they're getting married. They fall under the exception." Which I haven't added in yet, but I guess I should. "They were fooling around behind our backs before we hired her to help us."

Noah snorts another laugh.

"What's a good thing?" I ask TJ, happy to move away from discussing the company policy.

"I happen to know that Sophie's the kind of woman who's interested in having her own happily ever after."

"Happily ever after?" I sound out the words as if they're a foreign concept. "You've been watching those Disney Princess movies with Deacon and Violet again, haven't you? Has the Man Card Club demanded you surrender your membership yet?"

Once Upon a Cowboy now available.

ACKNOWLEDGMENTS

First, I want to say a big thanks to everyone who has fallen in love with my romantic comedies. Your enthusiasm for the books is heartwarming. This is especially true when it comes to the members of my Facebook reader group (Stina's Sweethearts). You guys are the best!

I want to thank my editor Bev Katz Rosenbaum (BKR Editing), as well as Hope and Jessica from Flat Earth Editing for their copyediting and proofreading expertise. All three individuals helped make this book sparkle. I especially have to thank Jessica for correcting my terminology when it came to the horse gear. I grew up in England until I was eleven years old, and took English riding lessons for several years. Western and English riding use different terms when it comes to equestrian equipment. Fortunately, Jessica is very familiar with Western-style riding. Naturally, I can't forget Brenda St. John Brown, who shared her own brilliant suggestions and wisdom when it came to this book and beyond. When I get stuck with a plot point, she's always there to give me suggestions.

Writing can be a lonely occupation if it weren't for the online author support groups. These are the places writers can go to get answers to their publishing and marketing questions.

And finally, I would like to thank my family. They put up with so much when it comes to my career. Between the hours I spend writing and marketing and searching through photo stock sites for the perfect sexy image that Facebook won't reject, it's amazing they still recognize me. At least I *think* they still recognize me.

ABOUT THE AUTHOR

Born in Brighton England, Stina Lindenblatt has lived in a number of countries, including England, the U.S, Finland, and Canada. This would explain her mixed up accent. In addition to writing fiction, she loves photography, especially the close-up variety, and currently lives in Calgary, Canada, with her husband, three kids, and their cat.

For news about her books, social media sites, and to sign up for her newsletter (which includes her exclusive giveaways), check out her website at stinalindenblattauthor.com